SWEET MEDICINE

¶ This book is dedicated to the spirit of toleration and the power of friendship.

The flower-fed buffaloes of the spring,
In the days of long ago
Ranged where the locomotives sing,
And the prairie flowers lie low.
The tossing, blooming perfumed grass
Is swept away by the wheat,
Wheels and wheels and wheels spin by,
In the spring that is still sweet.
But the flower-fed buffaloes of the spring,
Left us long ago.
They gore no more, they bellow no more,
They trundle around the hills no more,
With the Blackfeet, lying low,
With the Pawnees lying low,
Lying low.

Vachel Lindsay

Sweet
Medicine

SUE BODDINGTON

Privately printed for
Sue Boddington
Dacia, 99 Poulshot Road, Poulshot, Devizes, Wilts SN10 1RX
sue.boddington@virgin.net

by The Hobnob Press
8 Lock Warehouse, Severn Road, Gloucester GL1 2GA

Design and typesetting by John Chandler. The text is set in 14 point Doves Type, leaded 2 points. Doves Type is a digital facsimile, created by Robert Green, of the celebrated face made by Edward Prince in 1899 for the Doves Press, based on Jenson's 15th-century Venetian type.

Born and bred in Wiltshire Sue Boddington graduated from Bristol University in History, English, Theology and Philosophy. After flirting with teaching, acting and singing, she joined Wiltshire Library Service, holding the posts of Senior Librarian Adult Learning for the county and Community Librarian for the Calne area. Now retired, she still lives in Wiltshire and is the voluntary curator of Calne Heritage Centre.

Front cover design by Freda Jackson.

CHAPTER ONE

The creature paused for a second only, just long enough for the nose to twitch as the scent of man drifted into its nostrils and for the soft, brown eyes to flicker nervously. It was a fatal second in which the loosened arrow flew to its mark. The deer was in mid-air, springing away into the trees, when the arrow pierced it through the head. It seemed to hang suspended in the air, the delicate hooves quivering in time with the vibrating arrow burning in the animal's brain and then it fell with a crash into some blackthorn bushes, white with May flowers.

The hunter ran to the spot, but drew back when he saw the bright red drops of blood staining the white blossom. For a moment the sight startled him and reminded him how much he hated hunting- Bear Claw, the great hunter, who to save a child had attacked and killed a full-grown grizzly when he was only fifteen years old. The bear had ripped the boy's chest open and one great claw buried deep in his shoulder had snapped off. It was months before it had worked up out of his flesh. It had given him the name he now bore and he wore it around his neck on a leather thong. He had worn it for fifteen years.

He was the most successful hunter in his village. He could imagine the derision if he had tried to explain to anyone how he hated hunting. The chase, the stalking was good, the moment when he loosed the arrow and heard it sing in the air, his satisfaction with his marksmanship when it was true, all these things pleased him. But when the moment came to retrieve the kill, then he could not prevent a stinging sense of regret from welling up inside him. Now as he stared at the mottled, brown body of the deer and watched the red spots spreading over the blossom, he wished he had let the creature spring in to the forest. It was always the same. Yet his people must eat.

"Forgive me great leader of the deer," he murmured, "I am sorry that to feed our children we must kill your children and thank you for the gift of life the death of your children brings."

The prayer made him feel less guilty, helped to erase the bitter taste in his mouth. He drew the arrow from the deer's brain and wiped it clean on the damp spring grass. Then he lashed the body by the hooves to a long staff, slung the staff over his shoulder and made his way back to the river.

It was early. The sun had not long risen and the narrow, winding river glistened. The sunlight struck the multi-coloured pebbles lying on the river bed causing arcs of iridescence like miniature rainbows to hang over the water. Bear Claw splashed through to the opposite bank, then stopped to listen as he caught the sound of distant music, a thin reedy sound, but sweet and wistful. He smiled- Benjamin Barnett was playing his reed flute.

Instead of heading upstream out of the woods and on to the plain where his tribe was camped, he trotted down an incline towards the sound of the flute and soon saw the smoke of the Barnett homestead twisting through the trees. It was a small but sturdy log cabin with a ramshackle veranda strewn with domestic clutter and a sofa with the stuffing coming out. At the back of the cabin was a well -tended garden already showing signs of spring growth and the benefits of a mild winter. A pen with two milk cows grazing in it stood in front of the house, while a goat and a dozen chickens wandered around aimlessly.

Benjamin Barnett had been chopping wood. Logs were heaped around him as he leaned back against the rails of the pen playing that plaintive tune on the flute. An axe rested against his leg. Bear Claw had liked the look of Ben the very first time he saw him when the white man moved into the area three years before. There was something totally trustworthy about him, a calm honesty. The Cheyenne had no reason to trust the whites, but Ben was different.

He was a handsome man in his early thirties. There was an elegant air about him that did not match the rough homesteader's clothes and battered hat that he wore. His long face was finely boned and his dark eyes that appeared to be brown, but shaded into a deep green, were serious, almost melancholy.

Bear Claw stood in the trees for a moment, observing how lost Ben was in his playing. Suddenly the dog that lay at Ben's feet, a huge, bony wolfhound, caught sight of the shape amongst the trees. He leaped to his feet, snarling deep in his throat, the hair at the back of his shaggy neck rising stiffly. Barnett snapped out of his reverie. He stopped playing, his hand closing around the handle of the axe beside him.

Bear Claw sauntered out into the open, smiling his wide, encouraging smile and Ben recognised him at once.

"Oh, it's alright Caesar, it's Bear Claw. Go and meet him. Go on."

The dog rushed at the Cheyenne, who dodged aside, trying to keep the deer clear of Caesar's probing nose and licking tongue. He swung his burden across the top rail of the cattle pen and still smiling he said in English, "I don't see you around for some weeks Ben. Spring ceremonies take up much time."

He spoke with the guttural inflection of the Cheyenne tongue but his English was fluent and uninhibited. Bear Claw had a talent for languages. He could speak most of the dialects of the plains tribes and had soon picked up English from his conversations with the trappers and his trading visits to the forts higher up the river. He reached out, tapping the axe which was still in Ben's hand.

"You are nervous this morning to reach for a weapon so quickly. You have trouble?"

"No not trouble exactly, but a couple of visitors who did little to inspire confidence."

Barnett was an Englishman; his speech betrayed that instantly. He was well-spoken, his voice clear and melodious. The youngest son of landed gentry from the Wylie Valley in Wiltshire, Ben had been educated at Eton and Cambridge. His academic achievements were high, but when he left university, he could find no occupation that satisfied him. As much as he loved the arts, the academic world seemed xenophobic and false to him. He had no taste for trade and even less for idleness. He had married Frances Lucas, the daughter of a baronet from his home county and a year later had persuaded her to embark with him for America.

They spent two years with cousins in the gentility of Boston, but that was not what Ben had in mind when he sailed for America. He wanted land, a quiet place to farm and tend, where he could work hard, watch things grow and reflect on life free from the pressures of society. He made inquiries and came into contact with two brothers who had just returned from Montana and were offering a plot of land and a cabin for sale in an isolated spot about 40 miles from the small town of Baker. They had intended to work the land themselves, but the older brother had sustained a severe injury logging and could no longer cope with the rigours of a pioneering life.

They assured Ben that the cabin was in good repair because they had only left it two months previously. There was woodland nearby which provided plenty of fuel for the fire and cooking stove and the water from the deep well they had dug was pure and safe to drink. They had also begun to prepare some of the land for cultivation and it appeared fertile. There was a stage route that stopped at Baker and the town could provide all they would need, furnishings, tools, transport vehicles and livestock. Even allowing for a percentage of exaggeration on the part of men eager to sell, it sounded to Ben to be just what he was looking for and the price was reasonable. His enthusiasm conquered Frances' initial fears and they trekked west with three large trunks, by a network of stage coaches.

Now here they were. It was harder work than even he had imagined, but he did not regret it. His homestead in a fertile area, tucked in between the Tongue and the Powder Rivers, tributaries of the great Yellowstone, was all he could have hoped for. He was grateful too for friends like Bear Claw, who had brought some of his womenfolk to help when Fran's baby was coming. Bear Claw was proud of his self-appointed role as protector of Ben's eighteen- month- old daughter Sarah. He was regarding the Englishman now with a questioning look on his face, waiting for his friend to explain what he had seen that morning to make him so edgy.

"About six this morning I thought I heard that wolverine around the henhouse again, so I went out with Caesar to look round. It was the wolverine alright but he's too damn quick for me."

"You saw him?"

"No, he must have heard me unbarring the cabin door, but I could make out his tracks plainly enough."

"I understand why you worry." Bear Claw had heard many tales around the campfire about the voracious appetite and dangerous temper of the wolverine. Their medicine was strong and their influence bad. "The wolverine is not a good visitor. He often brings bad luck."

"It wasn't the wolverine that worried me Bear Claw." Ben had tucked his reed flute into his belt and was gathering up the smaller logs into a wicker basket. "I don't think he can bring me bad luck. It was what or rather who I saw when I went out to the edge of the woods following the track- Antoine La Farge- not my favourite spring visitor. Now he is bad luck."

Bear Claw made a noise in his throat that expressed very eloquently what he thought of La Farge.

"He is early this year," he said.

La Farge was a French trapper, who came down the Yellowstone from Fort Union every spring to ply his trade in the fertile, wooded areas along the river. He would go back upstream in the early autumn to trade off his skins and spend the winter in the relative comfort of the fort.

Ben nodded. "I had a brush with him in the autumn, just before he went back up river. I caught him several times hanging around the house talking to Frannie. I can't imagine any woman being safe with La Farge for very long. Besides she was afraid of him."

He glanced towards the house, as his wife appeared on the veranda for a moment, her auburn hair gleaming like fire in the strong sunlight. Bear Claw followed his gaze, half expecting Frances to acknowledge him, but she did not look in their direction. Ben sensed what he was thinking.

"It's me she's ignoring. I am very unpopular at the moment. I dropped my pipe on the rug last night and burned a hole in it- you know- her favourite rug, the one she brought over from England with her, traditional Persian Kashan."

He was smiling but seemed sorry that he had upset her.

"Anyway," he continued, "La Farge was dragging

a travois behind him stacked up with trade goods, including a generous supply of that vile rot gut he distributes around the local tribes. He had the affrontery to try to sell me some. By God I wouldn't touch that stuff. It could strip the bark off trees, so what must it do to your throat?"

"What did you do?"

"I told him what he could do with his whisky and he went off into the trees calling me foul names in French. It was like a sewer overflowing, probably didn't occur to him that I might speak French."

Bear Claw grinned, but he was uneasy about the trapper.

"Where was he heading?" he asked.

"I'm not positive but he could well have been going across the river towards your village- if he got as far as that."

Ben's wicker basket was full now. He rested his foot on the pile of logs.

"Which brings me to my second visitors this morning. Perhaps I should have told you this first. Just about an hour ago, your brother-in-law,

He-Who-Runs-Fast and his cousin Crow Dog came riding into the yard in a very fevered state. He-Who was in a rage. Someone from your village was killed this morning on Cottonwood Creek. Shot in the back with a rifle bullet according to him. I think he was ready to believe I had done it. I'm sure that if I had flinched or shown any fear, he would have run me through with that feathered lance of his."

Bear Claw put his hand on Ben's arm. "Ben

Barnett," he announced solemnly, "I have told He-Who-Runs-Fast that although he is my kin, if he hurts you in any way, I will kill him. I mean what I say. But who was killed? Did my wife's brother say?"

"No, I couldn't make out half of it. His English is about as good as my Cheyenne. But I think I convinced them that I wasn't the culprit. I also think they knew that La Farge was in the woods. He was clearly another prime suspect. It wouldn't be hard for them to pick up the trail of that travois."

Bear Claw was shouldering his deer. "I must find out what is happening. You, Fran and the little one must stay at home Ben. When there is death then there is anger and often the innocent suffer." He was already running into the trees, Caesar at his heels. "I will warn you if there is any danger."

"Take care of yourself," Ben shouted after him. "He-Who was almost out of his mind with anger."

The Englishman watched his friend disappear into the dark green shade of the woods and called Caesar back. The dog loped back and Ben rubbed the animal's bristly neck. He was moved when he considered that Bear Claw really would be willing to jeopardize his relationship with his own tribe in Ben's defence.

The man in question was considering too as he ran up through the trees, the deer swinging behind him. He was wondering, as he often did, just where he stood in the order of things. Bear Claw was not a full-blood Cheyenne. He was half white. His father, White Bull, was a great warrior amongst the Cheyenne and his fearless death at the hands of the Pawnee was still talked about with great pride in the village. His mother however was Hannah Marchak, the only daughter of a Jewish pedlar from Germany.

Jacob Marchak was peddling his wares amongst the Mandan and Hidatsa tribes on the prairie grasslands of South Dakota.

He travelled with his wife and seventeen- year-old daughter Hannah. The spring of 1829 was his second year following this route between the villages. He was welcomed in the earth lodges of the Mandan and saw little reason for fear on this lonely and vulnerable journey. He knew nothing of the fiercer tribes that had in more recent years taken up a nomadic existence on the high plains to the west and therefore showed little concern when one Tuesday morning, as he urged on the mule that pulled his livelihood along in a wooden cart, he saw a band of about thirty warriors approaching on horseback.

As they drew closer, he stopped the cart to wave to them, telling his women folk to unpack some of the wares. An arrow had pierced his heart before he even suspected any danger. Bear Claw remembered how the terror still lingered in his mother's eyes when she described the scene to him. The Marchaks had been unlucky enough to run into a party of Northern Cheyenne, returning home disappointed and angry because their horse-stealing raid on a Crow village had failed. They vented their frustration on the defenceless pedlar and his family, murdering both parents and the mule, but taking Hannah with them.

White Bull claimed her for his wife. She was

submissive and obedient, afraid of the taciturn, scarred warrior. She fetched and carried for his two Cheyenne wives, silent and despairing. Then something happened that changed her- her son was born. She saw in him her hopes of retaining her identity. Defiantly she sang Yiddish lullabies to her baby. She taught him to speak German, though warning him he must never use the language in anyone's hearing except hers. It was a painful process for it had to be done in snatches when none of the other womenfolk could hear and report it to her husband. He caught her once and beat her viciously, but the subversion continued. It would have been an impossible task without the compliance of White Bull's senior wife. Bright Moon was not openly friendly to Hannah. She hardly spoke to her except to issue commands, but if she heard her speak to her son in that strange language, she turned a deaf ear and did not report it. Perhaps it was because her grandmother was an Arikara, captured in a raid, who often expressed a longing for her own tribe.

The menfolk told the children stories of the Cheyenne heroes, the mythical ancestors, but Bear Claw heard stories of other heroes too, Abraham and Isaac, Jacob, Moses and Joshua, wise men and great warriors of his mother's people. He longed to tell the other boys these stories but knew they must remain secret.

Hannah Marchak's exultation grew when she saw that the predominant physical characteristics of her growing son were Jewish rather than Cheyenne. Night after night she had prayed for it, rocked and cried and prayed for revenge on the proud warrior that called himself her husband. She felt God answering her prayers when she saw the bright blue eyes of her son, the thick, curly hair that was impossible to braid and which also grew on his chest at such a rate that it could not be plucked smooth for long.

White Bull's other wives would lard the boy's head with bear's grease, hoping to straighten and flatten it. Their intentions were kind because they thought it would make it easier for him to fit in with the other children if he looked more like them. But when their backs were turned, Hannah would take him to the river and lovingly wash it all off.

In her triumphant defiance, she did not stop to consider what problems she might be creating for her son. Whether she liked it or not he must live as a Cheyenne. She was blinded by her obsession. He was always aware that he was different. He had not always borne the name of Bear Claw; before his brush with the grizzly, he was Stranger Among Us. He loved and admired his father, who treated him with equal favour alongside his full-blood son. He wanted to be a Cheyenne, but he loved his mother too and her emotional refusal to accept her life, her fierce grief, hurt him. He longed to help her, but the only consolation she would accept was his alienation from the Cheyenne community where he so much desired to belong.

Then there was his vision. As a boy on the verge of manhood, he had gone out in search of his vision, the spiritual revelation that would prepare him to be a man. After the usual purification ceremonies, he had ridden alone into the mountains near the Bighorn River and camped on a high ridge looking out over the plains. He fasted and prayed just as the old ones had instructed him. He gazed for hours into the endless sky until he felt so small, so insignificant that he was swallowed up in it.

It was perfect satisfaction, total belonging, something he had never known before, but his elation did not last long, for it was then that his vision came. Above him he could see a sword, not a sabre like the soldiers wore, or a cutlass such as he had seen in the forts on the Missouri River, but a huge, two-edged sword, a sword of fire. Tongues of flame danced along the double blade and the light from it was blinding. There was heat too; it seared his flesh, forcing him to step back. On either side of the sword was a feather, a russet brown one and a white one. They shone as brightly as the sword.

He had a desperate urge to take the feathers in his hand. He reached out for the brown one, but the sword barred his way, the flames licking around his fingers. Perhaps he was meant to take the white one- but again the sword was there, the angry tongues lapping over his hands. He had cried out in despair and then they were gone. The sky was as still, as blue and as constant as before. He did not understand immediately. He was too shaken by the vividness of his experience to think straight. He kept searching his hands for burn marks, finding it hard to believe the flames had not been real. But as he was riding home, he thought about his mother's face and then he understood.

The All-Knowing Father had told him that he

must forever live on the edge of two worlds, Cheyenne and white, never able to embrace either of them wholly. Bear Claw's vision quest had brought him no joy, but he knew he must accept it. When he returned to the village, he took his buffalo hide shield and painted on it the flaming sword and the feathers, wishing there was some way he could capture even half of their brightness, the vibrancy of their colours. He was a good artist and the distinctive design drew many eyes.

The old men asked him to explain the symbols. His friends were curious about his vision quest, but he would not open his heart to them. He could not talk about it even to his half- brother, White Arrow, who shared most of his secrets. He simply told those who inquired that they must observe the way he lived and perhaps they might understand.

He-Who-Runs-Fast would never understand. He had no time for anything that challenged the traditional Cheyenne way of life. Anything alien must be bad and his distrust of white men was paranoiac. He could never forget Bear Claw's white blood. It was a continual barrier between them, even when Bear Claw had taken his sister for his wife. The tension between them was heightened now by Bear Claw's friendship with Benjamin Barnett. It was useless to tell He-Who that Ben was a good man, who wanted only to live in peace with all men. He was white and that condemned him.

White settlers were rare in this corner of Montana in 1860. Over in the south west, towards the Rockies, the white man was beginning to make his present felt. Near the Bitter Root Mountains gold had been found in 1858. Settlers with beef herds and sheep ranchers were also infiltrating the valleys of the Bitter Root, but the Great Plains and the wooded areas along the rivers below the Missouri were still very much the preserve of the native population, penetrated only by trappers and traders. He-Who dreaded the coming of the settlers with some justification. A trickle could become a flood. He knew from experience that there were plenty of whites like Antoine La Farge, who would shoot an Indian in the back without provocation and boast about it and judged it wiser to trust none of them.

He had a grain of respect for the long knives, the soldiers because they were warriors – that was something he could understand, but the settlers puzzled and disgusted him.

He wondered how any man could stand up with pride when he spent much of his day digging in the earth, planting things, chopping wood and feeding livestock, tasks fit only for women and children. He regarded such men as weaklings without value. Bear Claw kept a protective watch over the Barnett family because he knew how quickly the scorn and anger that pulsed through He-Who-Runs -Fast could turn into violence.

His friendship with Ben had opened up a new aspect in his life, for he found that all the things he could not confide in his Cheyenne brothers, he could tell the Englishman. Ben was the only man he had spoken to concerning his vision quest and his identity confusion. He remembered then, as he leaped across a narrow ditch into the last stand of trees before he came out on to the open plain, that Ben had once suggested to him that his individuality might not be due solely to the fact that he was half white.

"A man may be born and live in a society all his life," Ben had said, "And in general he will abide by the rules of that society, adopting its habits as his own. He firmly believes that this is the right thing to do, but every so often he will see something that he cannot condone- an injustice- a code of behaviour, which is accepted quite happily by the rest of society, but which goes against his own nature, that which is essentially himself, irrespective of what influences work on him from outside. His soul -if you like- will not bear it. Who is to say Bear Claw that the centre of yourself would have been any different if you were pure blood Cheyenne?

Don't be too ready to lay the blame or the credit on your white blood, as if there were two separate halves of you, one that behaves like a Cheyenne and one that doesn't."

Bear Claw was thinking about it now as he followed the broad track that was clearly the mark of a travois dragged through the grass. There were other tracks too, unshod Indian ponies. Only a stand of cottonwoods lay between him and the edge of the plain. A movement in the trees caught his eye and he approached more warily, but as he drew nearer, he could see birds circling, rooks and crows dropping down from the branches to the ground, then whirling back up, their wings cracking against the branches of the cottonwoods. They scattered as he reached the spot, flying out into the open sky, melting away into the azure brilliance.

He saw the travois first, the hide bundle torn open, shredded with a knife, the contents scattered around the floor and hanging on the thorn bushes. There was a piece of bright green, velvet ribbon blowing in the blackthorn. For the second time that day he was struck by colours contrasting with the white blossom. He wondered if it was a sign of some kind. He was surprised to find himself thinking of Frances Barnett's fiery auburn hair when he looked at that ribbon. He could see her wearing it as he reached out to take it from the bush. Although he would hesitate to give it to her himself, he could offer it to Ben,

It was then that he saw La Farge. The big Frenchman lay sprawled on his back, his arms thrown awkwardly behind him. He was skewered to the ground with a lance like a beetle on an entomologist's collecting board. Bear Claw recognised the weapon as the lance of He-Who-Runs-Fast. Clearly, he had tried to draw it from the body, but the haft had snapped off high up, leaving most of it protruding still. That would not please his wife's brother thought Bear Claw. It was his favourite war lance.

La Farge had been scalped, neatly, economically and the raw circle on his skull dribbled blood into his open eyes and made garish red stripes in his beard. Bear Claw dragged what was left of the hide wrap from the travois and spread it over the body. He unleashed the travois poles, sharpening the ends of two of them with his knife and used them to peg the hide down at two corners. He had no respect for Antoine La Farge while he lived, but he knew that the whites abhorred the notion of leaving a body to be picked clean by the crows.

The sight of the dead trapper had taken his mind off the ribbon on the bushes, but now as he set off for the village, he took it gently from the flowers and tucked it inside his shirt. As he did so he thought how close Benjamin Barnett had come to suffering this fate instead of La Farge. The thought sickened him and he began to run to free his mind from it. Running always exhilarated him. He was thick-set and powerful, but light stepping. He covered the mile to the village in about six minutes, feeling the air hot against his skin as the sun rose higher over the treeless plain.

The Cheyenne village lay tucked behind a bluff, taking advantage of the protection from both wind and sun that the grassy ridge afforded.

Forty tepees were pitched in a rough circle, though not evenly spaced but in little groups of varying numbers. Bear Claw could hear the sound of keening before he climbed over the bluff to look down on the village. It was the thin, high wail of mourning women, piercing the still air, hanging on the heat haze. The soft pad of his moccasins seemed like thunder in his ears as he wove his way through the tepees. A crowd was gathered outside a large tepee decorated with red circles and yellow lightning symbols, the tepee of Man-Who-Cannot-Bend -His-Arm. The warrior's wife was sitting under the open flap of the tepee slicing off her long hair with a knife. Lumps of hair lay in her lap, on her shoulders and scattered over the floor around her, shiny black symbols of grief.

Now Bear Claw knew who had been murdered on Cottonwood Creek. He groaned aloud. Man-Who-Cannot-Bend-His-Arm was a generous man, much respected in the band. Wise and level-headed he could always be counted on as a friend. He was a loss indeed.

His wife, Blue Dress, continued her public display of mourning, criss-crossing the point of a knife across her forearms, causing thin rivulets of blood to start up, wailing and rocking as she did so. Bear Claw felt great pity for her, for he knew how much she loved her husband. He was He-Who-Runs-Fast's uncle and when Bear Claw had married into the family, the uncle had been very good to him, welcoming him warmly to his kin. Blue dress had been friendly too. She had given his wife, Crying Wind, many fine gifts on their wedding day. She was like a second mother to her.

She had comforted Bear Claw as best she could when Crying Wind had died in the terrible measles epidemic that had ravaged the band four years past. Even though her own brother had died, she had thought of others.

She had given Bear Claw her finest buffalo robe to wrap his wife's body in for her final resting place. Now she sat in the dust covered in drifting hair and blood. He wanted to go to her, but it was not the Cheyenne way to comfort a woman before her public mourning was finished.

He-Who-Runs-Fast was attracting much of the attention of the crowd to himself as he recounted the story of the events of the morning. In his hand he held La Farge's scalp. His face was animated as he talked, his black liquid eyes darting and shifting over the faces of his audience.

His rage had been somewhat abated by his killing of the Frenchman, but he was still very excited. Bear Claw had known him since boyhood yet there were times when the savage vitality of the man still took him by surprise. Beyond him stood Crow Dog, backing up his cousin's statements, while he kept guard over the goods they had looted from La Farge's pack, including the whisky-from the look of Crow Dog he had already sampled it. He was a gaunt man with a large frame, his face scarred by smallpox. He was usually taciturn and slow to react, but now he was as loquacious as his cousin, his face high coloured and hot.

Bear Claw pushed his way through until he stood in front of He-Who-Runs-Fast. His wife's brother turned to him, his face hostile and accusing.

"I have heard what happened today," Bear Claw said quietly, "I share your grief for the death of your uncle. When I married Crying Wind, he became my kin and we had great respect for each other. I loved him. The whole band will miss his wisdom and kindness."

The reply was almost a snarl. "He does not need your testimony to his character. We all know what a good man he was, but his goodness did not save him. He was shot in the back. He wanted no trouble, so when the trapper insulted him, he rode away. Because he was a man of honour he never once believed he would be shot in the back."

"How do you know this?"

"The trapper told us," Crow Dog interposed, leaning forward over his cousin's shoulder, "We held a knife at his throat and made him tell us the truth. He screamed and cried like a baby."

He grinned with satisfaction and Bear Claw could smell the whisky on his breath from where he stood.

"When I heard the truth, I killed him," He-Who-Runs-Fast announced to the crowd, who murmured approval. "I am not slow to avenge my kin."

"But why did he shoot him?" Bear Claw was puzzled. "What did they argue about?"

"Does a white trapper need reasons to murder an Indian? La Farge was like a rattlesnake."

A voice at Bear Claw's side said, "Man-Who-Cannot-Bend-His -Arm was carrying pelts, good ones, beaver, fox, ermine. The Frenchman stole them."

Bear Claw turned to see his brother, White Arrow, standing beside him.

"Now the whole thing makes more sense. So in return He-Who, you and Crow Dog looted a dead man's bundle."

"He won't need it anymore," guffawed Crow Dog.

Even as he spoke Bear Claw remembered the green ribbon inside his shirt and felt for it. It was still there. He too had acquired something from that bundle. He strode past Crow Dog to look at the pile of goods, axes, blankets, jewellery and ribbons.

"The Cheyenne don't need these. When did we become so poor that we needed to rob a dead man?"

He knew full well that the taking of trophies was a common practice, acceptable to the rest of the village, but he could not resist the urge to bait these two men, who were so pleased with themselves, as if they had done some brave deed. He-Who-Runs-Fast grasped Bear Claw's forearm so tightly that his nails dug into the flesh.

"Are you so sure that you know what the Cheyenne needs?" he hissed, his eyes two narrow, black slits. They contrasted markedly with Bear Claw's blue eyes that were now wide with indignation. He could not miss the inference.

"I am a Cheyenne," he said simply.

"Your father was, but what about your mother eh? She would have known about all these trifles wouldn't she, because her father was a filthy white pedlar."

Bear Claw tore himself away from the man's grasp, struggling to hold his temper. They had been through this so many times before. Every time He-Who lost control of himself he hurled insults at him, reminding him that his blood was a stain on the tribe. It was so familiar to him that Bear Claw wondered why it never ceased to sting him. He despaired of ever becoming immune to it. He turned his back on the sneering He -Who.

The crowd was growing excited, arguments breaking out, jostling and pushing. Bear Claw snatched up a jar of whisky, showing it to White Arrow, who shook his head sadly. Grunting, Crow Dog grabbed for it, but Bear Claw jumped back and the big Cheyenne almost stumbled over.

"Look," Bear Claw shouted to the crowd, "Look

what He-Who-Runs-Fast has brought back for you. Poison to burn your throats, rot your guts, destroy your senses and he says I do not know what the Cheyenne needs. I know what he does not need, this stuff."

So saying, he smashed the two-gallon jar on the ground. Crow Dog and He-Who leaped back as the glass shattered, splinters flying in all directions. Before they could gather their thoughts, Bear Claw and White Arrow were breaking up the remaining five jars. The earth wreaked and smoked with adulterated whisky. If the glass had not prevented him, Crow Dog would have thrown himself on the floor and licked some of it up. His distress was extreme.

He-Who-Runs-Fast pulled his knife from his belt. White Arrow saw the blade flash, reflecting off the last of the jars as he hurled it to the ground. He exchanged a glance with his brother.

"You have always tried to make me look a fool in front of everyone," He-Who was screaming, "Well this time you have gone too far."

"Put your knife away. I will not be provoked. You would like that wouldn't you? Well, I will not play your game- just as Ben would not play it this morning. He is never going to give you an excuse to kill him, so just stay away. Why did you go down there? You know Ben would not kill anyone from our village."

"My uncle was killed by a bullet from a white man's rifle. Why should I not suspect this man you call your friend?"

"Because Ben Barnett would never shoot a man in

the back. Your hate blinds you to all reason."

The crowd was in an uproar now, as the two men stood just a few inches apart, each daring the other to make the next move. But that move did not come. A man stepped between them, pushing them apart. He stabbed a lance down into the ground and it quivered between them. The handle of the lance ended in a carved crook of wood and it was wrapped down as far as the point with otter skin. Long strips of fur hung from the handle with pendants of eagle feathers swinging from them.

No man carried such a lance except Burning Fire, the head chief of the Elk Society. He was the principal warrior of the band, the leader of their military society. He seized He-Who by one of his long braids and with the other hand he took hold of Bear Claw's curly hair.

"What do you fools think you are doing, brawling and quarrelling in front of a grieving woman? Have you forgotten that your kinsman is dead and we should be mourning him? You insult his name to behave in this way right outside his tepee. We will discuss this quarrel at a more appropriate time. I should bang your heads together. If Lone Wolf were not lying sick in his tepee, he would be here teaching you some good manners. You behave like half grown boys, not warriors. Clear off all of you," he turned on the crowd fiercely, "Get back to your tepees and prepare yourselves. We shall soon be taking Man-Who-Cannot-Bend-His-Arm on his last journey. Go quickly, or I will call out the Elks to beat you back to your lodges."

He did not need to tell them again. The authority of Burning Fire was not challenged. Lone Wolf was their spiritual leader, their father, but Burning Fire led the warriors into battle. He policed the village with his Elk Society members and few men dared cross him. The crowd melted away, drifting back in groups to their lodges to discuss the situation amongst themselves.

Burning Fire pulled up his lance. He jerked it in the direction of Blue Dress. "She is a better Cheyenne than all of us. She does not forget her duty."

Through all the shouting, the commotion, the smashing of glass, Blue Dress had continued to keen, swaying rhythmically, trance-like. Her clothes were soaked now with blood from her self-mutilations, but she seemed to feel no pain except the pain of her loss. Bear Claw was ashamed.

"You're right Burning Fire, we were insulting Blue Dress and her husband's memory. That is the last thing I want to do. Come on White Arrow, we must go and prepare."

"This wound between us will not be healed easily," his wife's brother shouted after him. "One day your white friends will get you into bad trouble. I only hope it doesn't bring trouble for all of us."

After Bear Claw had presented the deer to his womenfolk, he sat for some time outside his lodge with White Arrow beside him. His half-brother allowed him his thoughts for a while. He sat cross-legged, regarding the porcupine quill patterns on his moccasins.

White Arrow was a small man, slight and sinewy. He was three years younger than Bear Claw. His face was amiable and he smiled a great deal. His bright, brown eyes watched everything with perception. He was very proud of his large, hooked nose that seemed almost too big for the rest of him. He regarded it as curved and handsome, a great source of admiration amongst the women. His dream vision had told him he must use only white-feathered arrows. If it had not been for that, he might have been named Big Nose rather than White Arrow. He watched his brother's face, studied the way his eyes darkened through several shades as he brooded, then he said suddenly,

"He-Who-Runs-Fast won't provide for Blue Dress. He has announced to everybody that he has enough dependent relatives and can't take on another one."

Bear Claw looked up. "But he is her closest kin now. She has no brothers, no children. It is his duty to provide for her. He is the one who is always sounding off about the Cheyenne way. Let him walk it. Blue Dress is proud. If she thinks he doesn't want her, she will isolate herself from the camp and mourn alone. I hate to see a woman do that."

White Arrow nodded. "I agree with you, but He-Who does have two wives and eight children in his lodge. I think he has some excuse. No one in the village will blame him for refusing."

"Well, I blame him and what is more, I will shame him." Bear Claw jumped to his feet. "I will provide for her." His face clouded when White Arrow began to laugh. "Why are you laughing?"

"I knew it would come to this. It always does. One day your heart will prove too big for your hunting skills and then what will all those women do? You know what they say in the village, that before long you will have another name, Lives with the Women."

Bear Claw smiled and looked back over his shoulder into the tepee, where Painted Shawl was sitting cross-legged stitching a parfleche. She smiled back at him. When Crying Wind had died, her sister Painted Shawl was already a widow with two daughters. Bear Claw had taken her into his lodge. Many people thought he would soon take her for his wife, but it did not happen. He was a father to the girls and loved them as if they were his own, but he could not make love to his wife's sister; they were too much alike and it hurt him.

He was regarded strange for this outlook for amongst the Cheyenne the sisters of his wife were always seen as potential second wives for a warrior. The family ties had been cemented already. The restricted and circumspect behaviour expected of a young man courting his first wife need not apply if he wished to marry his wife's sister.

But Painted Shawl and her daughters were not the only women under Bear Claw's protection. When a Cheyenne man married, he set up his new tepee in close proximity to his wife's mother. Little kinship groups formed as daughters married and brought their husbands to live around their mother's lodge. Tall Woman had three daughters, Crying Wind, Painted Shawl and Singing Linnet, the youngest, who was born with a twisted leg and deformed spine that bent her double. She was ashamed of her affliction, envying her beautiful sisters and her athletic brother, He-Who-Runs-Fast. She hated to be seen and rarely left her mother's lodge. No brave came to offer ponies for her; she could not expect it. She devoted herself to her mother and felt she was some comfort to her when her father died in battle.

Bear Claw found himself the only man left in this group of lodges. His mother-in-law was proud of him for his sense of responsibility and did not lose her equilibrium when he broke taboo to speak to her. A Cheyenne never spoke to his wife's mother. He respected her, provided her lodge with meat but he did not communicate with her and must never be alone with her. He was even obliged to cover his head in her presence. Bear Claw however had never seen the sense in this custom. He admired Tall Woman for her wisdom and the way she cared for her daughters. It seemed an onerous burden to him, never being able to speak to her. It was like Ben had said- his soul would not bear it.

He had tried to obey the taboo at first, certainly while his wife was still alive. He would bring food to Tall Woman's lodge, leave it outside and retreat in respectful silence. Singing Linnet would appear to take the food inside while he sat in the opening of his tepee irritated and dissatisfied. He went on doing this for a year after Crying Wind died, then one day he could bear it no longer. He had brought a brace of prairie hens, young and succulent, but this day instead of leaving his offering outside, he pushed back the tent flap and strolled in.

Once he was inside his resolve almost failed him, for Singing Linnet was hiding behind her mother, her eyes wide and Tall Woman's face made him feel he was on the verge of doing something very dangerous. But he had gone too far now for retreat.

"Mother," he said, aware that his voice was not as even as he would have wished, "I hope you and Singing Linnet enjoy your supper."

Tall Woman remained calm. She did not reply, but inclined her head very slightly in acknowledgement. Then he fled from the lodge, afraid of his own temerity, but from that day on he spoke freely to her. She did not answer, but she showed no hostility towards him and told no one about his taboo breaking, taking particular care that her son, He-Who -Runs- Fast did not hear about it. She knew what trouble that would cause.

She was grateful to Bear Claw when he agreed to add another woman without support to his little band. Shadow That Dances was Tall Woman's girlhood friend, but she had no kinship ties with Bear Claw. He had no duty to help her, never-the-less her lodge was set up next to Tall Woman's. Bear Claw never forgot how excited he felt when he saw his wife's mother coming from her tepee towards him. She was carrying a pair of exquisitely worked moccasin leggings, her gift to him for his courtesy to her old friend. For a moment he almost believed she would speak. He held his breath, watching her hesitate and was disappointed when she laid her gift gently on the floor outside the tent. Perhaps he expected too much; she had said thank you plainly enough without words.

So now Bear Claw had six women to support and was about to take on a seventh. White Arrow, although he joked about it, admired his brother for his generous heart.

"If Blue Dress sets up her lodge beside yours, I will help you provide for her. My wife will complain, but I'm used to her nagging."

Bear Claw put his arm around his brother's shoulder. "Well if there is anything left over after that growing band of children of yours have had their fill, I shall be happy to accept it for Blue Dress. I will risk Dawn Singer nagging at me too."

"Blue Dress might not come." White Arrow added as a sudden afterthought.

"She will come. But we had better get moving if we want to find some gifts to accompany my kinsman on his last journey."

In a Cheyenne village the dead were always disposed of quickly. They could not take the risk of the dead one's spirit ranging about the village, bringing bad luck. Man-Who-Cannot-Bend-His-Arm was dressed in full war dress with all his ornaments and personal decoration. He was then wrapped in two buffalo hides, bound tightly around him and taken out on a travois a few miles from the village to Raven Bluffs. They laid him in a hollow in the rocks and covered him with boulders to keep him safe from the depredation of wolves and coyotes. His nephews arranged his three lances in a stark tepee shape frame in front of the grave, on which they hung his war shield, his bow and quiver, his eagle feathers and his medicine bundle. Lone Wolf, was too ill to rise from his sick bed to honour his friend on his death journey, so Burning Fire and all the dead man's closest kin, laid gifts around the circumference of the three lances, gifts that symbolised the qualities of the man while he lived.

They recounted his deeds in song. The medicine man danced the prayers that would help release his spirit and send it on the journey to the realms of the All Father.

It was evening before Lone Wolf's band of Cheyenne returned to their village. All through the ceremony, He-Who had shown no sign that he and his sister's husband were at odds, but when they reached the village, he spurred his horse away from the main party and went to his lodge to avoid any contact with Bear Claw. It was as if he blamed him for the death of their uncle.

Bear Claw lay in his lodge that night with the tent flap open, watching the stars in a black sky. The air was very still. Apart from the call of a distant coyote, all he could hear was the gentle breathing of Painted Shawl and her daughters sleeping at the far end of the lodge. The air was cold, but he did not feel it. He fancied he saw trails of silver spread across the sky like a spider's web. He opened his clenched fist and in the dark, he could just trace the outline of the thing he held there. It was a golden star with six points, hanging from a delicate gold chain. He kept it in his medicine bundle and it was one of his most precious possessions. His mother was wearing it when she was captured. The Cheyenne had not taken it from her for they sensed it was a spiritual symbol of some kind, perhaps strong magic. When she was dying, she had pressed it into her son's hand, urging him to take care of it, to honour it and not forget the beliefs of his mother's people. He did not forget. There in his lodge, under the eyes of the stars, he repeated the prayers she had taught him, murmuring a lone kaddish for the soul of his uncle, squeezing the Star of David until the points pierced the flesh of his palm.

CHAPTER TWO

The sun was slipping down behind the trees. Fran Barnett liked to watch it disappear until there was only a vague, gold reflection where the fire had been only moments before. The trees were now bathed in pink light streaked with pale gold and a white dove flying up into the glory of it was suddenly transformed into an exotic, multi-coloured bird.

"Look Ben, the sunset is wonderful," she turned to her husband to find he was sleeping soundly in the rocking chair beside the fire, Sarah was asleep on his lap, her face pressed close into her father's chest. He had done a good job rocking his daughter to sleep-too good.

Frances smiled. She could understand why Ben was tired. He had been up all night guarding the stock from the depredations of that persistent wolverine. He had spent the day hunting, digging a drainage trench around a recently cleared patch of land, planting vegetables and just before tea he was up on the barn roof repairing the damage done by a heavy storm the week before. It was little wonder that when he settled for a moment in a comfortable chair, he fell asleep.

She lifted Sarah carefully from his lap and lay her down in her wooden cot, tucking her in with a bright coloured blanket, patterned with Indian designs, a gift from the women of Bear Claw's lodge. Then she picked up the book that had slipped from Ben's hand when he had dropped off to sleep. It lay on the floor open at a page decorated with leaf tendrils all along the edges, a book of sonnets. She had given it to him for an engagement present and had been well satisfied with his genuine pleasure in the gift. The book was open at a page where Dante's sonnet "For certain he hath seen all perfectness, who among other ladies has seen mine" was printed in curling italic.

She remembered only too well that evening at Lady Hartford's literary soiree, when Benjamin was asked to recite. He spoke verse beautifully and was always in demand at these gatherings. She had only met him twice but she had already convinced herself that she was in love with him and was in agony all week in case anything should prevent him from attending the soiree. He came. She watched him, charming, well-mannered, yet rather aloof and reticent. There was an air of sadness about him that attracted her. He smiled at her from the other side of the room, but he did not come across to her and she was disappointed. She could not have imagined that when he was called upon to recite, he would speak this sonnet of Dante's directly to her, as if there was no other person in the room.

"From all her acts such lovely graces flow,
That truly one may never think of her,
Without passion of exceeding love."

From that moment on there was to be no other man in the world for her but Benjamin Barnett. She recalled as she put the book of sonnets back on the shelf under the larder, that poetry had brought about their very first meeting. She had heard her parents talk much about Andrew Barnett's youngest son, about his achievement's at Cambridge, his fine mind and what a pity it was that such an amiable young gentleman was so restless and unsettled. He was then twenty-eight, high time he chose himself a wife; that would help him settle.

She was eighteen, the middle one of three daughters and easily the most beautiful. She had decided that she would not like Mr. Benjamin Barnett. He was bound to be insufferable if he was so clever and inclined to force his opinions on everybody. She had changed her mind very swiftly when they went to dinner at the Barnett's. He was the handsomest man in the room and his manner, far from being conceited and aggressive, was unassuming, gentle.

She often wrote poetry, modest little verses in the style taught her by her governess, but her father was inordinately proud of them. He had shown some of them to Benjamin, unaware of her acute embarrassment. Ben had read them with polite interest, complimented her on them and discussed poetry with her as if her opinion mattered to him. She had never felt so flattered, so intellectually valued in her life. He even asked if he might read some more of her verse someday and she knew he meant it.

She laughed as she thought about it now, her hands absently tidying the books on the shelf- Homer, Virgil, Shakespeare, Wordsworth, Shelley, Keats, great tomes of history and some novels. He had brought some from England, but most of them he acquired during their two years in Boston.

She was sure there could not be another log cabin in Montana with five shelves of books like these. This led on to another thought, one that had begun to nag her. It had crept up on her in an insidious, quiet way and now it would not leave her; why a man with an intellect like Ben's should choose a life like this one, isolated from society and filled with such back-breaking manual labour.

She wondered why he did not miss his parent's handsome country house in the verdant Wylie Valley in Wiltshire in the way she missed the town house in Warminster where she was brought up. She had not expected to miss her parents so much and her sisters' endless chatter. Ben wrote to his mother regularly but he rarely spoke about his previous life. He knew his eldest brother Samuel was interested in maintaining the family estate that he would inherit one day, so his father was well-supported.

Standing beside the chair, she stroked his hair, smoothing it tidy. It had grown long and was permanently dishevelled, lacking shape or style. It used to be so well-groomed, tapering neatly at the back of his neck. Now it irritated her to see him clawing it back with his fingers as if he had never been introduced to a comb in his life.

Just after they had arrived in Montana, he had tried to grow a beard, but this she would not countenance. Her opposition was so fierce that he abandoned the idea and shaved dutifully every morning. He was still handsome though she thought as she sat down at his feet, resting her head against his leg. He was leaner and more tanned but very handsome. She repeated the thought to herself because she was afraid she might prefer the well-dressed, elegant country gentleman that she had fallen in love with at eighteen.

She reached out, tracing her finger lightly along his full lower lip. When she had asked her sister Beatrice what she thought of Benjamin, Beatrice had replied, "he has very fine teeth," as if he had been a horse. But then Beatrice related most things to horses. She was right however; Ben did have good teeth. His face was irradiated when he smiled.

She was there again, back in the past. Why did she do it so much? She got up and walked restlessly around the room, wishing Ben would wake and talk to her, but at the same time not wanting to disturb his sleep. It was not that he neglected her. She could never accuse him of that. He discussed all his decisions and plans with her and respected her opinions.

When they made love, he was still as intense as he had always been. She felt no physical alienation.

She reminded herself that she had known full well what kind of life she was going to when she agreed to leave Boston. She had been dismayed at first by the small size and spartan conditions of the cabin, but after Ben had extended it and it was furnished more comfortably, she began to take a pride in keeping it clean and tidy and how she taught herself to cook on the iron stove. She was strong and active, quite able to help her husband with some of the outdoor tasks. The revelation that she could cope without servants was exciting to her.

The one duty she flatly refused to do however was to empty the bucket from the privy, a wooden cubicle just behind the barn. To be fair to him, Ben never expected her to do so. He dug the contents into the dung heap on the edge of the woods.

But her determination to be the perfect pioneering wife was weakening. The birth of Sarah had given her life a different perspective and turned her thoughts back towards Boston. She wanted to hear gossip, show off her daughter to her cousin and his wife, to walk down a street with Sarah free from the fear of cougar, grizzly or Indian. She had a childlike craving to be admired. It was more than just a shallow desire for new, fashionable clothes, she hoped she was above that and yet the more she tried to define precisely how she felt, the more it eluded her.

She loved music deeply. In Boston they had gone to concerts at least twice a week. She missed her piano; that would have been some comfort at least. Ben played his home-made flute, but there were limits to what he could play on a reed with six holes bored in it.

He seemed happy. She did not want to take that away from him, but she was aggrieved that he did not appear to perceive that she was not. His intellectual and spiritual resources were greater than hers; he did not need society. She would never understand how great a relief he felt to be free of it. Besides he could move around more freely than she could and he had his friendship with Bear Claw. She longed for some female company at times. Bear Claw's womenfolk were kind and friendly, but they spoke no English, remaining strange and alien to her. She had a fear of the Cheyenne that she could not conquer, but would not confess that to Ben.

The gardens and parks, the elegant houses and clean streets of Boston were in front of her now. They passed between her and Ben's face, blocking her view. Perhaps he would agree to her going back for a few months so that her relatives could see Sarah. But how could she be certain that once she was there, she would want to come back to Montana? She could not contemplate any kind of life without Ben, but now the doubt had been formulated in her mind, it was free to haunt her and she could not trust herself.

Just then she caught sight of a shadow flitting across the veranda. She heard no footsteps, but she was aware of someone standing in the doorway and she turned slowly, half afraid. Bear Claw stood there, silent, watchful. Her release of breath was audible and she was pale.

"I am sorry if I frighten you. A Cheyenne learns from childhood to make no noise. It is safer to be soft-footed." He glanced across at Ben. "Is Ben well?"

"Oh yes, he's just tired out that's all. He didn't get any sleep at all last night. That wolverine just would not go away. I wish it would leave us alone."

Bear Claw nodded. He had a bad feeling about that wolverine. Ben might deny it, but it could be a bad omen.

"Did you want to speak to Benjamin?" Fran asked

"Yes, but I will not wake him. He needs to sleep. I will come back later."

He hesitated for a moment, feeling in his pocket

for that piece of green velvet ribbon. It would be easy to give it to her now, but what would he say? How could he explain why he wanted her to wear it? He was afraid she would misunderstand. It was better that Ben should do it.

Barnett stirred, murmuring in his sleep as if something troublesome stalked his dreams. Frances began to stroke his hair again, light, soothing movements. She was pleased to demonstrate her affection for her husband. It assuaged her conscience a little over her yearning for Boston.

"I think the wolverine is in his dreams," said Bear Claw softly. "I will go now- come later."

He was gone as silently as he had come, slipping through the lengthening shadows of the trees. He liked the dusk, the shifting, mysterious quality of it. Sometimes he felt he could touch it with his fingers.

He walked deep into the woods, following some half-defaced tracks that looked very like a wolverine's. If he could find and kill it, life would be easier for his friends at the cabin. He was convinced now that bad medicine was involved. The darker the woods became, the more he felt it.

He walked for half an hour until the tracks just disappeared. It was strange; they just stopped. He looked at the bark around the bases of the trees nearby for claw marks, but there was no evidence that any animal had climbed up into them. His fear grew and he decided to go back to the Barnett's cabin.

As he turned, a sound froze him in his tracks. He crouched, listening, ready to move in any direction, his body tense and evenly balanced. The sound reached him again. This was no supernatural creature; it was a man's voice, but it seemed to coming up from the ground. He moved stealthily towards the sound and as he got closer, he could distinguish the words.

They startled him so much that he thought for a moment he was caught up in some vision, for the voice was speaking his mother's tongue. Since she had died, he had not heard it spoken and he had feared he would forget what he had learned through lack of use. Now he heard it rising up from the earth.

"God help me," the voice was muttering, "How am I going to get out of here? Please help me."

Bear Claw stopped on the edge of an animal pit, the kind that both trapper and Indian dug to catch larger game, particularly the grizzly. It had been concealed with moss, twigs and leaf fronds for they lay scattered around the sides. At the bottom of the pit was a man. His leg was twisted underneath him and even in the fading light, Bear Claw could see that it was badly swollen. He was scraping weakly at the sides of the pit, trying to pull himself to his feet, but succeeding only in bringing showers of earth down into his face. His blond hair gleamed white in the half-light and he was bathed in sweat. At that moment he gave up his fevered scraping to lean back against the wall of the pit. Only then did he see Bear Claw. He twisted, grunting in pain as he tried to pull his pistol from his belt. Bear Claw held up his hand in the universal sign of peace.

"No," he said in German, "Don't be afraid. I will not hurt you. I will try to help you."

If Bear Claw had been amazed a moment before, it was nothing to the shock of the man in the pit. He wondered if he was running a fever and was already in delirium. There above him was the strangest looking Indian he had ever seen, with a mass of curly hair down to his shoulders. It was bound with a wide, beaded band decorated with one eagle feather. Painted bone earrings hung from his ears. Under his buckskin waistcoat he had a scarlet linen trade shirt, but instead of trousers he wore a breach clout with moccasin leggings that came up to his knees, leaving his thighs bare- and this apparition was speaking to him in German. He began to laugh hysterically, half crying. He was dying in this hole, plagued by hallucinations.

"I'm going crazy," he muttered. "Crazy!"

"No," the apparition spoke again, "I am not in your imagination. I am here. I am a Cheyenne from the band of Lone Wolf, but my mother came

from your country long ago. She taught me to speak your language. It is good to hear it again after so long. I hope you understand me – I have to search for words."

The man was sobbing now, his face buried in his hands. He had been down that pit for three days and nights, with no food or water, his broken leg swelling more each day. He was afraid to shout too loudly in case it attracted some predatory animal. At night he heard them prowling around the top of the pit, yellow, unblinking eyes in the darkness and snuffling, panting noises that made his flesh creep. The knowledge that this German speaking Indian was a reality was too much for him. Any self-control he had left deserted him.

Bear Claw waited for a while, then he called,

"You have no horse, no equipment?"

Fighting back the tears of relief that caught in his throat and choked him, the German replied that his horse was frightened off by some wild animal and he was looking for it when he fell into the pit.

"Wolverine," thought Bear Claw, "He truly is bad medicine."

"My leg is broken. I can't stand. I don't see how you are going to get me out of here."

Bear Claw was working on it. He was unwinding the length of rope that was bound around his arrow quiver.

He tossed one end of the rope down to the injured man, fearing it might not reach. They were lucky; it proved just long enough.

"Tie that around your waist and hold on tight."

It was hard work pulling him up. He was a big man, over six feet tall and weighing at least twelve stone. It was clear that the pain in his leg was agonizing as he banged against the side of the pit. When he finally lay on the grass at the top, both men were fighting for breath.

"I didn't think you could do it," the German gasped. "I never thought I would be thanking an Indian for saving my life, thought they'd be more likely to take my hair. Let me shake your hand Indian."

He stretched out his hand, stained with earth. His nails were chipped and broken where he had been trying to claw himself up.

"My name is Lothar Klein."

The Cheyenne gripped his hand. "I am Bear Claw."

He was surprised at the way he churned over inside, feeling a strange excitement. This was the first time he had ever met anyone from his mother's country. But this was not the time for talking, the German was in great pain and his leg needed prompt attention. Bear Claw pondered what to do. It would not be safe to take him back to the village, not in the present circumstances, besides it was too far. The Barnett's cabin was the most logical place to go.

"This will hurt," he warned him, as he began to haul Klein to his feet. Once he had him in an upright position, he jack-knifed him over his shoulder like a sack of meal and set off at a jog trot towards the Barnett's.

❀

Frances Barnett had just lit the lamps. The soft glow of the oil lamps always heartened her. She liked the moment when the shutters were pulled together and the cabin door was barred. At dusk the trees were gloomy and frightening to her, but when it was dark everything could be shut out. Ben was still sleeping, more fitfully now, turning in the chair uncomfortably. She had felt his forehead, just to make sure he was not feverish, but it seemed cool enough. The first year they had come there, just after he had finished extending the cabin, Ben had a bout of fever. He was very ill for several days and she was terrified of that happening again.

She had shut the stock in for the night and now she whistled for Caesar. The dog padded across the veranda into the house and lay down beside Ben's chair. Now she could bar the door. The plank of wood that barred the door stood on end against the wall. It was five feet long and six inches thick, unwieldy for a woman as small as Fran to handle. It slipped out of her grasp as she lowered it into the door brackets and fell into place with a thud. Ben woke instantly, shuddering with the suddenness of it, sitting up in the chair, his face startled and uncomprehending. Sarah in her cot wriggled and fretted for a moment.

"Oh Benjamin, I'm sorry. That bar is rather heavy for me. It slipped from my hand."

Ben passed a hand across his face, as he tried to gather his thoughts. He had been dreaming, confusing, surrealistic dreams and the atmosphere still hung around him.

"Surely it's not dark already? What time is it?"

He reached into the top pocket of his shirt, pulling out a watch. The hands pointed to 8.30. It was a magnificent watch in a gold case, inlaid with coloured enamels. On the back of the case was an inscription, "To our dear son Benjamin from his loving parents." They had given it to him the day before he sailed to America. He studied the curling script.

"I intended to write to mother this evening. I must have been asleep for hours. Why didn't you wake me Frannie?"

"There was no need. I have done everything outside. You were so tired, I thought it would do you good to sleep."

She was leaning forward poking the fire and Ben was struck by the similarity between the colour of the flames and her hair. She wore it knotted at the nape of her neck in a thick chignon. It amused him because she was so particular about styling the front of her hair. She had brought some curling tongs with her from Boston and the fringe at her forehead and all the stray tendrils of hair that fell around her ears were a mass of delicate curls.

"You do feel well Ben, don't you?" she was saying as she jabbed away with the poker into a smouldering log, causing a spurt of flame and sparks to fly up the chimney. "You were so exhausted tonight that I was a little afraid that you might be sickening for something."

"I've never felt better in my life." He caught hold of his wife around her waist and sat her down on his lap. "But if I felt half as well as you look, I would live for ever. How do you manage to be a hard-working homesteader's wife and still look so beautiful?"

He played with the crystal earring in her ear, swinging it with his finger. She was still only twenty-four and seemed younger to him then, as she put her head against his shoulder. She had regained her figure quickly after the birth of Sarah; she was as slender and supple as ever. He deftly pulled out the three pins that held her hair in place and a cascade of sweet-smelling auburn fell all over him. Taking some strands of it in his fingers, he pressed it to his lips, brushing his mouth down the length of it in a slow, sensuous movement until he reached her shoulder, then he kissed her throat.

"Ben," she was stroking his cheek with the back of her fingers, "I really do think you have been working too hard this spring-that great irrigation ditch around the top land. It really was work enough for three men."

"You mean with my advancing years I ought to take it easy."

"Advancing years, rubbish. You're only thirty-four. What I mean is I think you should take a holiday."

He laughed in genuine amusement. "Holiday! What sort of holiday did you have in mind the Right Honourable Mrs Barnett?"

He often teased her about her right to a title. Here, the very irrelevancy of the fact that her father was a baronet was a pleasure to him. He smoothed his hand down her thigh, feeling the flesh under the crisp calico of her dress. To his surprise she pulled away from him and began to walk about in front of the fireplace.

"No Benjamin, I am serious now. I think we ought to take a trip to Boston to see Henry and Jane. Every time they write, they say how much they want to see Sarah and how much they miss us."

Ben stretched his long arms and yawned. He was still smiling.

"Well if they are so very eager, why don't they make a trip out here to see us? I can just imagine that. The trip out from Baker alone would just about finish off your cousin Henry. My dear boy I am utterly debilitated and do you seriously mean to tell me that there is no plumbing." He mimicked Henry's languid drawl with mischievous accuracy. "It wouldn't hurt Jane to hoe a row of potatoes though."

"Oh stop it! You won't even consider the suggestion will you? It is all a joke to you. Well, it isn't to me. It would do us both the world of good to go to Boston, only for a couple of weeks, not long."

He was taken aback by her earnestness, bordering on anger.

"But Fran my dear, are you seriously suggesting that I leave freshly planted crops to look after themselves while we go junketing in Boston. I suppose you think the animals could forage for themselves till we get back. This is not the kind of life you can choose to abandon at will. You knew that when you agreed to come here."

"I came here because you wanted it." She was twisting her hair around her hands.

"And you don't want it?"

"Yes of course I do, but it's only natural that I should want to see my relations sometimes."

He could not deny that; perhaps he was asking too much of her to live this enclosed life without some occasional relief.

"Well, would you like to go and take Sarah? I could put you on the coach at Baker or even take you up river to catch the steamboat. Sarah would love that. You could stay a few months then and eclipse all the Boston beauties."

Frances felt it again, the fear that she could not trust herself. She began to cry.

"Oh no, I don't want to go without you. I don't. I couldn't leave you on your own for all that time."

He had not expected tears. He took her in his arms in a protective way.

"Please, please don't cry Frannie. It's alright. Look, I tell you what, this weekend we will all go into Baker. If we start out early, we can spend the day there. There are probably letters for us at the post office. You can have a gossip with Mrs farmer in the general store, buy something for yourself and Sarah. Then there are those two old sweethearts who do the sewing, Miss Louisa and Miss Charlotte. You know they insisted that the next time we were in town you should take tea with them."

Frances could not help smiling in spite of herself.

"It's you they want to come to tea," she sniffed, "Not me. Ben, I do love you. I love you so very much."

"I know that, you have no need to convince me."

He was about to say more, when Caesar began to growl. It was his low, suspicious growl of warning. He stood up and edged towards the door, his head on one side, listening. Ben was listening too. Fran gripped his arm.

"There is someone out there," she said.

"Perhaps so. I had better take a look."

"Don't go outside, not without your gun."

"Fran there is no need to be so afraid. It's probably only a squirrel on the veranda"

He opened one of the shutters, peering out into the darkness. Caesar was barking now, his head pushed against the door, eager to get outside. As Ben's eyes became accustomed to the dark, he could make out a shape moving in the yard. It looked like a man carrying a pack, but as he stared harder, he could see that the pack was another man slung across his back. The outline of the carrying figure was familiar to him. He unbarred the door and reached down the lighted storm lantern that hung on the door post. Frances was taking his rifle down from over the fireplace.

"I don't think I shall need that," he said as he stepped outside, wondering why she was so nervous. She had not used to be so, not when they first came to Montana. Perhaps concern for their daughter's safety heightened her fear. He looked back at her standing with the gun in her hands, the light from the fire flickering across her face, which was strained and tight. He felt guilty and turned away, walking out into the yard, holding up the lantern. In its light he could recognise Bear Claw. The Cheyenne was feeling the weight of his burden, taking deep breaths and blowing hard in an attempt to keep up a rhythm. He was relieved to see Ben.

"Let me help you." Barnett lifted the man from Bear Claw's shoulder and between them they carried him into the house, supporting his swollen leg. He was still conscious, but only vaguely aware of what was happening around him.

"He fell down an animal pit," Bear Claw was explaining, as they lay Klein down on the bed. "His leg is broken. Ben, he comes from my mother's country. I speak to him in her language."

His eyes were shining, excited. Ben smiled, feeling the depth of his friend's pleasure.

"He was deuced lucky then that of all the people who might have found him it turned out to be you. How far have you carried him?"

"From the middle of the woods. Two miles maybe. I begin to wish for a horse."

Barnett poured a glass of water from the pitcher on the table by the bed and supporting Klein's head, he held the glass to his mouth. The German drank eagerly. It was his first drink in three days.

"Danke, danke."

"You needed it. How long were you in that pit?"

"Ah, Englishman," the German said in English, coughing and spluttering in his eagerness to drink, yet talk at the same time. "You are Englishman?"

"Yes."

"I am in England two years, in that damned pit three days, but that seems longer than my two years in England you understand!"

"I do indeed. If you were destined to fall into a pit, you couldn't have done so in a better place than in the territory of the only German speaking Cheyenne in Montana."

Klein tried to sit up, but cried out as a searing pain gripped his leg.

"We must help the leg soon," Bear Claw urged.

"Yes, better cut the boot off and try to reduce the swelling, then perhaps we can devise some kind of splint. Frances, could you get a cloth and bowl of cold water?"

There was no reply. Ben turned around to see that his wife was still standing in front of the fire, clutching the rifle, her amber eyes wide. He took the gun from her hands and repeated firmly, "Frances, cloths and water please."

She seemed to wake from a trance and hurried to find what was needed murmuring, "Yes, yes of course."

Between them they managed to cut Klein's knee-high leather boot away from his leg, although it was an awkward, painful process. The flesh was white and distended, suet-like to the touch. Cold water did not reduce the swelling markedly. Pawnee Killer, the medicine man, used particular herbs to treat swelling and Bear Claw knew that some of these herbs grew at the edge of the trees in Barnett's top-land. He raced out with a lantern and had gathered a bunch in minutes. The poultice they made from these herbs was more effective and gradually the swelling lessened to a degree. They then set the leg in wooden slats, bound in place with strips of rag. It was far from expert, but the best they could do.

Klein had slipped into semi-consciousness. Ben covered him with a blanket, shaking his head.

"I can't be sure we have done the best thing. I'm not much of a doctor."

"I think with time it will be well," said Bear Claw.

He was sitting cross-legged on the floor, rocking Sarah's cot, but studying the German closely. "The break does not feel bad to the fingers. My brother, White Arrow broke his leg like this. The break in the bone was much worse, but now he does not even limp."

He stared at Klein's face, hoping he might see something there to remind him of his mother, but there was nothing. She was raven-haired, with soft curls and dark blue eyes which glowed with intensity. He often feared that he might forget her face, that time would blur the image, but it was still as sharply defined as if she stood in front of him.

Klein was different. He had broad cheek bones, strongly angled down to the wide mouth. His pale gold hair was finely textured and silky, just beginning to thin a little at the crown of his head. His moustache was of the same quality, soft and light, trailing around the corners of his mouth.

"Ben, do you think he knows the town, Hamburg where my mother was born?"

"He may do, but don't count on it. Germany is a big country you know."

Bear Claw felt sure Klein would know it, but the man must be left to sleep now and jumping to his feet, he decided it was time he returned to the village. Ben followed him out on to the veranda.

"How did he come to fall into that pit? Have you any idea?"

Bear Claw nodded, his blue eyes troubled. "A creature frightened his horse. I think it is the wolverine." He put his hand on Barnett's arm. "Ben, I do not like it. That animal is bad, I feel it. Early this evening I come to see you, but you are asleep, so I think I will come back later. Frances says the wolverine is here all night, so I follow the tracks. In the middle of the trees the tracks stop, disappear, no signs, nothing. It is as if the wolverine goes up into the skies. I look at the trees but there are no claw marks anywhere."

"That is strange," Ben agreed, "But there must be some explanation for it. Perhaps something wiped out the tracks. Don't worry about it. I am sure it is just an ordinary, hungry wolverine with no malice in mind, except to sink his teeth into our hens. You can't blame him. It's easy meat. It is my problem; I will deal with it somehow."

Bear Claw grunted. He was unconvinced, but he did not argue. Something else came into his mind and he took from his shirt, the piece of velvet ribbon, pressing it into Ben's hand.

"What's this?"

"Ribbon for your wife. I found it." He did not reveal where. "The women of my lodge have decorations enough. Your wife has hair like fire, the ribbon will look well in it. Once when I was at Fort Benton, many years past, I see this white woman, a soldier's wife, her husband is an important man, general maybe. She wears around her neck beautiful green stones, also like fire, green fire-not like glass beads, many more times more beautiful. They seem to have many faces and burn as fiercely as the sun. Have you seen such stones Ben?"

"Yes, emeralds."

"Emeralds," Bear Claw repeated the word to himself, savouring the sound. He delighted in learning new words. "This ribbon is such a colour. You must give your wife emeralds one day."

Ben was chewing his bottom lip, thinking about his conversation with Frances that evening. He was hardly in a position to give her emeralds now. Once perhaps, but not now. His mother possessed an exquisite pair of emerald earrings. He could remember her remarking that they were perfect for Fran's colouring and that one day she should have them. He wondered if she ever would. Before this evening he would have been confident that she did not care about them anyway, but now he felt less sure.

"Well, thanks to you Bear Claw she will have emerald ribbon at least. Come back in a moment and give it to her yourself."

"No, you give it to her. I must go." -and he did.

Ben watched him disappear into the darkness before he went back into the cabin and barred the door. Caesar began to nose at the ribbon in his hand, curious about the foreign smell of it and Barnett pushed his head away playfully. Frances was watching Klein. His breathing was regular and easy enough, but his face was pallid and bathed in sweat.

"Do you think he will recover?" she asked her husband.

Ben thought there was every chance that he would.

"But look, here is a present for you," he held the ribbon out in front of her, "A present from Bear Claw. He was too shy to give it to you himself. You see, you do get admired, even here."

She took the ribbon, holding it against her cheek to feel the softness of the velvet, flattered that Bear Claw should bring her so pretty a gift. She pulled her hair together in her hands and tied the ribbon around it in a bow.

"How does it look?" She was reaching for the hand mirror on the mantlepiece.

"Beautiful," he said quietly, but he did not smile.

That night at least two men in Montana could

get no sleep. Bear Claw lay in his lodge rehearsing all the German he knew, murmuring the pronunciation to himself, recalling the inflections of his mother's tongue. There was so much that he wanted to ask Lothar Klein and he wished to ask it in German. It was only right that he should; he could not wait for the morning.

Benjamin Barnett was passing a second successive sleepless night. This time there was no wolverine to blame. He and Fran had made a bed up for themselves on the floor, having surrendered theirs to the injured Klein. Ben lay in the darkened cabin, watching the last embers of the fire die away. Caesar's bony frame was pressing against his side. Francis was in his arms, her body warm against his. She had fallen asleep quickly, tired by the emotions of the evening. He rested his head against the soft whiteness of her shoulder, trying to forget the look on her face as she stood there clasping that gun, the strain, the fear he had seen. He was more depressed than he had ever been since they came to Montana. He too was eager for the morning.

Chapter Three

White Arrow squatted on the floor outside his lodge painting himself, daubing long bands of grey paint down his bare chest. He wore nothing but a breechclout and moccasins. The paint was drying on his face already. He looked as if he had fallen face down in a chalk stream. The bowl of grease paint smelt rancid. Bear Claw was used to the smell of ancient animal grease, but this added an extra potency.

"The smell of you will frighten the eagles away brother," he said, pushing the bowl away from him with his foot and fanning the air in an attempt to disperse the stink.

White Arrow gave him a disapproving look.

"No, it will draw the eagles. It always does. Pawnee Killer always uses it and he has caught more eagles than any man I know. Besides, I have eagle power. Our father had it and he passed it on to us. I think you have it just as strong as I do, but you won't use it."

Bear Claw shook his head. He did not lack courage, but he had never relished the thought of being confined in a small pit, trying to strangle a furious, fighting eagle. He thought of the seven-foot wing span and the murderous curved beak and began to wish White Arrow would change his mind. His brother went on painting, his face concentrated and serious.

"You don't need that horse of Crow Dog's," Bear Claw told him. "You have plenty of horses. At least two of them are as good as that one. It's not worth twenty eagle feathers. He only said that to dare you into an eagle catching."

White Arrow knew that well enough.

"Of course he did and I am not going to back down. I will not stand for Crow Dog shouting it around the village that I have no faith in my eagle power."

"Crow Dog's mouth can do you no harm."

White Arrow did not reply. He stood up so he could daub his thighs and the back of his legs more easily. He was very confident that he could catch an eagle. He had sought the advice of Pawnee Killer, who knew about these things. He had observed all the rituals, sitting up all night to sing the eagle songs, his lodge had swayed with the vibration of it and took a sweat bath to cleanse his mind, body and spirit for the task. The hot stones still glowed inside the sweat lodge, showing brighter because it was not yet fully light. He must be ensconced in his pit before dawn, before any eagles were in the sky. They were sharp-eyed creatures and might see what he was up to.

The camp was silent and sleeping in the grey half-light. The wind that blew down constantly from the high plains tugged at the lodge skins and rattled the warriors' shields hanging on their tripods outside the lodges. The wind was always there. Out on the plains in high summer it scorched and seared the land, drying up the water courses, burning off the grass, cracking a man's skin and parching his lips. In the winter, when the temperature could drop below zero without warning and a mild late autumn day could turn into a biting winter night, the wind whipped up bitter blizzards with wet, blinding sheets of snow and sleet that ground all living things to a standstill.

The white men who travelled the high plains in winter soon learned to hate the Norther, that vicious wind. The Cheyenne had learned to live with it, seeing it as neither friend nor foe, just something to be borne. However, a band was always grateful to find a more sheltered spot to camp, lower down the plains, near the woods and rivers, partly sheltered by bluffs. Lone Wolf's band had found a good place to camp that would serve them well when winter came.

It was cold this morning, the sharpness of a dawn in early spring. Bear Claw was glad of the warmth of his buffalo robe, but White Arrow, intent on his purpose and eager to be gone, did not notice the wind across his bare shoulders. He picked up his leather noose and the piece of meat he intended to use as bait.

"I am ready," he announced, "Will you walk to the trap with me?"

His brother nodded and they skirted the village in silence, watched by two dogs skirmishing around the tepees. All around the bluffs, prairie dogs pulled their heads back into their burrows at the last minute, narrowly avoiding the stepping moccasins in their curiosity. A small band of antelope took off at their approach, kicking up their heels and springing across the short grass, strange and shining in the half-light.

The eagle trap was two miles away, but they dare not ride in case the sound of the horses alerted the eagles. They loped along at a trot, White Arrow murmuring a song under his breath, until they reached the rocky ridge where the previous evening, he had dug out his eagle trap. It was a shallow pit, just big enough for him to crouch in. He lowered himself in, wriggling around until he was comfortable, then Bear Claw handed him the rawhide noose. He let his hand rest on his brother's arm for a moment, before he began to cover over the mouth of the pit with twigs and grasses, leaving two clear spy holes for White Arrow to watch the sky. When the camouflage was complete, he fixed the bait in position and stood back to judge the effect.

"Go now," White Arrow's voice came up to him from beneath the twigs. "The light is coming fast. The eagles will be flying soon. They will see you."

Bear Claw had no desire to jeopardize his brother's chance of glory and left without another word. He walked back to the village, watching the sky banding with pink and pale blue. He felt discontented because his chief desire was to ride down to the Barnett cabin and spend some more time with Lothar Klein, but he did not want to be out of the village when White Arrow came back with his eagle feathers. Besides he wanted to be close at hand in case his brother's eagle power was not so strong as he thought.

It was four days now since he had pulled the German out of the pit. His fever had subsided on the second day and when Bear Claw arrived on the third day, Lothar was sitting up in bed, demolishing a plate of food and talking freely. He laughed loudly when Bear Claw asked him if he was a trapper or perhaps a farmer. He seemed to find it a great joke.

"Do I look like a farmer?" he had asked, wiping the remains of Fran's best pot roast from his moustache and pouring himself a second cup of coffee. Bear Claw found that difficult to answer. He had not realized that farmers had a particular form of appearance.

"No, my friend," Klein wagged his finger confidentially, "I mean to make myself a great deal of money. No farmer ever gets rich very quickly. I am in Montana looking for gold."

This surprised Bear Claw. He had heard that gold had been found to the west, near the Shining Mountains, the ranges that the white men called the Rockies, but he had never met anyone searching for gold on this side of the plains. He told Klein as much. The German did not contradict him, but smiled in the way a man does when he knows best, but is too polite to argue. His reasons for being in that particular area were very specific, but it was too early to discuss that with Bear Claw. He must know his man first.

Lothar Klein was very sociable. He had a ready, encouraging smile and laughed a great deal. He was willing to answer any of Bear Claw's questions.

"Hamburg," he had said, "Do I know Hamburg? But of course I do. I have an uncle there. He has a freight business on the river- owns a dozen barges."

He launched into a description of his uncle's house overlooking Hamburg's largest park. It all sounded very magnificent and elegant, not at all like the cramped, two-roomed houses in a dark, cobbled street that his mother had described to Bear Claw, but he said nothing about this. All he wanted to do was listen to Klein, who enjoyed an audience. The German was optimistic about his leg, sure it had been well-treated and would heal quickly. He could not find words enough to praise the kindness of the Barnetts and Bear Claw. His main cause for concern was the loss of his horse and all of his equipment, including a new, seven-shot Spencer repeating rifle.

Bear Claw as he ambled back to his village in the cold dawn was deciding which of his horses he would give to his new friend. The previous autumn they had taken forty Comanche horses in a raid down into Texas.

The ten warriors had four horses each. He decided that Klein should have the best one of these. He had planned to prepare it as his foremost war pony, but a gift was worth little if it did not involve the giver in some sacrifice.

The village was awake now. He could smell cooking. Outside his own lodge, Painted Shawl was stirring pieces of pommes blanche and dried strips of prickly pear cactus into a meat stew to thicken and flavour it. He leaned over the pot, sniffing appreciatively, dipping his finger in and sucking it clean. Painted Shawl rapped his fingers with her horn spoon.

"It's not ready yet. Keep your fingers out." Then she asked seriously, "Is White Arrow waiting for the eagles?"

He nodded, looking across to the tepee of his mother-in-law. Tall Woman, Shadow That Dances and Blue Dress, her hair rough and spikey, mangled in her ritual mourning, sat in a circle, scraping away at an animal carcass, removing all the surplus meat and fat. He could just see Singing Linnet sheltering in the recesses of the lodge.

A band of half-grown children, shepherded by two women, was on its way to the creek to fetch water. Bear Claw asked Painted Shawl's daughters if they wished to go. They did not hesitate, running after the other children, yelling for them to wait. He took great pleasure in watching his nieces grow. They were strong, healthy girls with happy temperaments. He was happy to be a father to them while they needed him.

After he had eaten, he spent a restless morning, not able to settle down to anything.

He began to dress his arrows and adjust the tension of his bow-string, but all the while his mind wandered to White Arrow in his eagle pit and Lothar Klein at the cabin.

He watched the women go off across the plain on a vegetable digging expedition, equipped with dibbles to prise out the roots of a variety of wild vegetables. They were singing and joking. Painted Shawl had promised to find him some red turnips. They were not so common as the white turnip, which the French trappers called pommes blanche, but they were much tastier and she knew Bear Claw loved them.

He had just made up his mind to go hunting as soon as White Arrow returned, when a party of young braves, who had gone out early that morning, under the direction of He-Who-Runs-Fast, came riding into the camp, whooping and shouting.

They milled around on their horses in the centre of the village, a tangle of snorting horses, waving arms, flying feathers and excited voices. When Bear Claw's eyes had penetrated the dust and movement, he saw that the centre of attention was a bay mare, saddled and loaded up with a pack. A rifle hung in a holster from the saddle. He knew this must be Lothar's horse; it fitted his description in every detail. He hurried across to the horsemen and asked what had happened. A youngster explained that they had found the horse drinking down by the creek. She had scratches all down her flanks as if she had been attacked by a cougar, but she was a fine horse.

"And look what was on her saddle," he shouted above the noise, "A rifle, a soldier's gun, one that fires bullets one after another. One like the Crow war party had when they attacked us last summer."

He-Who-Runs-Fast was taking the gun out of the holster. He held the weapon to his shoulder, testing its weight, squinting down the barrel, taking mock aim at his fellow warriors. His view came to rest at length on his sister's husband. He aimed the gun at Bear Claw's broad chest.

"How would you like to be my target brother? I have loaded the gun with seven bullets. Would you dare stand there and test my aim?"

He-Who's aim with a bow was deadly, but he had little experience with a repeating rifle.

"I would certainly risk it," Bear Claw replied coolly, "Because my life would be safe. You still have the safety catch down on the gun."

He -Who lowered the rifle, his eyes darting over the mechanism around the trigger and his group of devotees began to laugh.

"Besides," Bear Claw was standing close to him now, "You will have no time for target practice. That is not your rifle. I know who the horse belongs to and I shall take it back to him."

"Are you going to tell me it belongs to your precious white friend Barnett? A man who chooses to spend his life digging the earth and planting seeds has no need of a warrior's gun like this. I found it and I shall keep it, horse, gun and pack."

Bear Claw explained briefly about Lothar Klein and the animal pit, knowing that his wife's brother would not relent. He wondered why he continued to reason with him, for he barely had the patience to listen.

When the story was finished, he laughed contemptuously, asking what kind of man was fool enough to lose his horse and then fall into an animal trap when trying to catch it again.

"If you ask me, he doesn't deserve to own a horse if he cannot take better care of it than that. I owe no white man any favours. If he wants his horse back, let him come and take it from me."

Bear Claw would have liked nothing better than

to have knocked He-Who-Runs-Fast out of his saddle, for he sat there so arrogant, so confident in his reputation as a warrior. The roach of porcupine tail hairs that stood up on his head like a cock's comb and the strips of otter skin, decorated with trade mirrors, reflecting light from all angles, that swung from his shirt and leggings all heightened his aggressive, proud look. He really believed that he was the perfect warrior, the mode for all the youths of the band.

Bear Claw curbed his desire to unhorse him, declaring instead,

"Lothar Klein is not our enemy. He means us no harm. He was just passing through our territory when he had this accident. He has now become my friend and it is unworthy of a Cheyenne to steal from his brother's friend. Do I ever steal from your friends? The mark of a great warrior is generosity not greed."

He-Who spat viciously, his horse circling around, sensing the tension in the rider. Bear Claw stepped back out of range.

"I will take the matter to Lone Wolf. We will let him judge what should be done about this." and he headed straight for the lodge of Lone Wolf, leaving his wife's brother to fume and shout obscenities after him.

He was met by Lone Wolf's wife, Prairie Flower, at the lodge opening and asked respectfully if he might speak to her husband about an important matter. Lone Wolf had been ill for some weeks with a feverish coughing sickness that gave him no rest. It had left him very weak and the village had been instructed by Burning Fire, leader of the Elk Society, not to worry him with problems until he was well. Bear Claw however felt justified in taking this matter to him. Prairie Flower was reluctant to let him in, but his earnestness persuaded her and she stepped aside to let him pass. It was a large tepee, more than twenty buffalo hides had gone into the making of it, but it was gloomy for every flap was pegged down to keep out the wind. The floor smelt earthy, but there was another smell too, a sickly smell of soured herbs.

Bear Claw peered through the gloom to see Lone Wolf lying on the turf bench that ran around the outer part of the lodge. He was propped up against a back-rest of woven willow mat stretched over a frame and so swathed in buffalo robes that his face was just visible. Bear Claw was surprised to see how gaunt and grey he had become.

"I am sorry to disturb you father, but I have a problem on which I would like your advice."

The whole band called Lone Wolf father. It was no easy task to be a peace chief.

"Sit down and tell me your problem. There is a lot of noise going on outside. I was about to send Prairie Flower outside to find out the trouble."

His voice was dry as if there was a constriction in his throat. He was a man of perhaps fifty, an energetic, powerful man when in full health, but clearly suffering great pain now. His face was gentle, but his eyes were sunk back in his head and deep lines etched his forehead and the corners of his mouth.

Bear Claw squatted on the floor beside the bench and told his story, a concise outline of all that had happened concerning Lothar Klein. Lone Wolf listened without interruption, struggling to control his bouts of coughing.

"This man is from my mother's country. He is like my kin. We say all Cheyenne are brothers and I honour my father's kin, so surely I should honour my mother's too. He-Who-Runs-Fast insults me by refusing to return what belongs to my kin. He won't listen to me, so perhaps he will listen to you.

He seems to grow more unreasonable with age, instead of growing in wisdom as we are supposed to do. Will you speak to him father?"

Lone Wolf pulled himself up into a sitting position. He did not answer the question, saying, "I am worried about your relationship with He-Who-Runs-Fast. He is your wife's brother; you should help and support each other, but instead you wrangle constantly. Burning Fire tells me that you threatened to kill him if he harmed the white man Barnett, who lives down by the river. Is that true?"

Bear Claw nodded. He always felt ashamed when Lone Wolf's steady eyes searched his face.

"Then I hope it was only bravado, for you know very well what happens when a Cheyenne kills one of his own people. The sacred arrows are flecked with blood and the murderer must suffer. It is almost as if he rots inside so that his brothers cannot stand the smell of him. He pollutes the camp and must be banished from it. Such a killing involves the whole tribe. You would risk that for a white man?"

Bear Claw felt his colour rising and his retort

was sharper than he had intended. "I did not realise the colour of a man's skin mattered to you Lone Wolf, but if it does remember that I am half white and tell me so. It is certainly that which spurs He-Who on to jibe at me and try to block everything I do. Ben Barnett has been a better brother to me than He-Who-Runs-Fast. He has shown me kindness and hospitality. He is a good, honest man, who means well by the Cheyenne. He-Who would kill him if he had the chance, just to spite me and I've warned him of the consequences. It's not just bravado father, I mean it."

Lone Wolf attempted to reply, but he was wracked by a fierce fit of coughing that shook his whole frame. The violence of it frightened Bear Claw. He searched around in the dim light for some water and found a skin water bag hanging from the central lodge pole. He poured some into a tin cup and held it to Lone Wolf's lips. The water spilled, running down over Bear Claw's hands, as the older man continued to cough, but at length he managed to take some water and the fit subsided. It left him breathless and shaking.

"This illness is worse than I thought," Bear Claw said, helping his chief into a more comfortable position, "Can Pawnee Killer do nothing for you?"

"Never mind my illness, you came to me to discuss your troubles not my health and it saddens me to hear you confirm your threat to your wife's brother. As you know, a peace chief holds office for ten summers. When I became chief two summers ago I was strong and active, now I am not so sure I will live out the span of my office."

Bear Claw opened his mouth to protest but Lone Wolf lay a bony finger on his lips. "It is not for you to deny it. Only the All Father knows the truth of it, but I have a strong premonition; you must grant me that. I have had the honour to attend the Great Council of 44 and sit with the Sweet Medicine Chief and his four helpers. It will be my duty to choose the next peace chief and for some time it has been in my heart to choose you."

Bear Claw stood in astonished silence, hardly believing what he heard.

"A peace chief must put aside all thought of personal gain, all pride and selfishness. Whatever happens, he must keep his temper, always listen with a sympathetic ear, no matter how much he would like to tell the complainer to clear off and leave him in peace. It's not easy. He can never nurse a grievance, but equally he must be strong and energetic to protect the weak and make sure that justice prevails in the community. Not many men can combine these qualities, but I believe you can. We will have to come to terms with the white settlers and the soldiers in the future. It is no good just hoping that they are going to go away. We must try to understand the way they think. You will be in a good position to do that. I know that you have often felt the difficulty of your two blood streams, but perhaps they will serve you well in time.

Consider what I have said and think what a disaster it will be if you murder your brother. Take care Bear Claw, for my sake and the sake of the whole band, as well as your own."

Such a long speech exhausted Lone Wolf and he

lay back on the bench, closing his eyes for a moment, Bear Claw was dazed by what he had heard. He could not believe that a man who had seen his vision of the flaming sword could ever sit on the High Council of the Cheyenne nation. It did not make sense. Yet he knew it was unheard of for a man to refuse to accept the office when chosen.

"I know He-Who-Runs-Fast makes your life hard," Lone Wolf had gathered a little strength, "He aims to become leader of the Elks one day and sees himself as a great war chief.

He is a brave warrior, but he has no control over himself and is a bad example for the young ones. If he achieves his aim, we shall need a strong peace chief to advise the people wisely and stand up to him. You have had much practice in that."

Bear Claw smiled. "I have indeed father."

"I believe your friend Barnett is a good man. He has worked hard since he moved into the woods and has never done us any harm. You must bring him into the village one day to smoke a pipe with me, this man from your mother's country too. I have no quarrel with a man because his skin is lighter than mine. It is a foolish distinction to base a judgement upon. We all live under the same sky."

He began to struggle up. "Help me up Bear Claw. I'll see if I can persuade that hothead to return the horse and gun. You're right, it is dishonourable to steal from a brother's friend."

Bear Claw helped to pull the chief to his feet. As the buffalo robes fell away from him, the extent of his emaciation was fully revealed. All his bones were sharp, jagged, jutting through his clothes. He could not stand firmly without support. Bear Claw found it hard to hide his distress at the sight of Lone Wolf's body. He could remember as a boy, watching his father White Bull, ride out at the head of a war party with Lone Wolf riding beside him, a powerful, heroic figure that seemed to bear no relation to this ageing man, wasting away with sickness. Lone Wolf knew what he was thinking.

"If I can bear it, you can my son. Before we go out, promise me you will try your hardest to exercise control in your dealings with He-Who-Runs-Fast."

"I will do my best."

The sun was now high in the sky. As the two men came out of the dark lodge the brightness of the light blinded them for a moment. Supporting Lone Wolf with one arm, Bear Claw used his free hand to shield his eyes from the sun. He-Who was still waiting astride his horse, the rifle in his hands. Most of his followers had dispersed, but a few lingered on to see the outcome of this latest confrontation.

It was clear to all that their peace chief was very ill. He could walk only slowly, resting his weight on Bear Claw, but when they reached the defiant warrior, he stepped away and stood firm.

"It is good to see you out of your lodge again," He-Who-Runs-Fast said formally.

"It is cold and I would rather be inside it, but Bear Claw tells me you have taken the property of his friend and refuse to return it. I do not approve of this action."

He-Who gave Bear Claw a dark look. He swung down off his horse and took the reins of Klein's mare in his hands as if to emphasize his claim on her. The horse was fretting, worried by the unfamiliar smells of the camp and he stroked her muzzle to calm her.

"It is easy for you to say that when you have heard only Bear Claw's side of the story."

"That's true, so tell me the story yourself. Is there anything I have not heard?"

He-Who hesitated. There was nothing to tell except that he had Klein's horse and gun and wanted to keep them.

"I am sick of him saying that every stray white man is his friend. I found this horse without an owner down by the creek and by my reckoning that makes it mine. How do we know Bear Claw does not want it for himself?"

Bear Claw snorted. He did not bother to refute the accusation and He-Who realised he had made a bad misjudgement.

"Bear Claw is not a liar," Lone Wolf declared. "Sometimes he is stubborn and goes his own way, but he is a good Cheyenne in his heart and is no liar. Your father was one of my closest friends. I know you want to be as great a man as your father. His reputation haunts you. Well, remember that much of his reputation was based on his generosity. He would give away his last shirt. What would he say to you now if he knew that you would steal from a man who is not our enemy, chiefly to spite the son of White Bull?"

He-Who-Runs-Fast knew he was beaten. He hurled the Spencer rifle to the ground at Bear Claw's feet.

"Here, take this white man's rubbish. I do not need it anyway. Take it back to that fool who falls into animal pits."

He did not know how to take defeat graciously; his whole body quivered with frustration. At that moment there was no one, not a white man, Pawnee or Crow that he hated more than his sister's husband. He felt that the blue eyes mocked him now, those white man's eyes and he turned away, clenching his fists.

Bear Claw turned to help Lone Wolf back into his lodge, when a strange sound reached his ears, vague, drifting at first, then more distinct, singing and cheering. It was the sound of women's voices. He exchanged glances with his chief and then stared out across the plain, trying to make sense of the shapes hanging and shivering in the heat haze that fringed the horizon. Then he saw them, the women, running towards the village, kyiying songs of praise and admiration, the young girls shrieking and dancing. Running in front of them, with a smile that split his face from ear to ear, was White Arrow. He was clutching a bundle of eagle feathers. His arms were scratched, his head covered with earth, but his feet flew over the grass.

Bear Claw supported Lone Wolf into his lodge, much to the relief of Prairie Flower, thanked him for his intercession and her for her patience, then ran out to meet his brother.

"I told you," White Arrow was yelling, long before

he reached him. "I told you I had eagle power. Where's Crow Dog?"

Amid the excitement, He-Who-Runs-Fast leaped astride his horse and rode out of the village, brushing aside the running women in his eagerness to be gone.

❈❈❈

Ben was knocking in a fence post with a massive wooden mallet when he heard Fran scream. The mallet still in his hand, he ran down from the top land towards the house. Lothar Klein was sitting on the veranda playing with Sarah. He instinctively pulled the child to him when he heard the scream, protecting her with his arm from he knew not what. As Ben ran past he tried to pull himself up with the veranda post, but his leg would not take the weight and he sat down again heavily, cursing his incapacity.

Barnett skidded to a halt outside the hen house, where he found his wife standing just outside the door.

"Fran, for heaven's sake what is it? You frightened me screaming like that. I thought," He stopped in mid-sentence, seeing for the first time the state of the hen house. The door had been smashed in. The wood lay in long white splinters, sprinkled with speckled feathers that drifted on the dust motes in the sunlight. The carcasses of the hens were everywhere, ripped and bleeding, some of them headless. Entrails threaded the floor in serpentine patterns. He felt his stomach knot up.

"Oh dear God, the wolverine! Why did he have to slaughter them all like that?"

Then he heard it, the low, rumbling growl, full of fear and warning. In the dark recesses of the shattered hen house two green eyes glowed like jewels.

"Frances, get back," Ben pulled his wife away from the door. "He is still in there. No wonder Caesar didn't bark last night. The wolverine waited until Caesar wandered off hunting early this morning before he made his move. Keep well out of the way."

He stepped warily into the shed, grateful for the mallet in his hand, but not sure what he was going to do.

"Well, Mr Wolverine," he murmured, "I have finally got to meet you. I think this will have to be the first and the last time."

He could see the creature now, crouching back against the wall, its powerful body stiff with fear, the teeth bared. The growling was becoming more frenzied, the pitch higher. Ben took a step closer, one step too close for the wolverine, for it flew at him, knocking him off balance with the power of its rush before he could aim a blow with the mallet.

He could taste the strong smell of the fur at the back of his throat, then felt a stinging sensation as the claws ripped across his chest and trickles of wet blood ran down over his ribs. The jaws were snapping close to his face, saliva spraying all over him as he fought to push the wolverine away.

Fran snatched up the pitchfork that was propped against the side of the hen house and without any hesitation, drove the curving spike into the animal's haunch. It fell over on to its side, shrieking and spitting, a terrible sound that made her shudder and she dropped the pitchfork as if it had burned her hands.

Ben struggled to his feet and swinging the mallet high above his shoulder, crushed the writhing creature's skull with one blow, relieved to silence that horrifying cry of pain. He dropped back down on his knees, coughing, spitting bits of fur from his mouth. His shirt had been torn to shreds. Pieces of blue linen stuck to the blood on his chest. His throat was clawed and red wheals ran from his shoulder down to his navel, all beading with blood like a tattoo.

Frances knelt down beside him, running her fingers over the scratches on his chest, pulling away the bits of linen.

"Oh Ben, your favourite shirt!"

"What shirt?" He pushed himself up on to his feet, pulling Fran up with him and holding her face in his hands, he kissed her.

"Thank you Fran, that was a brave and resolute thing to do. I think I might have lost more than my shirt if you hadn't acted so quickly."

A smear of blood had rubbed off on her cheek and he wiped it away with his finger. "Come on, I had better clean myself up a bit before I sort this mess out."

He was glad to get away from the hen house for he suddenly felt very sick.

The smell of the wolverine was still in his nostrils and there was blood everywhere. Frances sensed his unsteadiness and took a firm hold on his arm.

"You are bleeding a great deal. I will wash the scratches with some spirit in case there is any infection and that should stem the bleeding."

She began to talk rapidly, releasing her nervous tension as they walked across the yard. Ben let her talk. So Bear Claw's dreaded wolverine was dead at last. He would plague their nights no longer, but Ben felt no elation. He was sorry to be the instrument of even more destruction.

The depression that had settled over him the night Bear Claw had rescued Lothar, still hovered around him. He tried to disregard it, but he could not shake it off. It lurked there in the back of his mind, throwing shadows over everything. He made an effort not to let it show, but sometimes those shadows would be reflected in his eyes and his face became dark and sombre. The sense of foreboding was strong now after that carnage in the hen house. Perhaps he was beginning to believe in the wolverine's bad medicine after all, he thought.

Lothar Klein was doing his best to keep Sarah occupied. He was relieved to see her parents walking towards the house. The savage snarling of the wolverine was audible to him up there on the veranda and he felt so helpless.

"Lieber Gott!" he exclaimed as he saw the state Ben was in, "What was it, a cougar? Are you hurt bad?"

Ben shook his head. "No, it's only scratches, just a lot of blood that's all. It was a wolverine. We have had trouble with it for months. It drove Caesar to distraction and now he has missed the denouement. But it finally achieved its aim, killed every hen we had."

"Ach, that is bad. The same damn creature that frightened my horse I bet and helped me fall into the pit. Well, good riddance!"

"It could well have been the cause of your horse running off. Thank you for keeping hold of Sarah."

The German shrugged to indicate that he had done nothing in particular, as he let Sarah waddle over to her mother, declaring that if he had two good legs he would have taken pleasure in finishing off the beast himself.

Lothar Klein had an even greater pleasure to come because around forty minutes later Bear Claw rode into the yard on a pinto horse, leading behind him Klein's mare complete with pack and gun. He was overjoyed, particularly about the rifle which was a new design, fresh to the market that year and had cost him fifty dollars. When helped to his feet, he hobbled precariously on the wooden splints, making a fuss of the horse and slapping Bear Claw on the back

"You are a marvel," he said in German, "A real marvel. I can hardly wait to see what you will produce next. A good full barrel of strong beer would be welcome. See if you can find me one of those."

The word bier was not in the vocabulary of her language that his mother had taught Bear Claw, but as the sound was almost identical to what the other whites called beer, he assumed he knew what Lothar wanted. He nodded, smiling and Klein put his arm around the Cheyenne's shoulder. He had a confidential, intimate manner with him, as if he had known him all his life, his broad, pale hands patting Bear Claw's arm or resting on his shoulder with a natural ease.

"You had better go in and see your friend Ben. He has been wrestling with a wolverine this morning. Lucky for him, he won."

Bear Claw started for the house. "Hey, wait a minute, you can help me in with you."

When the two men came into the cabin, Ben was sitting at the table drinking a cup of coffee. Frances had dressed his wounds and found him a clean shirt, so apart from the livid marks on the side of his throat, he looked none the worse for his encounter.

"You killed it?" Bear Claw demanded, unceremoniously dumping Klein into the nearest chair. "The wolverine is dead?"

"Yes, it's dead, thanks mainly to Fran. She attacked it with a pitchfork and gave me the chance to finish it off."

Frances was beating the rug as it hung over the window ledge. Bear Claw saw the circular yellow/brown burn mark on it and remembered what Ben had said about his pipe.

"That was brave," he told her.

"No it wasn't, I had to do something. It could have injured Ben badly. Look at these scratches."

She began to unbutton her husband's shirt, but he pulled her fingers away briskly and stood up.

"Bear Claw has seen far worse things than a few scratches Fran. I had better get that hen house cleared up."

She felt rebuked and showed it. Lothar's light blue eyes were studying her face. She was suddenly aware of it and went back to beating her rug.

Down in the hen house Ben and Bear Claw stood over the body of the wolverine.

"It is big," murmured Bear Claw, "I have never seen one as big as this."

Ben watched the flies crawling over the splintered skull and kicked out moodily at the mallet that lay by the corpse.

"I wish I hadn't been forced to kill it like that."

Bear Claw raised his eyebrows. "Why?"

"I don't really know; it just seems so wasteful somehow." He bent over, feeling the animal's fur with the tips of his fingers. It was thick and soft. "The fur is magnificent. Well Bear Claw, if you kill a wolverine does it cancel out the bad medicine?"

His voice was light-hearted, but his eyes were not. Bear Claw saw the trouble in his face.

"You feel it is bad too?"

"I'm not sure what I feel, but it certainly isn't good. I often used to feel like this a long time ago, back in England when I was living an aimless life, following my parents on their endless social round, being exhibited as their tremendously clever son. Everything was so shallow, so hollow it echoed. That was before I met Frances, before I came here and learned how to work. There were so many shadows then settling over all the light, bright places of the heart and mind, so cold." He hugged his arms across his chest as if he could feel the cold even then. "Fran banished them all, made everything so clear and warm. I thought," He stopped, catching sight of

Bear Claw's face, earnest, intent, following the words and trying to interpret the emotions that were passing through his friend. Ben smiled.

"Oh Bear Claw, I'm sorry. You can have no notion of what I am talking about. I'm not sure that I do myself. You know something, I don't think wolverine wrestling is very good for my constitution."

He straightened up with a long sigh, as if he were exhaling all the murky associations that clouded his thoughts.

"These shadows," Bear Claw asked, "They come to you again now?"

He knew he had hit the mark by the startled expression that flickered for a moment in Ben's eyes. He had never seen Barnett look so vulnerable.

"I see you found Lothar's horse," Ben had turned away, looking around for a sack to collect up the chicken carcasses. "How did you work that particular piece of magic?"

The moment had passed for Bear Claw to pursue his question. Ben had changed the subject firmly enough to make it clear he wanted to discuss it no further.

The Cheyenne took the wolverine and buried it out in the woods, far from the cabin, hoping this would help Ben. He buried it deep, at least five feet down, dropping spade full after spade full of earth upon it.

"If you are a bad spirit," he intoned as he shovelled, "Stay buried here in the earth, cool and quiet. Leave my friend Benjamin in peace. If you have a quarrel, quarrel with me."

⚜

A month later, Bear Claw had reason to believe that the wolverine had indeed opened a quarrel with him personally. It was a cold, bright morning. Lothar Klein had abandoned his leg splints the previous day and was eager to test his ability to ride and joined Bear Claw on a hunting expedition. They were trailing antelope across the edge of the plain, up towards High Craggs, a steep outcrop of rock to the east of the Cheyenne village.

Lothar found that his leg ached after an hour in the saddle, but it did not impede his riding and he pressed on, determined to give it a tough test. Ahead of him Bear Claw had picked up a trail, for he was urging his mount up the narrow path leading into the Craggs, sending showers of loose stones back down in front of Lothar's horse.

"What is it?" the German inquired, shifting in the saddle to ease the ache in his leg.

"A big buck antelope, too good to lose."

Lothar was surprised by the height of the rock formation as they approached the top. He enjoyed high places and sat for a moment, penetrating the darkness of the dizzying ravine that plunged down beyond the top of the ridge. He could see the luminescent, gauzy wings of a dragonfly lighting the black wall on the far side of the ravine and concluded that there must be water nearby. He was thinking that it was early to see a dragonfly, when his reverie was broken by a scrambling noise. He looked up to see Bear Claw's horse teetering on the edge of the ravine, the Cheyenne pressing his knees tight to the animal's belly to prevent himself from falling off.

Lothar urged his own mount forward, intending to catch hold of the reins and steady the floundering horse, but before he reached it, the horse lunged forward on to the track and safety. The lunge was so violent however that Bear Claw was thrown sideways. Lothar grabbed for him desperately, almost unseating himself, but he was too late for the Cheyenne went crashing over the top of the ridge in a cloud of dust and flying stones.

Klein slid off his horse and hobbled to the edge, dreading the prospect of seeing Bear Claw's body bouncing its way down that endless ravine. What he saw when he forced himself to stare out over the edge galvanised him into action.

Bear Claw was about thirty feet down, clinging with both hands to a scrubby piece of bush that grew out of the rock face. He was trying to swing his legs in to touch the surface of the rock, but it was just out of reach.

"Hang on. I'll get you up." Klein was not sure how and he closed his eyes momentarily in an effort to think clearly. The ridge tapered away to a line of boulders, where the bushes were growing, before the sheer drop of the ravine. He took a deep breath and slid down the incline, trusting in the boulders to halt his slide. It worked and he blew out his cheeks in relief. He was now just above Bear Claw and could touch his hands if he stretched forward. All the colour had drained out of the Indian's straining hands. Under the tanned surface was a strange whiteness.

"Bear Claw, I can just reach you." He put his hand over the top of one of the Cheyenne's. "I can help you only if you have the nerve to let go with one hand and catch hold of mine, then do the same with the other hand. You understand, my friend?"

Bear Claw grunted his assent and Klein braced his feet against a boulder, hoping his leg would take the strain.

"Alright, we will do it now." He grabbed hold of Bear Claw's left hand and felt the palm in his. "Now the other one, quick!"

He had not been prepared for the tremendous pull of his friend's full weight suspended in space. He felt as if an iron bar had clamped across his chest, squeezing the air out of his lungs. The pressure on his leg sent waves of pain up into his stomach.

Bear Claw attempted to get his feet planted on the rock face without jerking out of Lothar's grasp. Once he felt the hard surface against the soles of his moccasins, he used Klein as a pulley to anchor him as he walked up the rock. The German had great strength in his arms and broad back. He took a deep breath and with a supreme effort hauled him up level with the boulders.

He hardly knew how he managed to scramble up the incline to the top path above the ridge. His body was one great lake of pain. He sat down heavily at the edge of the path, bathed in perspiration, his face alabaster white.

"Lothar, I am worried about your leg. I must see if you have opened the break."

Bear Claw began to probe at the leg with his

fingers and Klein winced, but the Cheyenne was now making optimistic noises.

"The leg is still sound. You are lucky. You saved my life with great courage Lothar. I owe you a warrior's debt."

Klein shook his head. "You owe me nothing my friend. Now we are even. You saved me from that damn pit. I would have died there if you hadn't come along. But trust you, no petty little animal pit for you, no, you have to suspend yourself over a two- hundred- foot drop. The way of the warrior I suppose."

Bear Claw laughed.

"How did it happen though? One minute your horse was climbing like a mountain goat and the next it was slipping over the brink."

"It was the wolverine," Bear Claw replied simply, his eyes serious.

"Wolverine, what wolverine?"

"The one Ben killed in the barn."

Klein looked sceptical.

"No, it's true Lothar. I felt his presence. He scared my horse. His spirit medicine is powerful. I don't know how to explain it to you in your language."

Lothar patted his arm. "Never mind, I doubt if I would believe a word of it even if you could explain it to me. I'll tell you one thing though; we have lost that damn antelope for sure. Could you give me a hand up?"

Bear Claw helped him to his feet where he stood uncertainly for a moment, testing how much weight he could put on his leg.

"You are truly my brother now Lothar Klein. Our lives have touched; that makes me happy."

Klein gave him a hearty slap on the back and hauled himself into the saddle.

Bear Claw had taken on Ben's quarrel with the wolverine, but felt good that Lothar now shared it with him, even though the German did not understand how he did so or believe in the creature's spirit power.

CHAPTER FOUR

The spring wore on. April passed into May, the moon-when-the-horses-grow-fat. The horses of Lone Wolf's band fed well on the young grass, spoiled and pampered by their masters, who groomed and schooled them into readiness for the summer buffalo hunt. A fleet, skilful pony was essential. The buffalo hunter must run his mount close up to the right side of the great beast and controlling the horse with his legs alone, use both hands to shoot an arrow down through the ribs into the buffalo's heart. Some hunters used a lance, for it was more dangerous, more courageous, the jarring impact of the blow often unseating the rider.

The great hunt filled all the young men with excitement. It gave them the opportunity to display their prowess not only in front of their own band, but also in competition with all the young warriors of the Cheyenne nation, for the great hunt was a communal affair. All the separate bands of Cheyenne came together at a prearranged rendezvous on the high plains to perform the sacred ceremonies that ensured a successful hunt. Once the ceremonies were over, no man was allowed to hunt on his own.

The summer buffalo kill was carefully organised

and policed by the military societies.

The plains tribes were so dependent on the buffalo that a sufficient kill was vital to ensure survival through the winter and it must be done in early summer, before the sun and burning winds dried up the grass and the buffalo herds dispersed. This was why the rules governing the great hunt were so strict. Nothing must jeopardize its success. Retribution fell swiftly on the man who ignored the plan of attack and rode out to strike the buffalo alone.

Bear Claw could remember two young warriors who were whipped by the Elk Society men until their backs were raw because they broke ranks and charged the buffalo before the signal was given. He described the incident to Lothar, as the German sat on a boulder, watching Bear Claw wading in the stream, scanning the clear water for fish.

"Quite right too," approved Klein. "Nothing will work without discipline. What's the use of having a plan if people are going to ignore it?"

He laughed as Bear Claw pushed his arm down into the water and with one scoop lifted a fish, throwing it up onto the bank just below Lothar's feet. It thrashed around, gleaming pink and silver in the bright light. Klein finished it off by clubbing it with a piece of wood.

"Hey, this is a big one. It seems that fishing is easy in this place."

"Easy for me," the Cheyenne retorted, "Not so easy for you."

"What are you talking about? Anybody can hook a fish off the riverbed. Look, I'll show you."

He jumped off the rock and waded into the river. His leg had healed rapidly and although he limped, his balance was now firm, even when the river current tugged at him as the water came up to his knees. Peering into the water he saw the dart of a fish pushing into the sand of the river bed. He groped for it clumsily, swearing as it slipped through his inexpert fingers and sand clouded the surface of the water. He splashed after it, making another snatch only to miss again and stepping hard into a depression in the sand, he fell headlong into the river, spraying water all over the laughing Bear Claw.

"I told you it wasn't so easy," he mocked.

His German was becoming smoother and more certain with every day he passed in Klein's company.

"Damn fish, "Lothar spluttered to the surface. "I'll have you frying in a pan before this day is out."

"No you won't, not unless you get out of the way and let me catch it."

Bear Claw was not ready for what happened next for Klein made a lunge at him, grabbing him around the waist and pulling him down into the water.

"I'm going to make sure you get as wet as I do my friend."

They splashed about, each trying to hold the other under water, horsing around like half-grown boys, until Klein who was getting the worst of it, struck out for the bank and hauled himself up. He sat there coughing, spitting out grains of sand and smoothing his lank hair out of his eyes. When it was wet, the thinning patch at the crown of his head was emphasised. He ran his hand over the patch as if he was conscious of it.

Bear Claw was beside him now, shaking himself like a dog.

"This country makes you people pretty tough," Lothar said.

Bear Claw nodded. "It is not easy to survive, but it is a good country."

Lothar lay on his back, his hands behind his head, feeling the sun begin to dry him off.

"It's a beautiful country by God. I like it down here by the river in particular. A man could hang around here for ever, but I really ought to be moving on soon."

"Where would you go?" Bear Claw was not eager for him to leave.

"I know where I want to go, but I don't know how to get there."

Lothar Klein had been very patient. He had held back the question he had been longing to ask all these weeks while he took stock of this most unusual Indian. He could hardly believe his luck in finding such a man, honest, trusting, eager to help his friends and the link with Germany was such a bonus. He emphasised the link as much as he could, drawing Bear Claw to him. Now he felt the time was right. When the Cheyenne asked him where he wanted to go, he sighed.

"Oh, I suppose it's just a dream, one of those hopes you cling on to, but they are never realised."

"Sometimes they are," Bear Claw encouraged. "I always dreamed that one day I would meet someone from my mother's country and now I have. Tell me your dream."

"Gold is at the heart of my dream. I want to be rich. You may not understand that, not with your way of life, but even your people take pleasure in owning more horses than their neighbours. In Germany you are nobody if you don't have money. You can't do anything worthwhile, go anywhere and really enjoy it. All the people you would like to know don't want to know you.

My uncle in Hamburg is well off in a modest way. He has no children, so If I had gone into the business, I would have inherited it one day maybe. But I don't want to be that kind of rich, hardworking, thrifty, middle-class rich, in church twice on Sundays, a pillar of the community. No, that's not for me. I want to be extravagantly rich, to have enough money to live in luxury on the Mediterranean coast. It's warm there you see Bear Claw; doesn't freeze your arse off in winter like it does back home or out here. I want to stroll on yellow beaches with a pretty girl on each arm, entertain my friends with the most expensive food and wine. I want to own a string of racehorses and be pointed out in the street, be accepted in the highest society. That's what gold could do for me."

He looked at Bear Claw, expecting him to speak, trying to read his expression, but his face was enigmatic. The Cheyenne was thinking of something Ben had said about the way of life in England. It seemed strange to him that Ben had come to America to escape the kind of life that Lothar desired above all things.

"I told you before," he said at last, "There is no gold this side of the plains."

"Ah!" Lothar was wagging that long index finger. He poked it into Bear Claw's shoulder. "There have been no gold strikes recorded this side of the plains. That is a different matter. It doesn't mean there is no gold. When I was up on the East Coast last autumn I met this man who told me a fascinating story. He had been prospecting in Idaho the previous summer and camped one night with an old prospector. This old fellow was going across Montana, down into Dakota to join his brother who had found a cave in the Black Hills that was the entrance to a gold mine. His brother had written to him to tell him you could see the gold shining up in the seams of rock and you had only to knock bits off with a pick as if you were mining coal. He said the Cheyenne Indians called it a sacred cave and were always talking about the treasures that came from it. Naturally they wouldn't tell any white man where it was. The old man promised to meet up with the man who told me the story in the autumn, but he never did.

He and his brother were never seen again. I would guess the Cheyenne caught them in their sacred cave. Do you know where this cave is?"

A dismayed expression had been spreading across Bear Claw's face as Klein's story unfolded.

"You are talking about the Sweet Medicine cave, where our ancestor Sweet Medicine received the sacred arrows. There is no gold there."

"Have you been there?"

"No, only the five sacred chiefs and the medicine men go in there. It is not a gold mine; it is a holy place. You must satisfy your dream elsewhere. Only bad things could happen to you if you insulted the spirits of that place. I don't wonder that the prospector and his brother were never seen again."

Klein sat forward, drawing his knees up under his chin. He could see that Bear Claw was deeply disturbed by any suggestion that the sanctity of the cave might be violated. He patted his friend's thigh reassuringly.

"Alright, don't worry. I wouldn't do anything to offend your spirits. It's an interesting story though, you must admit. I mean, why would the old man's brother say he had seen all that gold if there was none?"

Bear Claw shrugged. He began skimming stones across the river, wishing Lothar would change the subject. He could do nothing to help him on a quest of this kind.

"Stories are distorted in the telling," he said. "When they have passed through many different mouths. Amongst the Cheyenne a good story is the property of the man who first tells it and the people in his family. Nobody else can tell it unless the story owner gives them permission, makes them a gift of it. This way the story remains a good, true one."

"So you think it was a pack of lies?"

"Maybe, or a dream. A man's dreams are very powerful. The Cheyenne have received great treasures from that cave, but not the kind you are looking for."

"Ah well, I must search for my Eldorado elsewhere then." Lothar was smiling amiably. "Still I should like to see this cave just out of curiosity. You say you don't know where it is?"

"No."

"No one in your tribe knows?"

"Oh yes, Lone Wolf and Pawnee Killer, the medicine man. They have been there to pray and ask for power on special occasions." He hesitated for a moment, studying Klein's face.

There was little sign that the German was disappointed by the dashing of his hopes. His expression was placid and unruffled.

"Pawnee Killer drew a map on buffalo hide after his first visit to keep as a sacred thing for the band. Then if there is no man left who knows the way, the cave will not be lost to us for ever. No one must look at the map while Lone Wolf and Pawnee Killer are alive though."

If Bear Claw had not turned to throw another stone across the river, he would have seen something flicker in the pale blue of Lothar's eyes, something that as a hunter he might have recognised. But all Lothar said was, "It must be near dinner time. My belly's empty. We had better get back to see if our good friend Benjamin has finished hoeing all those vegetables yet. He's a funny one that Ben, talks like the lord of some English manor house, yet works like a navvy. If I were him, I would spend more time with that wife of his. She is wasted out here. She needs a glowing chandelier to set her off, an elegant silk dress, real gems on her lovely neck."

He stopped, afraid he had overstepped the mark, but Bear Claw was not listening. He had gone over to the horses hobbled in the grass by the trees and was taking something from a hide bag that hung from his horse's back.

Lothar eased himself to his feet and strolled over to him. Bear Claw too had been holding back all these weeks. Although he had learned much about Germany, he had spoken little about his mother to Lothar. Now he held out his open palm to the German. In it was the Star of David.

"This is what my mother always wore. She gave it to me when she was dying, as a symbol of her people."

Klein looked at the gold star. He turned it over with his fingers, then let it drop into Bear Claw's palm again.

"Jews," he said, "You find them everywhere."

Bear Claw found his tone hard to interpret. It was vaguely hostile.

"Jews, yes, my mother's people from Germany. Do you have a star like this?"

Lothar laughed. "Good God no, I'm no Jew. Germany is a Christian country. My family is solid Lutheran stock."

"Christian," Bear Claw repeated, his voice bewildered, "Like Ben?"

"Yes, I suppose so, in a way."

"And they are not all Jews in Germany?

"No, of course not. Jews don't have a home. They are all over Europe. They find themselves little areas to hole up in, where they won't be too bothered by the local population, then go about making a nuisance of themselves." He patted Bear Claw on the back. "Believe me, you're lucky you were brought up a Cheyenne, much better off."

He was mounting his horse now, eager to head back to the cabin for his dinner. Bear Claw stood gazing at the star in his hand.

"Come on then," Klein urged, "I told you, I'm damned hungry."

"Wait, I don't understand. My mother's people and Christians do not believe the same things, worship the same god?"

Klein scratched his head; he was not in the mood for comparative theology.

"Well, I suppose it's the same god, but they are no friends to the Christians. You've heard of Jesus Christ haven't you?"

The Cheyenne nodded.

"Your mother's people murdered Jesus Christ, got him nailed on a tree shaped like a cross. That's why Christians don't like the Jews. Now I'm going back before I starve to death. Are you coming?"

He jabbed his heels into his horse's flanks and moved off at a gallop. Confused, Bear Claw gathered up the fish they had caught that morning and set off after him. Despite Lothar's head start, the two men rode into Barnett's yard together. The German raced into the cabin, to find Frances by the stove, stirring something in a saucepan. It smelt good and he said so,

"I can smell that half a mile away," he said in English. "I have good instinct for food. Always I know when it is ready."

Frances smiled. Lothar's appetite was enormous

and she enjoyed cooking for him. On the other hand, Ben's appetite was uneven. Sometimes he ate well, but just as often he had no interest in food at all.

"I wish Ben had such a good instinct. He never knows when dinner is ready."

Bear Claw, lingering on the veranda, offered to fetch Ben. He needed to talk to him. If anyone could explain this puzzle to him, Barnett could. He found the Englishman on the top land still hoeing and weeding. The sun was penning down in the clearing and Ben had discarded his shirt.

His body glistened with sweat. Bear Claw scanned the rows of healthy looking vegetables.

"You work hard here."

Ben turned at the sound of Bear Claw's voice. He leaned on his hoe and took off his hat, brushing the beads of perspiration from his forehead and thick, brown hair with the backs of his fingers. He had little idea of the time. He never did when he was working hard. Once his body had got into the rhythm of the work, he let his mind range free. The whole of the world's mysteries were open to him then; there were no limitations. He could dwell on the complexities of existence and still hoe vegetables on his small parcel of land. He had been very absorbed in a philosophical problem he had come across in his reading the other evening when Bear Claw's voice broke his train of thought. He stared at the Cheyenne for some moments before he spoke, bringing his mind back to the present.

"Did you have any luck fishing?"

"Yes, four big fish. I leave you one. Little Sarah

likes fish."

"She will eat practically anything Bear Claw."

"Time for you to eat now. Frances sent me to tell you dinner is ready."

Ben pursed his lips, surprised that it was so late. He had hoped to finish his work on the vegetable patch before dinner for he planned to take Fran and Sarah for a ride in the wagon that afternoon.

"I'm too hot to eat. Tell her I'll not bother just now."

"She will be angry."

"Yes, I suppose she will. I had better come. I could do with a drink anyway."

He laid down the hoe, took his shirt from the fence and stepped out of the vegetable patch, slipping his arms into his shirt as he went. Bear Claw touched his forearm with the tips of his fingers, a gesture that was delicate and respectful.

"Ben, before you go in, tell me if it is true, did my mother's people kill your Jesus Christ?"

The question took Ben by surprise. "Who told you that?"

"Lothar."

"I might have known," Barnett's top lip curled with distaste, "Where is Lothar? Feet well under the dinner table no doubt."

Benjamin Barnett took no pleasure in the company of Lothar Klein. He was convinced it was high time the German stopped living on their hospitality and moved on.

He had been more than willing at first to help

the man in his misfortune, but as the weeks wore on, his mistrust of Lothar's jocular, easy-going manner grew. When there was hard work to be done around the farm Klein was nowhere to be found, but he was always ready enough to ride off hunting with Bear Claw and readier still to hang around the house and help Frances. He lifted and carried for her, teased and flattered her, gloried in her cooking, constantly praising Sarah. He lavished much attention on the child, declaring how much he enjoyed playing with her.

Now when Ben paused in the middle of some back-breaking task to see Klein lolling on the veranda, tossing Sarah in the air, tickling her and making her laugh and scream with pleasure, he wanted to snatch his daughter away from him and hold her close in his arms.

He could not fail to see that Frances enjoyed Lothar's attentions, his ever- present interest in her domestic affairs. He was always encouraging her to talk about the good life in England and she basked in it.

Those cold shadows that Benjamin so feared became more frequent. The brooding melancholy showed in his dark eyes. Frances had begun to complain that he was much shorter tempered than he used to be. Only the previous day she had accused him of not smiling all day. Perhaps she was right, for there were days when he did not feel much like smiling. Lothar does enough smiling for everybody, why does she need me to smile too, Ben thought.

Lothar's leg was fit enough for travel now; it had been for some time. Barnett knew he should have asked him to leave, but he did not want Fran to accuse him of jealousy. Besides, Bear Claw was so involved with Klein, still intoxicated with what he believed was a link with his mother. He took genuine pleasure in being with Lothar. He did not see what Barnett saw and would find his attitude hard to understand. So Benjamin brooded in silence. At that moment he could well imagine Lothar sitting at the table in the cabin, beguiling Fran with compliments. He was aware that he was scowling and looked at Bear Claw with a softer expression.

"Please answer my question," the Cheyenne was urging, "I must know if my mother's people did this thing."

"Oh Bear Claw, how can I explain it to you? It is a long story, so much more complicated than that bare statement of fact that you have just given me."

"Tell me the story!" Bear Claw squat down on the floor, legs crossed, as he would have done at the campfire for an evening story telling.

Ben gave one quick glance towards the cabin, thinking again of Lothar in there with his wife, then he sat down opposite Bear Claw.

"You told me once," he began, "That your mother told you stories about the heroes of her people, about Abraham and Isaac, Moses and Joshua, so perhaps you remember that many, many years ago, long before Sweet Medicine brought the arrows to the Cheyenne, the tribes of Israel, the Jewish people, passed into the land of Israel over the River Jordan, led by Joshua."

"Yes, I remember. Moses died on the mountain and

could not pass over with his people. That always made me sad, when he loved them so much and led them so bravely for all those years."

"Your compassion does you credit; it must have been a very hard thing to bear, to be able to see the Promised Land, yet not set foot on it. Well, the land over the Jordan was fine land, fertile and well worth fighting for. Many tribes of people lived there already, just like the different tribes live here in America. The Jews conquered these tribes one by one or made treaties with them and eventually they possessed most of the land."

Bear Claw tried not to interrupt. It was bad manners around the campfire to speak before a story was finished, but he knew Ben would not be offended.

"This land, you have seen it?"

"Part of it. When I was at Cambridge, a group of us students spent one vacation on an archaeological dig near Jerusalem." He paused, realising that his listener would not understand him. "What I mean is that we went there to dig up some ruins left by the Jews of the old time, to try to understand how they lived by what was left behind, to get some notion of what they were really like."

"I would like to see this country."

"You would appreciate it. It has a compelling atmosphere and made me think hard about the purpose of my life. But to continue the story- you must realise this is a very shortened version- the Jews themselves were split into family tribes. They managed to come together for a while, but the confederacy wouldn't hold and they split into two separate large tribes, each with its own leader. Society in both tribes became very corrupt, the rich misusing the poor and profit pursued at all costs. Prophets, holy men speaking the truth tried to warn the people that their way of life would lead to disaster, but they would not listen and disaster did indeed fall on both tribes. They were conquered by foreign powers and taken into captivity away from their land"

He paused, gathering his thoughts, searching for the quickest, clearest way to come to the point he hoped to make. His audience of one was enrapt by the story. Ben cleared his throat and continued,

"While they were in captivity, they began to dream of a man who would rescue them, who would be the greatest of the prophets and the finest of the priests. They began to call him Messiah, which means saviour."

Bear Claw repeated the word. He liked the sound of it on his tongue.

"Through good fortune, many of the Jews were able to return to their land and start again, but after some years they were conquered once more by another foreign people called the Romans. This time they were allowed to stay in the land, but the Romans occupied it with soldiers and forced the Jews to pay heavy tribute to their chief, the emperor. In these circumstances, the dream about the Messiah grew stronger and it was believed that when he came he would free them from the Romans. During this time Jesus was born."

"Jesus Christ was a Jew?" Bear Claw sat forward, his eyes opening wider. Ben could not prevent himself from smiling. The Cheyenne was like an astonished child.

"Yes, he was proud to be a Jew and any Christian who would try to deny that is a fool. He had a dream vision Bear Claw, just as you did and in his dream he heard God, the All-Father telling him that he was special. You see, he was the Messiah. He was to be the perfect prophet, the ideal priest, the greatest leader all in one. But he was sent to preach about mercy, love and forgiveness. He was not the people's idea of what the Messiah should be. They expected a warrior to drive the Romans out of their land, but instead he was the most magnificent peace chief of all time. They did not understand him and refused to believe he was the Messiah.

The Jewish priests were afraid that he would stir up unrest among the people, foment rebellion against the Romans and cause bloodshed, so they got him arrested on a trumped -up charge and he was executed."

"They nailed him to a tree Ben, like Lothar said?"

"The Romans did, yes, but it was the Jewish priests who set them on to do it."

Bear Claw was thinking of the Sun Dance pole, that ritual test of a warrior's endurance. He could remember seeing his father hanging from the pole, wooden skewers piercing his breast, straining and swinging to break the skewers through the flaps of skin, while the sun lit the dry ground with a redness fiercer than the blood seeping from White Bull's wounds. His father had proved his courage that day. He wondered if it was like that for Jesus on his cross, the ultimate sun dance. Then he was aware that Ben was speaking again with that clarity of his, every word weighed, every end letter sounded. The story was not quite finished.

"Christians believe that Jesus conquered death, that he came back to his friends after death, transformed, yet more than just spirit. He came back to assure them that there was something beyond death and that we too could pass through it, along the way he had opened to God. Most Jews however never believed in him. They continued to wait for the Messiah; they are still waiting. That's where the two paths divide, but Jews and Christians are very close together in many things. Their roots are in the same traditions. They both honour the great men your mother told you about."

"But Lothar said that Christians and Jews are enemies."

"Lothar cannot speak for all Christians. People live in great ignorance, enclosed in their own little world, they fear anything that seems different from them. The Jews were finally forced to leave their country again because an armed revolt against the Romans failed. They spread out all over the world and because they were living amongst strangers they kept together, practising their own customs and keeping up their traditions. They learned to speak the language of their host country, in your mother's case German, but they also developed a language of their own known as Yiddish, which is closely related to German but has elements of the ancient Hebrew language which was spoken by the Jews in the old time when they lived in Israel. Hebrew is still used in Jewish religious ceremonies."

"Lothar understands when I speak German," Bear Claw stated, "So it cannot be this Yiddish or Hebrew that my mother taught me."

"No, it appears she taught you German. Perhaps her parents were not Yiddish speakers. Anyhow the people that the Jewish settlers lived amongst in all countries did not understand them and were frightened by their strangeness. Also many Jews were talented and hard-working, particularly astute with money and did well for themselves, which caused jealousy." Ben did not try to explain the complications of money lending. "So Jews were often scorned and hated in Europe by Christian people who should be treating them as brothers. Now do you understand what a half-truth it was that Lothar told you?"

He did understand and he was relieved. He stood up and held out his hand to help Ben to his feet. It was a gesture of friendship that Ben accepted.

"But I cannot believe," Bear Claw said, "that Lothar meant to tell me only a half truth. Perhaps he does not understand like you do. Some men are given wisdom to understand things of the spirit and others have different gifts. You are a man of wisdom Benjamin Barnett."

Ben gave him a wry smile. "How I wish I was. But perhaps I'll have time to gain a little wisdom as I grow older."

They heard Fran calling before they saw her. She was standing on the veranda, staring down the yard towards the top land. Her face was red where she had been leaning over the stove, stirring the saucepan for so long and she was irritated.

"Ben, Bear Claw where are you? Are you coming in

for this food or are you not? If you don't hurry yourselves I will give the rest to Lothar. He will soon finish it up."

"Oh he would, he most certainly would," muttered Ben under his breath as they headed for the cabin.

"I ask you one more thing," Bear Claw said. "Do you believe that you will pass through death, go along the hanging road of stars to the All-Father?"

It was a question Benjamin found hard to answer.

"I want to Bear Claw, I want to very much, but I have periods of grave doubt. Yet I do believe in divine mercy and goodness, so triumph over death must be part of that, though I couldn't guess at the form it might take. Not a very positive answer I'm afraid. I don't have your confidence."

"You must believe it. I know there is life at the end of the hanging road. It is good to know that whatever happens here, you and I will meet again before the All-Father."

The Englishman wanted to say something, but it caught in his throat and he swallowed it down. Instead he motioned Bear Claw to precede him up the veranda steps, glad that his friend stood between him and the shadows for a while.

CHAPTER FIVE

They were perhaps twenty miles from the village when they saw the first signs of the Pawnee war party. The tracks showed fifteen horses. There were only six Cheyenne, He-Who-Runs-Fast, Bear Claw, White Arrow, Crow Dog, Old Hat and Horse-Kicking-Hard. When the news had reached him, passed on by two friendly Arikaras, that a bunch of Pawnee, adorned for war, were in the area, He-Who decided to investigate. It was more than likely that the Pawnee were looking for Lone Wolf's village. The Cheyenne had not ridden out intending to do battle, but most of them hoped in their hearts that there might be a chance to win some glory against their enemies.

They followed the trail for half a mile, leading their horses, walking soft. It was dry and silent. Dust whirled in the wind, but the wind made no noise. A few hundred yards ahead the ground dropped away into a gully, the bed of which was not visible to the Cheyenne, but they could hear voices, Pawnee voices.

White Arrow handed the reins of his horse to Bear Claw and ran in a low crouching position to the edge of the gully. Before he reached it he dropped down to the floor and crawled the remaining distance to the edge. It was a wide depression in the earth, like a dried up river bed and White Arrow saw a party of Pawnee lounging around on the grass, chewing pemmican, unaware that they were being watched. Their horses were tethered on the far side of the gulley. The men were confident, elated, laughing and joking, their weapons thrown carelessly on the ground beside them.

White Arrow with a satisfied grin on his face dodged back to the waiting Cheyenne and described the scene in whispers.

"I knew this was a good day."

He-Who-Runs-Fast had been certain that something significant would happen. He had dreamed strange dreams the night before. His coup stick and lance had danced in the air in his lodge. When the Arikaras had brought them the news of danger he was filled with excitement. He opened up the hide bag that hung on his belt and took out a pot of ochre. Yellow was his battle colour. He pushed his finger in the ochre and began to paint his face, deftly tracing zigzag designs across his cheeks. The others followed suit, each using different colours and designs.

A man's war paint was a personal thing; no two designs were exactly alike. To make a mistake in the pattern might mean disaster in battle. They prayed their own prayers too, the words reinforcing the strokes of the finger, sealing in the protection they sought with the paint.

"We will walk the horses as close as we can, then mount swiftly and ride down through them to count coup. If you fail to touch a man, you must be content with that for we must drive off the horses and take them back to the village."

He-Who looked directly at Bear Claw as he spoke as if he expected some challenge or contradiction, but his sister's husband was silent. Bear Claw's face paint was blue, a broad bar across his nose and smudges the shape of tear drops running across his forehead and down his jaw-line on each side of his face. His father had taught him to paint this design. A medicine man had shown it to White Bull and told him it was powerful, but warned him not to use it himself or it would bring him bad luck. He must pass it on to his son. Bear Claw had come through many skirmishes with the enemies of his people without a scratch and never forgot to thank his father in his heart for the gift of the paint signs.

The six men crept closer to the gully, coaxing their horses behind them and when they were almost visible to the enemy, they swung on to their mounts and thundered down the incline, singing their war songs. There was confusion at the bottom of the gully as the astonished Pawnee warriors leaped to their feet, snatching up their weapons.

Bear Claw, his coup stick clutched in his left hand, bore down on a young warrior who was already on his feet, spitting out the remains of his pemmican, angry to have his meal so violently interrupted.

He was wielding a short lance, but Bear Claw ducked inside the sweep of it and touched him full on the chest with his coup stick. Wheeling his horse around on the spot, churning up the ground, he went past the man again before he could regain his full balance and touched him once more, this time on the shoulder. Then he urged his mount away, up towards the Pawnee horses as He-Who had suggested.

He looked around to see if he could pick out White Arrow in the melee, but what he saw instead was He-Who-Runs-Fast pitch over his horse's head and hit the floor with a thud. His wife's brother had ridden down the slope like a devil in torment, so fast in fact that he missed his quarry completely. He tried to wrench the horse's head around to turn back for another stroke, but he was moving too fast to turn smoothly. His mount stumbled, almost falling and He-Who was thrown headlong. He landed on his back and lay stunned by the impact. Bear Claw could see the raised blade of a Pawnee hatchet and urged his horse back into the fracas, riding into the man threatening He-Who, knocking him off his feet. Still dazed, He-Who was struggling to rise now and catching him under the arm, Bear Claw hauled him up behind him on the horse.

Their fellow Cheyenne had already stampeded all the grazing horses. They were driving them on, shrieking and shouting to keep them moving, looking back over their shoulders, anxious about the fate of their companions. Arrows and lances sung past Bear Claw's ears as he drove his willing pony on. The sturdy pinto flew over the grass, despite carrying double weight and they were soon amongst their brothers, putting mile after mile between themselves and the outraged Pawnee.

When they felt they were safe, they stopped to catch breath and He-Who-Runs-Fast remounted his own horse, which had run behind them as if it had been on a lead rope. Old Hat and Horse-Kicking-Hard had counted one coup each. Like He-Who, White Arrow and Crow Dog had missed. Only Bear Claw could claim to have struck twice. Old Hat confirmed it; he had seen it happen.

"You were lucky that Bear Claw saw you fall," he told He-Who. "I saw it too, but I was too far away to help you. That Pawnee would have lifted your scalp to hang outside his lodge long before I reached you."

Crow Dog, angry because he too had failed, mocked his cousin for such a wild rush on the enemy.

"You rode so fast you would have missed them if they had all stood in a row and waited for you," he sneered.

He-Who-Runs-Fast ignored him. He was bitterly disappointed. His dreams had not told him the whole truth. He had led a successful attack, but there was no personal glory for him, all that would go to Bear Claw. That man forever stood in his path. He felt no gratitude towards him for saving his life. He knew how to die. If he had died fighting that Pawnee, the story at the camp fire would have been a good one and his name honoured for ever. But now he would have to listen to men singing Bear Claw's praises and laughing at him because he had caused his horse to stumble. Bear Claw felt the vibrations of hate come out towards him and turned away. His rescue had been instinctive. He would have done it for any of the group and none of them would have hated him for it.

The ride back to the village was a silent one for He-Who's stony face killed all conversation, but their arrival with the stolen horses caused much excitement and rejoicing in the camp. Bear Claw handed his sweating pony over to White Arrow's eldest son to rub down and take up to the grazing land and disappeared into his lodge, thinking it better for the general harmony to keep out of the way.

He was playing a dice game with his nieces, tossing the antler bone dice up in a basket and pretending to bet all his ponies on each throw, when White Arrow stepped into the lodge.

"I'm glad to see you," Bear Claw said with a grin, "I have only one good pony left."

But his brother's face was serious.

"I've come to warn you. He-Who-Runs-Fast is up to something, He has just found out that Lone Wolf has invited your two white friends to his daughter's wedding feast. You know what kind of mood he was in after this morning. He has ridden out of the village and Crow Dog said he was muttering something about discovering if these white men were worthy to sit beside Lone Wolf."

Bear Claw jumped to his feet. "How long ago?"

"Only a few moments. I came straight to you."

"All my ponies are up on the grazing ground."

"There are two outside my lodge, take one of those."

Bear Claw was already running across the camp towards his brother's lodge. White Arrow called, "Shall I come with you?"

"No brother, thank you but this is not your quarrel."

White Arrow shrugged and watched him ride out of the camp.

He-Who- Runs-Fast was only ten minutes ahead. He was riding down into the trees and splashing across the river. When he came into view of the Barnett cabin he dismounted, tied his horse to a tree and went on foot his lance in his hand,

The scene in the yard was very tranquil and domesticated. Frances was hanging out washing. Lothar Klein sat on the veranda peeling potatoes. He was chatting away to Fran as he peeled, taking maximum pleasure in the brief view of her ankles that were revealed as she stretched up to reach the taut washing line. Ben was on the other side of the yard, sharpening his bill hook on a grindstone. Caesar paced around him, irritated by the harsh sound of the blade rubbing on the stone.

He-Who-Runs-Fast saw someone else, Sarah Barnett, who was playing in the grass very near him, reaching out for an orange and white butterfly that eluded her grasping fingers. She lost her balance and dropped on her knees, beginning to crawl after her quarry, determined not to lose it as it pitched on a purple clover, sunning its wings.

She bumped into He-Who's legs as he stood silently watching her. Sticking his lance down into the ground, he picked her up in his arms. Sarah was not a nervous child. She saw Bear Claw often and was accustomed to Indians. Her inquisitive fingers began to play with the soft otter skin that wrapped his braids of hair.

"White man," he shouted at Ben, holding Sarah

out, "You have pretty baby. What I do with baby?" His command of English was minimal but the situation did not need much explaining. Frances dropped the half empty washing basket as she called her daughter's name and began to run towards Ben who was coming across the yard with the bill hook in his hand.

"Damn savage," muttered Lothar Klein, reaching for his rifle that lay on the veranda, but he knew he could not fire at the Cheyenne while he held Sarah in his arms.

It was Caesar who took the initiative. He rushed at He-Who, circling around him, snapping and growling, tearing at his leggings. He could not take up his lance to ward off the angry wolfhound without letting go of Sarah. She was struggling and kicking now, eager to get to her father who was running towards them. He-Who let her go with a frustrated snarl and snatched up his lance. In that moment Ben took hold of his daughter and carried her back down the yard, handing her over to Frances.

"Take her into the cabin and shut the door," he told his wife. She did not hesitate.

"I kill that bastard," Lothar snapped his finger on the trigger of his gun.

"No you won't. Do want to make things worse?"

Ben was anxious for Caesar as He-Who lunged at the dog with his lance and Caesar backed off, still growling. Then Bear Claw rode into the yard.

He had heard the commotion back in the woods and had driven his pony on, frantic to reach the cabin. Now he swung off his horse and landed beside Ben, his hand on the knife at his belt.

"Ah, so you come to protect your white friends," He-Who sneered. "Are they such children that they cannot stand for themselves?"

"What does he want Bear Claw?" Ben asked, his face taut. "Has he come to kill me at last? Ask him."

In response to the translated question He-Who-Runs-Fast smiled. It was a mirthless smile.

"I have come to see if this Barnett is worthy to be a guest at Lone Wolf's lodge. He is a great peace chief, his hospitality is famous, but to sit in his lodge a man must be a warrior, not a digger of the soil." He glanced contemptuously at the cultivated gardens bordering the yard. "If he has the nerve to stand while I count coup, I shall be satisfied."

"You give me your word that you will only count coup and not strike to kill," Bear Claw demanded.

"I give my word. You saved my life today, son of a white woman. I did not ask for it nor wish it, but our brothers saw it and will expect something of me in return. My word is what I give you in return."

Bear Claw searched his face, trying to decide if he dare ask Ben to risk his life. He-Who had lied to him before, but this time he was sure his wife's brother would keep his word for the sake of his reputation. He turned to Barnett.

"Ben, he wants to count coup on you, test your courage to stand and show no fear. It is a hard thing to do, but if you do it I think he will be satisfied. This morning we had a fight with a party of Pawnee. Some of us had one strike, I was lucky, I had two, but He-Who-Runs-Fast did not count coup. This will help to heal his wounded pride and he will leave you in peace."

Ben was nodding thoughtfully, but Lothar laughed.

"You must be crazy to believe that savage will not kill Ben. Look at him, he's like a wild animal. Ben, let me kill him now."

Ben however was not listening to Klein, He gave He-Who a quick look, then said to Bear Claw in a quiet voice, "Do you really believe he won't try to kill me?"

"I cannot make you do it, but I do believe he will not kill you."

"Then I will stand."

Bear Claw signalled to He-Who that Barnett would let him strike. He seemed surprised, but he acknowledged it with a motion of his hand and began to walk back into the trees to fetch his horse. As Frances Barnett came out on to the veranda she could see the Indian retreating and began to hope he was going away. Perhaps Bear Claw had persuaded him.

"What's happening? Is he going to leave us alone?"

Ben turned towards her. "Frances, I thought I told you to stay in the house."

"Yes, but I must know what is happening."

"I tell you what happens," Lothar blurted out, "This crazy husband of yours is going to stand there and let that Indian kill him. This is what happens."

"What does Lothar mean Ben?"

Looking up, she could see the Indian cantering through the trees and her husband stepped out right into the centre of the yard, where he stood very erect.

"Oh God, Benjamin, what are you doing?"

"It's alright Frances, he won't kill me."

He did not look at her for his eyes were fixed on the mounted Cheyenne approaching him. He-Who-Runs-fast had reined in and was lowering his lance. Ben ran his tongue over his lips; they felt very dry.

Fran ran down the steps, but Bear Claw raised his hand in front of her, indicating that she should keep away from her husband and the look on his face stopped her. Lothar Klein put his arm around her shoulder.

The roan stallion of He-Who-Runs-Fast reared up as his rider urged him on. Ben became aware that his fists were clenched and he relaxed his hands. He could hear his daughter crying in the cabin because she wanted to come out. The sound echoed in his head, mingling with the hoof beats of the on-coming horse. Fran's voice was there too, high-pitched, beseeching, but he could not distinguish the words. He only knew that however much he wanted to run, he must stand. It seemed an age before the horse reached him, almost as if it were moving in slow motion, the rider's supple body swaying with the movement of his mount, the garlands of feathers fluttering from the lance. In reality it was only a few seconds. Ben was staring defiantly into the Cheyenne's face when the lance struck him.

Frances opened her mouth to cry out, but no sound came and she buried her face in Lothar's shoulder. She would have fallen if he had not supported her. Ben half expected to feel the pain of the lance point in his flesh, but there was none, just a light prick as the point pressed against his chest and was gone. The horse and rider thundered past and He-Who-Runs-Fast had counted coup.

Barnett closed his eyes and made an effort to stop himself from shaking, suddenly appalled at the risk he had taken. He was not entirely successful and Bear Claw put a hand on his arm. Lothar had seated Fran down on the veranda and levelled his rifle at He-Who. He could bear this craziness no longer. It infuriated him. He had a spot between the Cheyenne's shoulder blades in his sights and his finger tightened around the trigger, but he never fired the shot. Ben turning to look for Frances saw Klein taking aim.

"No!" He stepped over and cracked the German across the side of the head with his fist, a violent blow that sent him sprawling on the floor. "Damn you Klein, don't you ever think? We have been struggling for three years to be accepted by Bear Claw's people and show that we mean them no harm. It has not been easy, but we are still alive. How much longer do you think we would remain alive, any of us, if you shot that man in the back?"

Bear Claw was startled by Ben's vehemence, the violence of his action.

The Englishman was trembling all over, as if wracked by some pain in the centre of himself. All his repressed dislike of Klein had gone into that blow. Bear Claw reached out to steady him, but he moved away as if he could not bear to be touched. Instead the Cheyenne began to help Lothar to his feet. He was coughing and spitting, his mouth full of earth and grit, a red wheal beginning to colour the side of his face. He was swearing in German and vowing he would never try to help a man again.

He-Who-Runs-Fast had not even looked back after he had counted coup. He had given his word and was satisfied. The white man had shown courage, that made his coup all the more worthy and he had no less a man than Bear Claw to be witness to it. He was already well into the trees, unaware of Klein's attempt to kill him.

Benjamin covered his face with his hands for a moment, trying to control himself. He could hear Frances sobbing. She was lying along the veranda steps, her face pressed into the cool wood. Ben knelt down beside her and gently stroked her shoulders.

"Fran, my love, I'm sorry."

He took her in his arms and turned her around to face him. She had not known if he was alive or dead, for she had all but fainted when that lance struck home, desperate to shut the inconceivable out of her mind. When her senses cleared she did not have the courage to look and face the truth. Now, hearing his voice and seeing the anxious expression and concern in his eyes, at first she could feel only relief. She kissed his face everywhere, his lips, his eyes, his forehead, his cheeks, his hair. But when the first moments of her relief were spent, she began to feel something else, anger that he had been willing to risk his life in that way.

"Why did you do it Ben? How could you? He could have killed you so easily. You had no right to take that risk."

"I know it was frightening for you, but Bear Claw assured me that he only wanted to count coup. I trust Bear Claw and you see, he was right."

"And what if he had been wrong? That vile Indian has always hated us. He would like nothing better than to kill you. You should never have taken the risk. It was irresponsible."

Ben felt that irresponsible was an ill-chosen word when the chief motivation for his actions was to ensure their safety for the future.

"I didn't do it to prove how brave I was Fran, far from it. It is not an experience I would wish to repeat. I did it because I thought it would be the safest course in the long run. Bear Claw is certain that He-Who will leave us in peace from now on."

"I'm sick of what Bear Claw thinks." She pulled away from her husband and got to her feet, Ben rose with her. "You should have protected us and killed him before he had the chance to hurt you. Lothar had a gun. I'm sure Lothar would have killed him if he had been in your place. I just cannot believe that you stood there and gave him the chance to murder you. How am I supposed to come to terms with that? If he had succeeded, what would have happened to us, Sarah and I? How would we- oh Benjamin- I don't know how I can forgive you for this."

He tried to explain that if they had killed He-Who-Runs -Fast, none of their lives would have been worth an iota, but he was flustered by her emotional attack. He was offended by her failure to understand his motives, yet felt guilty at the same time. Nothing he could say would sooth her; she truly believed that she would never forgive him for it. She was aware that both Bear Claw and Lothar were watching her. Right then she felt that Lothar was the only one who cared about her feelings. She saw sympathy in his eyes. Her response was to reach out and touch the red welt at the side of his face. Then frightened by her own actions, she fled into the cabin.

Ben stood helplessly on the veranda steps, not sure what to do next.

"She is right." It was Lothar who spoke. "I say you are crazy to do this thing. All you English are crazy. Serve you right if he skewer you with that lance. When a man tries to knock my head off I am not sorry for him you understand. You don't know how to treat that woman. What do you think she is, some Indian squaw, who can live like an animal?"

"Oh, leave me alone!" Ben followed his wife into the cabin and slammed the door behind him. Caesar, who was about to follow, just managed to pull his nose back in time.

"Why do you talk to him like that Lothar?" Bear Claw demanded gravely.

Klein was fingering the red mark on his face. It was painful and he was aggrieved.

"Well, he didn't have to hit me in that way," he replied in German. "Not as hard as that. I was only doing what any man would do. That brother-in-law of yours is a menace."

"But Ben is right. If you had harmed He-Who, his

kin would have taken their revenge. Maybe burned down the cabin and killed all of you. You would not have shot him in the back Lothar?"

Klein shrugged, wondering how he could deny it.

"Well, I'm sorry, I lost my temper, that damn Indian interfering with people when they are minding their own business. Perhaps I was a bit hasty, but I still don't like the way your friend Benjamin hit me."

Bear Claw could appreciate Ben preventing the shot being taken, but he did not like the way he had hit Lothar either. He was equally troubled by the memory of Klein's gun pointing in the middle of He-Who's back.

"Do you do anything to hurt Ben, not today, I mean on other days?"

Klein looked as if he could not understand what Bear Claw was talking about. The fair, openness of his face often gave him an innocent, boyish air. He held his hands out, palm upwards, in a gesture of incomprehension.

"What could I do to hurt him? I like the man, even if he is crazy. He helped to save my leg didn't he? I can't forget that. He's too serious about life that one, head too full of learning. That's why I feel sorry for his wife. She needs something to laugh about now and then. I make her laugh and I suppose he's a bit jealous. It's only natural. I would be jealous if I had a woman who looked like that. Don't worry Bear Claw." He put his arm around his friend's back. "All this will blow over. Tomorrow we will all be on good terms again, you'll see. At least now we can go to your chief's feast without worrying about your brother-in-law. Perhaps it's a good thing this happened. It will clear the air."

"You will not hold it against Ben for hitting you?"

"No, of course not. I am an easy going fellow. I don't hold grudges. Besides before long he will apologise to me."

Bear Claw nodded, but somehow he was not sure that Lothar would let it go that easily and he did not feel that Ben would ever apologise.

❋

Lone Wolf took pleasure in inviting the white men to his daughter's wedding. He-Who-Runs-Fast had called him a hospitable man and so he was. He had promised Bear Claw he would smoke a pipe with his white friends and this was a good opportunity to keep his promise.

His daughter was to marry Burning Fire's brother, who had courted her for five years. It was the linking of two powerful kin groups and the village was looking forward to the magnificent feast that would be laid on.

It was early evening, a few hours before dusk. Bear Claw had come to fetch his friends to the wedding. Frances Barnett was combing her husband's hair and he was trying not to laugh at the discontented expression on her face over the result.

"I wish I had some good scissors," she complained, "Then I could cut this for you more stylishly."

"When we go into Baker tomorrow, you can buy some more scissors and then you can cut it as short and stylish as you like, that's a promise. Now stop fussing over me Fran. Bear Claw's waiting. I'm not being presented at court you know."

"Perhaps not, but all those Cheyenne will be decked out in the finest things they have. It would be an insult to Lone Wolf not to make an effort. I don't want my husband to look at a disadvantage."

Benjamin Barnett would not have looked at a disadvantage anywhere that night. He was wearing the only elegant suit of clothes he possessed. Frances insisted that he buy them during the last month they were in Boston, despite his protesting that he would need nothing so smart for farming in Montana. She brought them out West never-the-less, carefully wrapped in tissue paper. He wore them on her birthday and at Christmas, just to please her, but apart from that the clothes remained in their protective tissue.

The cream shirt was silk and fastened at the neck by a pale blue cravat. The chocolate brown jacket and trousers fitted him perfectly, the thigh length flared coat emphasizing his upright stance and lithe walk. Bear Claw stood in the doorway admiring the effect. He looked pretty good himself in his beaded buckskin shirt. The designs were geometrical and intricate, a mixture of quill work and pony beads in white, blue, black, red and yellow. He wore the leggings that his mother-in-law had worked for him.

"I feel like Cinderella before the good fairy comes," said Lothar Klein. "Everyone has such fine clothes but me."

He was leaning against the mantelpiece, watching Frances fuss over Benjamin. He envied the way her fingers brushed over her husband's shoulders, picking off any stray bits of tissue paper still adhering to the cloth.

"Don't worry Lothar, you look fine," Fran assured him.

She moved across to him and straightened the collar of the blue shirt he was wearing. He bowed in acknowledgement of the compliment and they smiled at each other. She had taken great pains to make her husband look splendid and was proud of the result, but she had to admit that Lothar looked well enough in his faded waistcoat and trousers patched on the knees with squares of leather. The hot spring sun had tanned his face, emphasizing the blondness of his hair. He continued to look at her with open admiration and she found it hard to draw herself away from his gaze.

Ben, glancing across at the German, forced down an urge to make some acid comment. Instead he walked over to join Bear Claw at the door and Lothar followed him. As the others went to mount their horses, Ben turned back to kiss his wife goodbye and ask if his daughter was asleep.

"I wish you were coming with us Fran."

She could not resist one last fidget with his cravat.

"Well someone has to stay with Sarah. Anyway I wasn't invited was I? I can't sit in their circle and smoke that dreadful pipe. Squaws must know their place. Don't worry, I shall be quite happy."

"You won't be frightened?"

"No, I have Caesar for protection, although he would much rather go with you and I shall bar the door as soon as you have gone." She kissed his cheek. "Go on now and enjoy yourself."

As she watched the three of them ride out of the yard, she did not feel as resigned as she sounded. She longed to go to the wedding; it promised to be such a happy occasion. Even Ben seemed happy this evening, much more himself. His brooding had troubled her for weeks and she knew Lothar was at the root of it. She thought it was unreasonable of Ben to be jealous of Klein, for she was sure she did nothing intentionally to encourage him. He was always so pleasant and understood so well how she felt. She could not help responding to that.

She tried to supress her sense of the lust Lothar had for her, as she did not want to acknowledge it. Yet it was her awareness of it that caused her to choke back all her anger at Ben for the way he had jeopardized his life two days before and behave as if nothing had happened. She did not want to stimulate Lothar's desire to sympathise and comfort her, convincing herself that she was careful for Ben's sake, not wishing to add to that dark, troubled look that distressed her so. But this was only a half- truth; it was the old fear of going to Boston alone and not coming back.

Lothar talked of travelling, of cosmopolitan society and he was a constant reminder to her of Boston. He was a born city man with every intention of going back to the urban life. It was a pleasure and relief to listen to him. It astonished her how accurately he could put his finger on her emotions, how he could know just what she yearned for and play on it. When he talked of going away she felt her heart sink because she would feel cut off again, buried deeper than ever in this lonely corner of Montana.

She sat by the window, watching the wild birds swooping down to eat the grain that she had scattered for them. There were no chickens to eat it now thanks to the wolverine. They intended to buy some more poultry in Baker the next day. The thought of Baker cheered her and she began to darn some socks, wondering if Lone Wolf's daughter would like the present Ben was taking her.

Barnett was at that moment feeling in his pocket to make sure that the gift was safe as the three wedding guests rode out of the trees on to the plain. He and Frances had thought long and hard over the problem of what would be a worthy present for the daughter of a chief. Eventually he had decided to give up the Chinese lacquer box in which he kept his pens and charcoals. It was his grandmother's and he would miss it, but he had little more of worth to offer. Frances, not wanting him to be the only one to make a sacrifice, put her crystal bracelet into the box. When Ben had protested, she had shut down the lid firmly, insisting that she never wore it anyway.

Lothar intended to offer the copper kettle he carried around in his pack. It had a small dent in one side, but after he had buffed it up until it shone, he felt it looked respectable enough. Bear Claw assured him that kettles were much prized in the lodges of the Cheyenne.

The sun was setting as they urged their horses up over the bluff that masked the village from view. The colourful lodges of Lone Wolf's people were painted on a backdrop of a gold-streaked sky. Smoke curled in spirals from the smoke holes of the tepees, wreathing in and out of the lodge poles, soft and dreamy. A strange peace came over Ben as he gazed at the village, a warmth enveloped him. The others were riding down the side of the bluff, but he reined in at the top. He sat there absently stroking his horse's neck, letting the warmth steal all over him, as if he were soaking in a bath. He could feel all his muscles relaxing. It was a state that had eluded him for some time now, sleeping or waking held little peace. He felt drowsy, as if the village was part of a gentle dream that was drawing him into its welcoming centre.

"Ben!" It was Bear Claw's voice breaking into his reverie. He and Lothar were at the bottom of the slope, twisting around to look back at Barnett. "Come on, what is wrong?"

Benjamin smiled. "I was just admiring your village. It looks so beautiful from up here." He rode down to join them. "Bear Claw this is a good place to be tonight. There is a good atmosphere here. It is so strong it reached out and touched me."

As they approached closer to the village the dream-like illusion evaporated, for it was a very busy place indeed. People dressed in their finest clothes were passing between the lodges. In the centre of the circle of tepees two men were building up a fire and the whole place was pervaded by the smell of cooking from the lodges.

The three newcomers dismounted outside Bear Claw's lodge where White Arrow, his wife and a host of children were chatting with Painted Shawl. Lothar was soon involved in entertaining the children. He had an instant report with the younger ones and enjoyed himself hugely chasing them around the lodge.

Ben standing a little apart watching the activity, saw He-Who-Runs-Fast talking to his mother in the open doorway of her tepee. The Cheyenne saw him too and pointed, making some remark to Tall Woman. He seemed surprised however when he saw the Englishman walking towards him. White Arrow drew his brother's attention to the fact and Bear Claw followed Ben.

Barnett greeted Tall Woman in Cheyenne, then extended the greeting to her son, who stared at him, unblinking. Ben was working hard to learn enough Cheyenne to hold a proper conversation with his neighbours, but he did not yet feel confident enough to express anything complicated. He feared being misunderstood, so it was in English that he continued.

"He-Who-Runs-Fast I don't know how much of this you can understand, but I hope you will listen to me at least. This is a happy evening for your village and Lone Wolf has invited us here as friends. I know you don't trust me, but my wife and I have always tried to live in peace with your people. We will always try to do so. I wish I could convince you of that. Let us try and bury this enmity between us in honour of Lone Wolf's daughter on her wedding day."

He turned to Bear Claw, asking if He-Who had understood him. Bear Claw was certain that he had, but his wife's brother did not speak. He stood with his arms folded, his face an impassive mask. Ben held out his hand.

"Let me take your hand and we will both try to trust each other better."

But when he looked into the eyes of He-Who-Runs-Fast he could see no signs of relenting, not a flicker of sympathy. They were cold, glittering circles of jet. He-Who spoke rapidly to Bear Claw, a torrent of guttural sounding words, then he turned his back on Ben's outstretched hand and walked away. The Englishman sighed, making a gesture of resignation with his hands.

"Well, I did try Bear Claw. What did he say to you?"

"He said you had more courage than he expected from a farmer and he believes that you have some honour, but he will never shake hands with a white man."

"Beats me why you take the trouble to try." Lothar was beside them now. "Easier to make friends with a rattler. You waste your breath my friend."

Barnett gave him a sidelong glance, a look that betrayed how little he felt like Lothar's friend, but he said nothing, moving away before Klein's hand could come to rest on his shoulder. The significance did not escape Bear Claw. He had noticed before how Ben stiffened if Lothar touched him.

"We must go to Lone Wolf's lodge now," he said, "The wedding is beginning."

Tethered outside Lone Wolf's lodge were ten fine ponies that Strong Heart Man had brought when he asked to marry his chief's daughter. Lone Wolf, his wife and several more female relatives were standing outside the lodge. The chief stepped forward to receive his guests, raising his hand in welcome. He was still grey faced and stooping, but his cough was not so violent and came less often. The warm spring had eased his complaint, but he knew it was not cured. He expressed his pleasure that the white men had accepted his invitation and prompted by Bear Claw, they in turn presented their wedding gifts. Lone Wolf thanked them and handed the gifts to Prairie Flower, who took them into the lodge to show her daughter.

The wedding ceremony proper began when Brown Crane, the eldest daughter of Lone Wolf, was led out of her father's lodge by her mother. She was a small girl with an oval face, not particularly striking, but her almond eyes glistened and clothed as she was in an exquisite beaded buckskin dress, her waist-length black hair shining loose about her shoulders, most of the bystanders thought her beautiful.

She mounted the finest of the horses outside the lodge and an elderly woman took the reins. One after another, women emerged from inside the tepee, sisters, aunts, cousins and each took the reins of a horse. Then the little procession began to wend its way towards the lodge of the groom's parents.

As they passed Tall Woman's tepee, Benjamin saw a pair of eyes peering through the tent flap, sad eyes, eager to see but afraid to be seen. He stared directly at them and the eyes lowered self-consciously, shielded by long lashes.

"Bear Claw, who is that in your mother-in-law's lodge?"

Bear Claw did not need to look to give an answer.

"That is my wife's youngest sister, Singing Linnet."

"Why does she not come out? She will miss everything. Her eyes plainly show how much she wants to see the wedding ceremony."

He looked back over his shoulder, but the eyes had gone, the tent flap closed.

"She has a crippled leg and back. It makes her feel ashamed to be seen. She does not come out of the lodge unless she has to. I try to persuade her that no one looks at her to mock, but she has hidden too long and has no courage"

Bear Claw's explanation was interrupted by Lone Wolf who asked if his white brothers wished to help carry the blanket. The procession had halted outside a big tepee, brightly painted in red and green and a group from inside had brought out a blanket which they spread on the ground at the feet of the bride's horse. She dismounted and sat in the centre of the blanket. Bear Claw told his friends that it was an honour for strangers to help carry the blanket. Young men were stepping forward to take up the edges of it in their hands and following Bear Claw's example, Ben and Lothar did the same.

Brown Crane sat still and serene, her hands folded in her lap, as the men carried her into the lodge and put the blanket down on the floor. Her husband's parents took her hands and raised her to her feet, then all the men shuffled back outside.

"What happens now? Lothar asked in German.

"Is that all there is to it? Are they married now? I haven't even seen the groom yet."

Bear Claw replied in English, not wishing to exclude Ben.

"No not yet. His mother and her relatives will take her to the back of the lodge and dress her in different clothes, different ornaments, for they are receiving her into a new family. Then she and her man will sit at the centre of the lodge and eat food prepared by his mother. They sit side by side and when they have eaten together, then they are married. Yesterday the mothers of them both made a fine lodge for them."

He pointed to the tepee set back behind the red and green one, set well back so that the new husband would not have to come in too close contact with his mother-in-law.

"All the kin have given gifts to furnish it and when the meal is over, the two of them will go to their lodge together."

"And what do we do?" Lothar wondered.

"Go sit around the fire and celebrate. Come!"

Men were already squatting around the fire, the flames burning up as the wind rose, glowing vermillion in the dusk. The cracking and roaring of the dry timber reminded Ben of bonfire nights, when he was a boy. He would go down to the village green with the farm labourers' children, whose fathers worked on the Barnett estate. His parents did not approve of him playing with these children, but bonfire night was an allowed exception.

He remembered how Jack Brown had tied a

firework to a cow's tail on the common and the terrified animal had plunged into Milsom's dairy, upsetting five milk churns and treading in a vat of cheese. If Benjamin had not been with them the boys would have been soundly beaten, but because he was the son of the squire, he had saved them from a fate they richly deserved.

He could also remember how he always dreaded the moment when the flames of the bonfire reached the sad, stuffed effigy of Guy Fawkes. The villagers would cheer and shout, "There he goes. Burn, Guy, burn!" hurling sticks into the fire, singing and chanting. But Ben always felt a great sadness when he saw the body crumple and disintegrate in the charring flames. He had studied history avidly and perhaps he identified too closely with the real Guido Fawkes, the scapegoat, tortured and stretched on the rack until his attenuated, spidery fingers could barely scrawl his name under his confession.

The villagers thought nothing of the real man whose effigy was burning before them and were also only half aware of the ancient symbolism that went back into the distant, pagan past. As a child Ben could never explain why he should feel so melancholy and lonely as he watched Guy burn. He never lost that feeling, even in manhood, when he joined the villagers in their celebration at the end of autumn, the funeral for the warm, bright year past, although the knowledge that out of the ashes the new year would rise and flourish was a message of hope.

He stared at the campfire flames as he recalled those autumn evenings in Wiltshire and Annie, the blacksmith's daughter who had coaxed him into her arms in the big barn near her father's forge on the edge of the common. He was sixteen, she was four years older and very experienced. She knew it was the first time he had been with a woman and eased him into it with gentleness and skill. Her black hair was thick and springy, her brown, freckly skin had a warmth and vitality that made it such a pleasure to touch. He had gone home that night full of conflicting emotions, appalled by his readiness to succumb to the desires of the flesh, but also intoxicated by the strength and the joy of it. It was a dichotomy that he never fully resolved until he married Frances. He wished his wife was beside him now.

He noticed that Lothar had seated himself next to Lone Wolf in the circle around the fire and Bear Claw was beckoning him to join them, as he sat beside Lothar. Klein was eager and attentive, interested in all the proceedings. He asked why there was an empty space the other side of Lone Wolf.

"That is for Pawnee Killer, the medicine man. He will come soon with the pipe so we can all smoke in friendship."

"Pawnee Killer, oh, that's the man who drew the map that you told me about when we were fishing that time. Where is he then?" Lothar was conversing in German on purpose, enjoying the fact that Ben could not join in the conversation.

"Still in his lodge." Bear Claw pointed out the tepee painted white, without pattern or design, conspicuous amongst its colourful neighbours. "He will bring out the pipe soon."

Lothar concentrated on the lodge, taking detailed

mental photographs. As he did so an old man stepped out of the tepee, carrying a bundle, which he placed on the ground and began to unwrap. The German again asked questions, prompting Bear Claw to reply

"That is his medicine bundle. In it he keeps all his precious things connected with his vision quest and the things that help him with his healing powers. The sacred pipe is one of them and the map you spoke of because it is so important to our band."

Klein smiled his satisfaction, but did not show it in his voice.

"A big responsibility," he commented. "He must keep that in a very safe place. I would be afraid of losing it. I lose everything."

"It is tied to the central pole of his lodge. He cannot lose it."

"Does he live in that big tent all alone?"

"Yes, his wife died many years ago. He has no children, but it suits him to be alone with his thoughts."

Lothar was sitting with his arms around his knees, rocking backwards and forwards very gently, as he studied the medicine man, who was now coming across to the circle on his bent, stick-like legs. He had already filled the pipe with his own tobacco mixture, some trade tobacco mixed with red willow bark and sprinkled with powdered buffalo chips to make it catch light easily. He lit it with a stick from the fire and handed it to Lone Wolf.

"Remember," Bear Claw whispered to his white friends, "My people think it is unlucky for the stem of the pipe to touch anything during the smoke. You must not pass it sideways with the stem or the bowl first, but hold it upright, with the bowl pointing to the ground. Watch how Lone Wolf does it."

The peace chief was offering his prayer to the spirits of the cardinal points. He pointed the pipe stem to the sky, the earth and each of the four directions in turn, before he began to smoke. After he had taken a long, meditative draw, he passed it to Lothar, for the pipe always followed the circle of the sun from right to left.

As Bear Claw passed the pipe to Benjamin, Barnett offered up his own prayer that this day would cement his relationship with the Cheyenne, so that his family could continue to live in their secluded corner without fear. The red willow bark had an aromatic scent that stung the nostrils with its grey smoke. Through the haze, at the other side of the fire, Ben could see He-Who-Runs-Fast sitting with Crow Dog, the orange light from the fire making their faces glow yellow and unreal. He wondered what the warrior would do when the pipe reached him. He had already declared that he would not shake hands with a white man; would he also refuse to smoke with one? Ben looked at Bear Claw, who was also watching He-Who.

It was a long time before the pipe reached the far side of the fire. He-Who held it in his hands as if his prayer was a long one. Bear Claw would have given much to know what he prayed for. He feared for a moment that his wife's brother would not smoke, but after a pause that seemed calculated for its dramatic effect, he put the stem to his lips and smoked. Bear Claw saw Ben's mouth form a sigh of relief.

When the pipe was smoked out, the feast began. Dishes of roasted buffalo ribs in a vegetable stew were passed around the guests, who had been provided with horn spoons. Lothar was sucking on a rib bone when he spotted Strong Heart Man and Brown Crane coming out of the marriage lodge together to make their way to the new lodge that was to be their home. He grinned and elbowed Bear Claw.

"There go the newly wed ones," he said in English. "They have a good night tonight eh?"

"Not tonight Lothar, she will still wear the rope."

"Rope?"

"We would call it a chastity belt." It was Ben who answered. "All the young Cheyenne girls wear them. They have a fierce regard for their chastity. But I thought you would have found that out by now. You have been here at least two months haven't you?"

Lothar could not fail to miss the sarcasm in Ben's voice, but he did not rise to it. He just smiled as if he did not understand the implication and avoiding Ben's critical stare, he said to Bear Claw, "But they are just married, surely she will take it off now."

The Cheyenne shook his head. "You do not understand. Although Strong Heart Man has courted Brown Crane for five years, they have not spent time together alone. They talk a little now and then, they look at each other often, but they must go their separate ways and do not really know each other. It is not like with white people. They do not kiss and touch before they marry. So tonight they will sit together and talk and learn more about each other, so when the time comes to make love, they are not strangers. Sometimes it is several days before a new wife will take off the rope and give herself to her husband."

Lothar was shaking his head and laughing at what he considered was absurd.

"I think that is a concept that Lothar is totally unable to grasp," said Ben with a quiet emphasis. "I believe he is used to taking what he wants when he wants. Am I not right, my friend?"

He mimicked Klein's habitual endearment with obvious distaste, the dark eyes again searching for a response. This time he got one, for Lothar looked directly at him, fingering the side of his face where Ben had struck him on the day He-Who-Runs-Fast had counted coup. The mark had disappeared, but right then he could still feel the smart. Every time he saw what he considered to be a look of patrician hauteur on Barnett's face, when that top lip curled just enough to give Lothar the impression that the Englishman thought him beneath contempt, then he felt the urge to strike back, not physically, but in a much deeper, more lasting way. But he knew he must not show it yet. It was essential to remain the injured party in the eyes of Bear Claw. His time was coming; he would not have to wait long now. In that knowledge he could still force himself to smile.

"Perhaps you are right. A man who does not look out for himself is a fool. He deserves misfortune. Only the fittest survive."

"I did not realise you were a disciple of Darwin Lothar. His book on the origin of the species was published late last year, but the copy my brother sent me from England arrived only a few weeks ago so I haven't had the time to study it fully, but I do see that there are aspects of the theory of evolution that are admirably suited to your temperament."

Bear Claw put his hand on Ben's arm. He did not understand what he had just said, but his tone was clear enough.

"Ben, this is the wrong time for bad words between you. When we rode into the village you said it was a good place to be tonight. This is a feast, a time to be friends. Even He-Who-Runs-Fast has smoked with us."

"I'm sorry, you are right, it isn't the place. Perhaps I should have sat farther away from Lothar."

Klein burst out laughing and slapped Bear Claw on the back.

"Oh don't worry about him my friend, I pay no attention to him. These fellows who read poetry and deep books about the soul of things, they have funny moods you understand. They never give their minds a rest. Now me, I don't care for such headaches. Is there any more of that buffalo meat to be had?"

Ben turned his head away, as if to indicate that he had withdrawn from the proceedings and indeed he said nothing more for the best part of the evening. Lothar went on enjoying himself, doing his best to make conversation with Lone Wolf and partaking liberally of meat stew. Bear Claw's appetite had gone however. He was destined always to be in the middle. Trapped between two cultures, he was now caught between these two men, both of whom he called friend.

Over the past few days he had seen clearly how much Ben and Lothar disliked each other. Barnett made no secret of it and Bear Claw could now see through Klein's assurances. He had been observing far more than the German realised. His high regard for Ben prompted him to search for a reason, He could not believe Ben would dislike Lothar on a whim or that it was a simple case of jealousy. He could not forget that Klein had been ready to shoot He-Who-Runs-Fast in the back. The image haunted him, no matter how he tried to excuse it. He had also been more disappointed than he realised about Lothar's attitude to his mother's people.

He was very ignorant about them, yet spoke as if he knew everything, told damaging half-truths, with no understanding that they were hurtful.

The knowledge had dawned on Bear Claw that being Jewish was separate from being German and that Klein was no closer to his mother's people than they were to the Cheyenne. It had been a puzzling discovery at first, but he was growing used to it. Benjamin Barnett, who had never visited Germany, could not speak the language, had more sympathy for and knowledge of the Jewish people than Klein would ever have. Lothar had told him much about the country of Germany, but all the deeper insights into what it meant to be half Jewish had come from Benjamin.

He looked at the Englishman, who sat in silence

staring into the fire, the flames reflected in his eyes and then across at Lothar, laughing with Lone Wolf and he knew he would be glad when Klein was gone. It was not how he wanted it to be and he was unhappy about the admission. It was a relief to him when the story telling began.

Every Cheyenne feast ended in a story-telling. It was the favourite past time around the campfire. A man could draw attention to himself in double portion by recounting his deeds and telling them skilfully. They were not all boastful stories of mighty deeds in battle or hunting. Many were strange tautologies and folk myths or simple domestic incidents, laced with much down-to-earth humour and vulgarity.

Bear Claw was busy interpreting the stories in an undertone to his friends and Klein found plenty to laugh about. He knew some good funny stories himself he said. Perhaps Lone Wolf would like him to contribute. The chief was very willing and with Bear Claw's help, Lothar told a story about his cousin Helmut, who after indulging in too much wine in a Berlin café, wandered into a brothel in the mistaken belief that he was entering his aunt's house. Once inside his adventures were hair-raising. Klein had a gift for comic description which even survived translation into Cheyenne and his story was well received. He sat down, his face flushed with success and the heat of the fire.

"Well Benjamin, my friend, now it is your turn," he announced loudly, knowing that Barnett was not expecting to speak. "Let us hear what good stories they have in old England eh!"

Ben was taken by surprise and the expression on his face showed it. The last thing he wanted to do then was to stand up before all those attentive faces and tell a story. What could he tell them that would strike a responsive chord? A dart of panic passed through him for he could not recall one story; his mind had gone blank. Every plot of every book he had ever read, every stirring tale of courage, every risqué joke all deserted him. He glanced desperately at Bear Claw, hoping he could save him.

"I-I didn't expect this Bear Claw. I know it sounds foolish, but I really cannot think of anything. Must I tell a story?"

Bear Claw nodded. "Now you have been asked to refuse would be misunderstood. It is a thank you to Lone Wolf for his feast."

"Come on now," Lothar goaded. "Do you mean to tell me that a man with his head crammed full of so much learning knows no story to tell a bunch of Indians? This disappoints me."

There was a glint of triumph in his eyes that stung Ben. He slowly rose to his feet, looking around at the expectant faces, hoping that something would come. Then in his mind's eye he saw another face, the face of Jeremiah Collins, his father's gamekeeper and he knew what story he would tell. It had been a favourite of old Jeremiah's and had made the children's hearts beat with a strange excitement every time he told it to them. It concerned Ben's grandfather George Barnett and his pursuit of the ghost fox of Manley Hollow, an obsession that finally led to the squire's death.

Ben began tentatively at first, but he soon became involved in the story finding that it still moved him, just as it had when he sat on the stile by the wood and listened to Jeremiah tell it. Bear Claw, relieved that Ben had responded to Lothar's challenge, did his best to pass on the full weight of his words to the audience, resisting the urge to embellish.

"That particular morning dawned cold and grey. A thin drizzle was falling and the wind moaned around the house. George had dreamed of that fox all night, long, sleek, red with eyes like yellow moons. It ran before him in his dreams, beckoning him with its brush, on and on. Squire George had more fox tails nailed around his stables than any man in Wiltshire, but he had never seen a fox as big as this one. The day he had chased it across the downs, then again when he saw it in the woods, something deep inside him warned him to leave it alone. 'This one is not for you. He's more than you can handle. He's not for the barn door George.' But my grandfather was not a man to listen to the quiet promptings of an inner conscience.

He acted impulsively, as his emotions drove him and more than anything in the world he wanted that fox. He was ready to believe that he would never get another night's sleep again until he drove those great moon eyes out of his dreams.

The hunt began ordinarily enough, the beaters pushing through the thickets, the pack of hounds and the horsemen following after, when suddenly my grandfather saw him, posed on the horizon as if he was waiting for them. I don't know if anyone else saw that fox, but George

Barnett gave the view halloo, the horn sounded and the hounds began to bay.

George could see that fox as clearly as he could feel his horse beneath him and he rode like a madman. Soon all the others were left way behind, until only grandfather and the dog pack were within reach of the fox. On and on they went, over fields, hedges, stone walls, hills, valleys, gardens and streams. He had no idea where they went, only that he must pursue.

At last they reached the coast, many miles from their starting point. He could hear the sea crashing against the rocks somewhere below. There was the fox standing on the edge of a ridge up ahead, beckoning it seemed with his magnificent red brush. Then he was gone as if he had evaporated into the air. George urged his horse on in one last desperate spurt up over the ridge and down to destruction, for it was a sheer cliff face, dropping down to the sea below. Horse, rider and every one of those thirty faithful hounds plunged over the cliff into the waiting sea.

No one ever found the body of a fox, but my grandmother told me herself that about the time the tragedy occurred, she was standing on the terrace at home when she saw a massive fox with the biggest yellow eyes she had ever seen. He stood there looking at her, nodded his head and disappeared into the bushes.

My father, Squire George's son, refuses to believe that there was anything special about that fox and contends that grandfather was the victim of a terrible accident. But perhaps the Cheyenne will see more in this story than my father can. I myself have never hunted the fox and no tails hang on my barn doors."

Ben stood for a moment, allowing Bear Claw to finish translating his words, then he sat down. There was a murmuring and nodding of heads amongst his listeners. They were impressed.

The words had rhythm and they were convinced that Squire George had met the Spirit of the Foxes that November day.

Lothar laughed. "Some story for a man who can think of nothing to say. I wish now that I do not ask you. I say your grandfather was a pretty crazy old man to go leaping off a cliff like that for a fox. You English gentlemen do some strange things, I think maybe you have inherited some of his craziness to leave what you have in England to come and live here."

"I think I have gained more than I have lost. It all depends what you are searching for."

Lothar nodded slowly. "Yes, we all search for something Benjamin. I have a hunger too, but maybe my horizon is more easy to reach than yours. I do not set my sights on life's meaning, I try only to live it."

Ben sat forward, half smiling, pleased that he had once again drawn the German out from behind his camouflage, but the conversation was not continued for another story was beginning.

It was very late, around one in the morning, when the guests left Lone Wolf's camp. Bear Claw rode with them for he intended to travel to Baker with Ben and Frances the next morning. He had some furs and bead work he wanted to trade and the business of the town always attracted him. He liked to see the shops stocked with goods and the big coaches come in from the east with their dust-streaked passengers.

After the story telling had finished, Pawnee Killer had invited Bear Claw and his friends to his lodge for another smoke and a drink. He had been intrigued by the story of the ghost fox and wondered if the elegant white man with his command of words, had any more good stories to tell. He was a collector of stories and could always persuade a man to make him a gift of a particularly good one. Ben was no exception; he willingly gave permission for the old man to repeat his story. "The story is yours," he said with a smile and Pawnee Killer nodded his satisfaction.

As they rode home, all three of them began to feel the effects of the brew Pawnee Killer had given them. It was potent, startling at first swallow, but becoming more palatable with each sip. Now their throats felt scorched and their thinking was none too clear.

"What the devil was it Bear Claw?" asked Ben, loosening his cravat. He could feel the heat rising in his face.

"No one knows," the Cheyenne replied, laughing. "Only Pawnee Killer can make it. It is his secret and he guards it well."

"He has many secrets, that old man," Lothar murmured. He had a clear picture in his mind of the medicine bundle tied to the central lodge pole of Pawnee Killer's tepee. He had memorized every inch of the inside of that lodge. "But that secret I would like to know. I wish I had a barrel of that stuff to take home with me. It is damn good."

"It's damn strong!" Benjamin did not feel entirely secure in the saddle. "A couple more of those and you would have needed a travois to get me home. I've had some drinks in my time, but never anything quite like that. Perhaps it's a good thing that we don't know what it's made from."

The others were inclined to agree with him. Lothar sang the rest of the way home, trying to teach the song to Bear Claw and after a while even Ben joined in the chorus.

The cabin was silent when they reached it, but a light still burned inside and soon Caesar was barking at their approach. Ben tripped on his way up the veranda steps and the three of them sat on the steps for about ten minutes laughing and shushing one another before the Englishman felt able to face his wife, who had not yet unbarred the cabin door.

Bear Claw and Lothar went off to bed down in the barn. Once Klein's leg was well enough for him not to need the Barnett's bed, he had made himself a cosy sleeping quarters in the barn. Bear Claw was happy enough to lie in the warm hay. It smelt sweet. The discontent that had troubled him earlier that evening seemed far from him now. He was looking forward to his trip to Baker and it was good to be there with Lothar as the German sang them both to sleep with a gentle folk song that suited his light tenor voice.

CHAPTER SIX

Benjamin jerked the horse to a halt with an unexpected suddenness, throwing Caesar from one end of the wagon to the other, his claws scraping along the wooden planks as he tried to stop himself from sliding. Barnett turned, looking over his shoulder into the sun haze behind him.

The prairie was green, the grass more lush than the plain they had left. Big white daisies with sun-shaped centres and red star-like flowers coloured the grass. Ben would have appreciated the beauty if he had been in a better frame of mind, but he was too anxious to take it in. His head ached, the pulse beating at his temple, the result of Pawnee Killer's hospitality, but it was more than a hangover that bothered him. He banged his open palm down on the wagon seat beside him.

"Damn it Bear Claw, I shouldn't have come! We should have abandoned the idea and waited until tomorrow. Sarah would be perfectly well by then I'm sure."

Bear Claw was sitting next to him on the narrow plank that formed the seat of the wagon. "Do not worry," he said soothingly, "We will not be gone long, only away one night, back tomorrow. She is safe enough."

"That's not the point. I didn't want to go to Baker just to stock up. I wanted to take Frances because it would be something different for her, some women to talk to for a while. She loves people to make a fuss of Sarah. The whole point of the thing was to please Fran and here we are going to Baker and she is back in the cabin. I don't know why I did it. I must have been mad to let her persuade me."

He paused, glancing at Bear Claw who was contemplating his moccasins.

"Oh, what's the use of pretending? I do know why I did it and so do you. You sit there with that expression of extreme delicacy on your face as if you would never dream of suggesting that I set off for Baker this morning without my wife because I wanted to prove to her that I wasn't too jealous to leave her with Lothar. I do believe that she was testing me when she insisted that we go on as planned. She expected me to make a big fuss about it and then she could accuse me of being unfair to Lothar. Well, I didn't feel like giving her that satisfaction. Isn't that the truth Bear Claw? Your observation is unerring."

The Cheyenne shook his head. "I think she wanted us to go for my sake. She knew I was eager to visit the town and did not wish to spoil things. Your wife is kind"

Ben was not so sure that kindness was her chief motive in this case. That morning Sarah had parted company with her breakfast and had been subject to several bouts of vomiting.

Her temperature was no cause for alarm, but it would have been foolish to take her for a long journey on so hot a day. Frances would not consider it and Ben was ready to postpone the trip. Fran however would not hear of it; he and Bear Claw must go and fetch the supplies. The sooner the chickens were replaced the better. She and Sarah would be safe enough, Lothar would be around to keep an eye on them. She said this with a certain defiant uptilt of her chin, an unspoken challenge, one he had been too proud not to take up. He had climbed aboard the wagon without even kissing her goodbye and now he regretted it. He touched his forehead with the back of his fingers, wishing his head would stop aching.

"Well," said Bear Claw, "We can go back. It does not matter to me."

A lark shot up out of the long grass just in front of them, working its way up in the sky almost vertically, music bursting from its throat, pouring notes down on them with a wild joy. Ben looked up into the sky trying to follow its flight, but it was already too high to be distinguished in the bright sunlight.

"No, we won't go back. We are half way there now. I feel better now I have complained about it. This headache has put me in a foul temper. Remind me not to drink with Pawnee Killer anymore."

He flicked the reins and the horse moved on again towards their destination.

They were hot and thirsty when they arrived at Michael Farmer's store. It was a wooden framed building, painted white. Bear Claw liked the steeply sloping roof with the gables that jutted out into the street and the bow window where a variety of goods were on display. Ellen Farmer, a stocky Irishwoman with a high colour and a warm smile, was brushing the frontage of the shop with a broom. She was delighted to see Ben, coming forward to meet him, wiping her hands on her apron.

"But where's that lovely wife and daughter of yours Mr. Barnett? Don't say you haven't brought them."

Ben was sorry to admit that was the case and explained why.

"What a shame. I bet the child will be right as rain when you get back. But you must be thirsty after that long ride. Come in and have something to eat and drink." She gave Bear Claw a long look, but added, "And your friend too."

They ate boiled meat and potatoes in the parlour at the back of the shop. The coffee was freshly ground and perfumed the room. Bear Claw studied the dresser that took up most of the wall in front of them. It was made of pine and the shelves were overflowing with crockery and glass. Along the edge of each shelf was a row of brass hooks from which hung mugs and cups. He fully believed in the semi-nomadic life of the Cheyenne, when a family's entire possessions could be packed on a travois in less than ten minutes, yet he took great pleasure in the manifold objects the white man collected in his more settled existence. Standing on the bottom shelf of the dresser were four porcelain cups with matching saucers. They were good quality with gilded edges and hand painted with a design of violets. Next to them was a long stemmed vase of blue glass. He thought them very beautiful and was stirred by a desire to hold them in his hands, but dare not touch them in case Mrs Farmer might be offended.

When the meal was over, they walked to the yard at the back of the livery stable where Jack Parkin sold livestock and picked out twenty hens and a rooster, arranging to collect them in the morning when they started for home. Back at Farmer's store Bear Claw traded the beadwork that Painted Shawl had taken hours to embroider for two copper saucepans. She had given him clear instructions concerning the kind of saucepans she wanted. They must be bigger and shinier than the ones White Arrow got for his wife with some of his eagle feathers. He was relieved to find two that came up to her standards.

Ben had loaded up the wagon with supplies and fastened a tarpaulin over them. He came back into the shop dusting himself down, holding the door open for a woman with her arms full of goods. The shop was busy now, several women buying and gossiping. They were discussing the latest dress material, bolts of cloth that Ellen Farmer had arranged at one end of the counter to catch the customers' eyes. He stood watching them, half smiling, wishing Frances was there enjoying it. He had kept some money back for presents and was trying to decide if Fran would like some material for a new dress, when he remembered something else he must buy.

"Have you any good, sharp scissors?"

"We sure have, best Sheffield steel, all the way from England." Michael Farmer pulled out a drawer from under the counter, filled with scissors. "For dressmaking are they?"

"Well partly, but their prime function will be for hair cutting." Ben ran his hand through his hair. "My wife thinks I need tidying up."

If he had noticed the expressions on the faces of the women gathered by the material display he might have been convinced that they would have been more than willing to take him in his present untidy condition. He was certainly the centre of interest. As he had his back to them, he was blissfully unaware of the stir he was causing.

"Wives always believe there is some part of a man that needs tidying up son," pronounced Mike Farmer as he took out the pair of scissors that Ben indicated. Barnett felt the blade and the points, nodded his approbation and dropped them into his pocket. Then he bought a brightly dressed rag doll with hair made from strands of yellow wool for Sarah.

He hesitated over inspecting the bolts of cloth, for the women were still congregated around the area. As he gazed casually around the store, waiting for the right moment to manoeuvre his way nearer the cloth, he saw something in an open leather box that made him look hard. The box was on a shelf just behind Mike Farmer, tilted at an angle to display the necklace inside. Reflecting light from its green depth was an emerald necklace, each stone set in petal shaped collets of silver. He stepped closer to the counter, thinking he had misread the price tag, for it seemed ludicrously low. He could see Bear Claw at the back of the shop, sorting through a heap of kettles and buckets, grunting with dissatisfaction when he failed to find what he wanted.

"Bear Claw, come over here a moment."

The Cheyenne came, followed closely by Caesar

who was tired of chasing cats about the street.

"Look at that!"

"Emeralds!" Bear Claw had not forgotten the word. "They are very like the ones I see on the soldier's lady at the fort."

"They sure are beautiful ain't they?" Mike Farmer turned to look at them himself. "Not real of course, wouldn't be offering them at that price if they was. Belonged to my wife's great aunt. She was a traveller and had these made up by some Paris jeweller years ago. Wonderful copy, hard to tell from the real thing. The old girl died a few months back and left these to Ellen. The trouble is she won't wear anything green, thinks it's back luck. Ain't that crazy, her being Irish and all. You know how the Paddies are always going on about the Emerald Isle and all that Celtic blarney. Green is their national colour. But Ellen is so all-fire superstitious about that colour that she even worries about touching cabbages. So we decided we best sell the necklace."

Ben and Bear Claw looked at each other. Barnett knew now what he wanted to take home for his wife. He thumbed through the money he had in his pocket. Farmer was asking a fair price, but it was more than Ben had left. He had indulged himself by purchasing a generous supply of pipe tobacco and two bottles of brandy. He had not tasted a glass of good brandy in months and was eager to erase the memory on his palate of Pawnee Killer's special brew. Even if he returned those items it was still not enough to make up the money. Bear Claw could not understand why he hesitated. It was such a perfect gift for

Frances.

"What is wrong? Is it too much to pay?" There was disappointment in his voice.

"Well, although it is nowhere near the price of real emeralds, it's still rather expensive and I didn't bring that much extra with me. I doubt if it's the sort of thing Mr. Farmer would let me have on account."

Farmer was eager to sell the necklace and Ben was a good customer. He asked how much he was short of the price. Benjamin spread the money out on the counter.

"A fair bit I'm afraid."

"Wait!" Bear Claw rushed out of the shop to the wagon and returned with two fine pelts. "Will these make up the money?"

"No Bear Claw, you need those yourself. What about all those buckets and kettles you promised to bring back for your womenfolk?"

"Not important. They have buckets, they just want better ones."

Farmer was turning the pelts over, calculating their value.

"This is good fur. I reckon that would make up the money just fine, with a bucket or two thrown in as well."

Ben was still hesitating, but Bear Claw urged him so eagerly that he could not refuse.

"Very well, but I will pay you back in some way when we get home."

The Cheyenne shrugged his shoulders, as if it was immaterial to him.

"Since I know you Ben, you have given me many

things, not so much things to touch, but things from the heart. You owe me no debt."

Ben did not reply, but he took the necklace out of its box and handed it to Bear Claw. He turned it over in his hands and then held it up to the light. Ben could not help thinking that Frances could hardly be more pleased with it than Bear Claw.

"I suppose I had better book a room for the night at the boarding house," he said, half to himself, "It's getting late."

Mike Farmer took hold of Ben's arm and drew him to one side. "I don't reckon they'll accept him in Casey's."

Ben did not comprehend. He thought Mike was referring to Caesar.

"Oh, I shouldn't think they will mind. I know he's a big dog, but he's very obedient."

"No son, didn't mean the dog, I meant the Injun. Luke Casey likes dogs, but I see him help hang an Injun once, calls them the lowest of the low. Now that's not my opinion," he added hastily, seeing the look on Ben's face which was a mixture of incredulity and distain. "I believe in giving all men a fair chance. He's a breed ain't he?"

"His mother was white, yes."

"Seems a reasonable, civilized kind of a fella to me."

"If you mean that he is not likely to go around Casey's boarding house scalping the guests, you are right."

Ben was beginning to walk out of the shop.

"Where are you going?" Farmer called after him.

"To book a room."

Bear Claw had been so engrossed in the necklace, he was not aware of what had passed between Ben and the store keeper. He looked up to see his friend leaving and ran after him.

"Why are you angry?" he asked as he caught up with the Englishman. "I can see it in your walk."

"It seems that the good people of Baker are not yet advanced enough to offer Indians board and lodgings. I've just been warned off Casey's boarding house because Luke Casey likes dogs but not Indians."

"So why do you go there?"

Ben stopped in the middle of the dusty street.

"Because there is no earthly reason why you can't stay there for the night and I am going to make sure the proprietor knows it."

"No Ben, no trouble." Bear Claw was shaking his head. He had long learned that his white blood did not earn him any favours amongst the whites. They did not have the same concept of kinship as the Cheyenne. "I want you to have no trouble over me. People like you here. Let it stay so. I can sleep with the wagon tonight."

"Who's to say they would allow you in the stables either. It's a ridiculous situation. I've a good mind to drive back overnight."

Mrs Farmer was hurrying down from the store, her face colouring with exertion. She was a stout woman with short, heavy legs and running did not suit her.

"Mr Barnett, please don't go over to Casey's. That man has the devil's own temper. Nobody around here likes him. It's a marvel he ever gets any custom in that boarding house of his. He can be mean and violent and I wouldn't want anything unpleasant to happen. I'm sorry that fool of a husband of mine offended you."

"Your husband didn't offend me Mrs Farmer. It was the idea that the people of this town do not regard Bear Claw as their equal, that was what offended me. In fact it is one of the most offensive things I've heard in a long time."

Ellen Farmer took hold of Ben's arm and began to steer him back towards the store, her voice soothing.

"Well, you know how it is around here. People don't know much about Indians and they imagine all kinds of things. Bad things have happened, murders and such and it's only human nature to be suspicious." She reached out and patted Bear Claw's shoulder in a friendly way. "Now you understand that don't you?"

The Cheyenne nodded his assent. He knew about these misunderstandings all too well from both sides of the fence. He-Who-Runs-Fast could teach these whites a few things about misunderstandings and intolerance.

Ben was not inclined to be so acquiescent, but between them they persuaded him back to Farmer's Store.

"But I want you to know that we're not all like Luke Casey," Ellen continued, stroking Caesar's head as the dog pushed against her skirts.

"As far as I'm concerned, any friend of yours is welcome in my house, be he Chinaman or Turk. We have a spare room and I'd like you to stay there for the night. No charge of course, as compensation for this unpleasantness. I'm sure we'll all get on very well."

She tugged at Bear Claw's hair in a motherly way. "Such, pretty curly hair, you don't see many Indians with hair like that. Was it your Ma or your Pa that was white?"

He was about to say that his mother was Jewish, but he stopped himself, remembering that even here Jews might be as unpopular as Indians. He said simply that it was his mother.

It was only when Ellen offered the free accommodation that Ben recalled he had spent all his money. The thought that he might have made a fool of himself by causing a row in Casey's only to discover that he could not pay for the room, deflated his indignation somewhat. In the circumstances he accepted Ellen's offer with gratitude. The room was small and neat, sparsely furnished with a table, three chairs and two narrow beds covered with blue eiderdowns. A heavy oak cupboard stood in the far corner, but the floorboards were bare except for a rug between the beds.

Late that night Ben sat on the wide window ledge, smoking his pipe and staring down into the dark street below. At the far end of the street the saloon was a blaze of light, the sound of a poorly-tuned piano drifting up as far as Farmer's Store, mingled with shouting and laughter. A couple had come out of the saloon and walked down the street, their arms around each other. Ben could just see them in the shadows of the doorway opposite, laughing and kissing. She had a strident, teasing laugh and the way her hands moved over the man's back suggested she was used to pleasing. Her bare, white arms stood out in the darkness and there was something about the way her hair fell across her shoulders that reminded Benjamin of Frances. He turned away.

"Why not go to Bed?" Bear Claw had done just that an hour before, but he could not sleep. He was too aware of Ben's restless presence at the window.

"Get some sleep, you will be tired."

"You sound like Fran."

"You think about her?"

"I think about her most of the time Bear Claw, but perhaps I don't make that clear enough to her."

The couple across the street had moved on. He watched them disappear down an alleyway, then he stood up and extinguished his pipe with his thumb, knocking out the ash into the empty fire grate.

"I suppose I had better get some sleep."

He took off his shirt, boots and belt and lay on the top of the bed without disturbing the bedclothes. It was a sultry, airless night and he felt claustrophobic. Bear Claw was enjoying the softness of the sheets. He had never slept in a bed like this before. A buffalo robe was warm and comforting, but it attracted all manner of unwelcome guests, insects of every variety. The sheets caressed his skin and he began to understand why his mother had talked so often of her longing for clean sheets.

Ben turned out the oil lamp and the room was pitch black until the cloud passed from the moon. Then a shaft of light through the window illuminated the far corner of the room like a pale spotlight.

"I'm sorry Bear Claw," Ben's voice came from the darkness, "Sorry about how it was today, the room and everything. I shall never understand why human beings wish to humiliate each other so."

"They are not all so. Mr and Mrs Farmer are good friends to us."

"Yes, but folks like them are too rare. It often seems strange to me that the native tribes are willing to refer to themselves as Indians, when it can't be a word in any of their own languages. Have you never wondered where the word comes from, why the white men call you that?"

Bear Claw admitted that he was curious. "I have always thought it must mean something in your tongue. We do not use it amongst ourselves, only when talking to whites because it is something they understand. In our tongue we are Tsehestano, to you Cheyenne. That part of the Cheyenne nation that lives in the south call us Notameohmesehese, Northern Eaters, because we hunt for food north of them."

"I like the visual quality of your language, the way your words for things form pictures, although I am finding it hard to learn." Ben replied. Bear Claw was considering Barnett's original question. "I have noticed that you do not use the word Indian very often. You never call me an Indian, always Cheyenne."

"Well, mainly because it is so frequently used as a term of derision now. It wasn't so when the name was first used. When early adventurers from Europe first sailed to America they were looking for an easier route to a country called India, where many spices and other goods could be bought that sell for high prices back in Europe. When their ships landed on the shores of this country they first believed they had reached India, so they called the local people Indians. Even when their mistake was realised the name stuck."

"Do the people of India have brown skin?"

"Yes, they do."

"How do you know all these things Ben?"

"By reading and study. There is so much to learn about the world. I feel privileged to be granted the chance to observe the customs of the Cheyenne. There is much to admire in the way your society is organised. It angers and saddens me that so many white Americans make no effort to distinguish between the different tribes and the wide variety in their customs and languages, but lump them all together as Indians and dismiss them as mere ignorant, bloodthirsty savages. I know your way of life can be harsh and violent, but white men are equally capable of brutality. I shouldn't have given in so easily about Casey's boarding house. I should have made an issue of it."

The Cheyenne was not so sure about that.

"Someday maybe it will change," he suggested

"Not if we let people get away with it without challenging them, just as you challenge the attitude of He-Who-Runs-Fast. It will be a hard struggle to bring a spirit of toleration to towns like these."

Bear Claw, as he turned over on his side to attempt to sleep, was wondering if it might be part of his destiny to help bring that about.

❈❘❈

Frances Barnett had viewed her husband's trip to Baker that Friday morning with mixed feelings. Her disappointment at not going was allayed by her success in forcing Benjamin to accept her martyrdom. It would have been easy to agree to postpone the trip; no one would have minded that much, but she was embarrassed that Bear Claw had stayed the night to no purpose and might consider her a fetter on Ben's freedom of movement. Then there was the question of Lothar.

Ben was right to believe that she was testing him, trying to gauge just how jealous he was of the German. She had seen that look pass across her husband's face when she suggested staying, half accusing, half insecure and she was determined to show him he was foolish and mistaken. The more he hesitated about going, the more she urged it.

She had not been pleased the previous night after sitting up into the early hours, to find that he was not quite sober when he finally got home. She had the well-bred young lady's distaste for drunkenness instilled in her by a severe governess. She had always admired Ben's control in company when the drink was flowing. He could enjoy his brandy, but always knew when to stop. This was the first time she had seen him in any state of intoxication and it pained her to an unreasonable degree.

That night he was embarrassed by his condition, chiefly because it had taken him by surprise. He had felt himself growing more confused by the minute as he rode home, He had tried to make a joke of it, but she would not respond, just went about her wifely duty by helping him to undress, her face a picture of gentle reproof. He had never found buttons so hard to undo and he let himself be put to bed like an errant child, struggling to stay awake as he watched Fran do all manner of unnecessary jobs around the room. Clearly she had no intention of getting in to bed until he was asleep.

She refused to show any sympathy with the headache that he woke with next morning. She intended to later, but the events of that early morning had overtaken her. Sarah started to be sick almost as soon as she was taken out of her cot and two hours later, there was Fran, holding her daughter in her arms, watching Ben and Bear Claw on their way to Baker. Bear Claw was waving to them, but Benjamin did not turn as he drove out of the yard. She could tell from the set of his angular shoulders that her challenge had hurt his pride. She had never known him fail to kiss her goodbye.

As the morning wore on her pleasure in her success was overwhelmed by her regret. She could imagine herself running after the wagon, asking to be forgiven. She began to busy herself in the house, fussing over Sarah, washing clothes, cleaning things twice over with vehemence.

She was frying flapjacks in a battered pan, when she felt someone stroking her hair. It startled her, for she had heard no footsteps. For a moment she imagined that Ben had changed his mind and driven back home. She turned, ready to be contrite, happy to see him and stared into Lothar Klein's pale blue eyes. He was rubbing the strands of her hair between his fingers, appraising the texture of it.

"By God, your hair is so beautiful! All these weeks I want so much to touch it. I am not disappointed."

She stood very still, but he could see her grip tightening on the fork in her hand. He let go of her hair, smiling reassuringly.

"I smell the cooking from the barn, so I know it is dinner time."

She was still frozen to the spot, so he stepped around her to sniff at the flapjacks in the pan. "They look good. How do you learn to cook so well? I bet you do not do this in England eh? Daughter of a baronet, you have cooks and maids at home. That is right for such a lady as you. See how this cooking, washing and cleaning hardens your hands." He took hold of one of her hands. "Hands like these must not be spoiled."

His touch unfroze her and she pulled her hand away, turning back to the stove where she jabbed nervously at the flapjacks, lifting them off the bottom of the pan to prevent them from burning.

"I have learned so many useful things since we have lived here. I was so helpless before I married Benjamin, no use to anyone."

Lothar laughed and went over to Sarah's cot, peering at her solicitously and arranging the bed cover.

"The little one is sleeping now. I think her sickness is not serious, but if it was, I worry about you so far away from doctors. This is no place for a little one. No place for you. That man of yours makes me mad, a strange way to show his love to bring you to this godforsaken place just because he wants to be alone, to hide from the world. Maybe he expands his soul as he says, but what does that do for you and the little one? You have no friends, no one to talk to. It hurts me to see it."

She tried to speak, but nothing would come. Lothar drove home the shaft.

"This is not love he gives you, your fine English gentleman. I see how he looks at me, how that proud mouth of his curls at me. He thinks I am scum.

Well this scum knows how to love a woman, I am telling you. I would not waste you here. I am going to be one damn rich man Frances and if you are

my wife, then I am proud to show all the gentlemen in Europe what a beautiful woman you are. I will not hide you, I see you dressed in silk, sitting in fine gardens or at the opera, admired by everyone, that is what you are to me. I will give you everything you want."

Without any warning he put his arms around her and pulled her close to him. "I am going tomorrow. After tonight I shall know how to reach my treasure. It will make me rich for the rest of my life and you will share it with me, you and the little one. We will have a house in Paris maybe and one in London. Bright comfortable houses, with servants to keep them so, Velvet curtains, big, soft beds."

His hands stroked her breasts. She did not struggle; she was hypnotised by his words. "The little one will have a nanny and then a good governess, so she will grow into a fine lady like her mother. What does she do here eh? Run wild with Indian brats. Do you want that? Come with me Frances, you can have anything you want, anything."

He pulled her down on the bed, kissing her throat and breast, caressing her hips with his fingers. She did not respond, neither did she resist, just lay passively staring beyond him. He had expected her to struggle at first and was puzzled by her stillness. It was only when he lifted her skirt and began to pull at her cotton underwear that she showed any signs of distress. She sat forward, pushing him away.

"No Lothar, no please, I don't want to. I will not do it. Please don't force me."

She seemed filled with great strength and he had trouble holding her down. He was breathing hard for he had almost gone too far to stop, but Lothar's calculating mind was still in control. He had seen the perfect way to assert his superiority over Benjamin Barnett and his kind, he would take his woman from under his nose, but the success of his scheme depended on Frances' willingness to come with him. He might jeopardize the whole plan if he went too far now. He must show himself to be gentle, there would be plenty of time later. He smoothed down her skirt and kissed her face, his soft moustache rubbing against her cheek.

"Alright, I do nothing you do not want. I only want to make you happy. Can you blame me if I lose control when you are so beautiful?"

"Let me up, please let me up. The pan is burning. It will catch fire."

Indeed smoke was pouring from the stove as

the flapjacks burned to a crisp. She got up from the bed, running to the frying pan, clutching the handle as if it was a saviour. Lothar believed for a moment that she was going to hit him with it and flinched involuntarily. There was a wild look on her face that he could not interpret. She plunged the pan with its smouldering contents into the water bucket by the door and gazed into the bucket as the steam rushed hissing upwards. She was trembling, but there were no tears and Lothar decided to accept this as a good sign.

"I am sorry that I upset you. Forgive me, but I hold so much within me for so long. Just remember that I long for you. I will go pack for tomorrow. I leave you to think about it."

He left the cabin confident that the seeds were well sewn.

Frances sat in Ben's rocking chair all afternoon in a strange torpor. If Sarah was restless, she played with her, but she did so as if she were sleepwalking, unaware of what she was doing. She wanted Lothar to come back into the cabin, yet was terrified that he would. She needed to reason, but could not think clearly. Her mind was a whirling kaleidoscope of sensations. Ben was there amongst those fast moving pictures, her honest, handsome Benjamin, who had been everything to her since she was eighteen. She reached out for him. Everything would have been alright if she could have held him, but the pictures were moving too fast and he had moved past before she could touch him. She spoke his name, hoping it would bring the circle round again, but instead she could feel

Lothar's moustache brushing against her face and she could not explain to herself why she had let him go so far.

She was tingling with shame, not just because of the physical confrontation with Klein, but also she had allowed him to call Ben selfish and self-absorbed without defending him. How dare Klein suggest that Benjamin did not love her? How could he presume to know? Yet the more she tried to reason, the more she knew she could not let Lothar go without her. He had offered her what she dare not offer herself. The chance would not some again.

The hours passed and it grew dark, but she did not get up in her customary hurry to bar the cabin door. She did not go out to tend the cow and put the goat into the barn. The fire was burning low, but she did not notice.

It was the sound of hooves that first stirred her. She roused herself and went to the window. Lothar was riding out of the yard. She thought he was leaving and ran out on to the veranda, calling after him, but even in her agitated state, she could see that he carried no pack. He would not leave without his belongings.

She wandered back into the cabin and lit the lamps, but their cheery yellowness did not give her the usual pleasure. Her lethargy was gone now, replaced by a fierce nervous energy. She put Sarah in her cot and sang her some nursery rhymes. Then she paced about the room picking up things, Ben's piece of charcoal, the half-finished sketch of Sarah he had begun a few nights before, his clean shirt that she had washed only that morning and the old hat he wore when he worked on the land that she had tried to throw away a dozen times. She held them in her hands one by one as if she were performing a magic ritual that would make her husband appear in the room. She opened the bottom drawer of the cupboard and pulled out the box where she kept his best suit, the one he had worn last night. She had put it away so carefully, but now she unfolded it and replaced it all, spreading the tissue paper obsessively.

Then it was the turn of the precious book of sonnets. She could not bear to open it, to re-read that sonnet of Dante's, but held the book in her hands, tracing her fingers over the tooled lettering on the spine. Round and round the room she went, like a mechanical canary in a cage, touching, moving, listening. She could hear crickets grinding out their harsh song, owls in the woods with their long, mocking hoots, even the distant groan of a bear, but not what she prayed to hear, wagon wheels rattling across the yard.

Benjamin might have driven straight back from Baker if he was anxious enough. She knew that if he walked in the door then she would throw herself into his arms and never think of leaving him again. He did not come. He was sitting in the window just then in the top floor room at Farmer's Store, watching the couple across the street, wanting her as much as she wanted him, but he would not be home.

Another hour went by. Horse's hooves again, a single rider. Lothar had come back. She began to shiver, despite the mild air. He was running up the veranda steps, surprised to find the door unlocked. His face was flushed and he was short of breath.

"We must get out of here now, while it is safe. In the morning it will be no healthy place to be."

She stepped back from him, shaking her head.

"Lothar what do you mean? What have you done?"

There was an excited glow in his eyes that frightened her. He held up his hand and she saw that he was clutching a piece of buffalo hide. He opened it out in front of her. It looked like a map, crudely painted, but with directions clearly marked.

"This is our guide to the treasure. This little thing will make us rich, but we must go now. The owner did not part with it of his free will. His friends must not discover who has taken it."

"Lothar, you have stolen it. Who from? Not the Cheyenne, not from Bear Claw's village?"

She realised it must be so even as she asked, for there was no one else within miles and he had not been two hours away. He was gathering up some of Sarah's things.

"Hurry, get your clothes and the things you need for the little one and all the food you have." She still stood there shaking her head. "Damn it," Lothar shouted, catching hold of her arm, "If those Cheyenne find out I have the map, they come down here and kill us, the little one too. You know what those Indians are like. It is crazy to think you can live with them."

"But Bear Claw is your friend. He trusts you. This will hurt him so much. Don't you care about that?"

"Ach!" Klein shrugged his shoulders. "I am sorry

about Bear Claw. He is a good fellow and I like him, but when a man dedicates his life to becoming rich he cannot turn aside for friendships. This is my one chance. I take it while I can and you must do the same. I will make a new life for you. I promise it will be a good one."

He kissed her, then continued his feverish collecting. She watched him, appalled at the situation she was in. She thought of the way He-Who-Runs-Fast had held Sarah out in his hands. "White man you have pretty baby. What I do with baby?" She had heard those words over and over again in her dreams. She must get Sarah away from this place, away from those strange, unpredictable Indians that frightened her so much. Now there was no choice; Lothar had cut off all retreat. She began to help him pack.

He went to the barn and hitched his horse to a small cart, little bigger than a pony trap, but sufficient to carry the three of them and their belongings. Then he roped Ben's horse to the back of the cart. When Frances came out on to the veranda, Sarah in her arms wrapped in her Cheyenne blanket, Lothar had everything packed.

"Come," he called from the seat of the cart, "We must waste no more time." He was holding out his hand to help her up, but she hesitated.

"Not Ben's horse Lothar, you must not take his horse, not Sandy. Ben loves that horse and he loves Ben."

Lothar snorted contemptuously. "Horses love nobody. They are happy as long as they get enough to eat. We need an extra horse, a good strong one like this. He still has the wagon horse to ride. If you look over your shoulder all the time for that damn Englishman, you better not come with me. Stay here and moulder away, seeing no one, knowing nothing, that is if the Cheyenne let you live long enough."

"But what about Ben? When he comes home he will not know what you have done. He won't expect any trouble and they might kill him."

"He is the fool who chooses to live next door to savages. Let him reap the rewards. He is a big fellow, he can look after himself, besides Bear Claw is with him. He will protect him. Now do you get up on this cart or not?"

Her feet would not move. Even now she clung to the forlorn hope that the wagon might come down past the top land. Lothar flicked the reins.

"Alright, suit yourself. I am going."

"Lothar, wait! Stop! Don't leave me here. I am afraid to stay here. I want to come with you."

He looked over his shoulder and smiled to see her running down the yard behind him. He pulled the horse to a halt and took Sarah from her while she climbed up beside him.

"I know you see sense in the end. You are a clever girl. I will show you what it is to live. You will not regret it."

She could not help herself from looking back at the cabin as they sped out of the yard, straining her ears for the sound of a wagon.

CHAPTER SEVEN

Bear Claw struggled down the slope towards the village. If Jacob Marchak had been able to see his grandson at that moment, he would have believed the boy had gone into the family trade, for he was hung with pans and kettles. They banged together as he walked and it made him laugh. Ben had dropped him off beyond the woods, close to the village, because Bear Claw was eager to get back to Painted Shawl and show her that he did listen when she talked about pans. He intended to walk over to the Barnett cabin in the evening and collect his horse, which he had left in the stable when they took the wagon to Baker. He was keen to see Frances wearing her necklace.

It was barely midday, the sun not at its height, but it was already hot. The Cheyenne was so thirsty he thought he could drink the creek dry. The air was alive with insects. Long, brown horseflies with furry abdomens settled on his hair, flitting across his vision and irritating him. When he swat at them the array of pans jangled even louder.

They had left Baker very early that morning. Ben had spent a restless night, finding sleep impossible. Around five a.m. he had at last slipped into a light sleep, but he awoke abruptly after ten minutes, certain that he had heard Frances calling him. He knew it must be a dream yet it was so distinct , as clear as if she was there in the room. He got up and dressed, eager to set off for home as soon as possible. He had not enjoyed his trip to Baker. Bear Claw was sorry because he had enjoyed it. The hospitality of the Farmers, the good fortune of seeing that necklace, the soft bed with its white sheets, the ride back in the early morning over the prairie grass, all these things felt warm inside him.

The moment he stepped within the perimeter of the camp his happy mood dropped from him. An air of gloom pervaded the lodges, so strong it was tangible. It came out to meet him and wrapped around his shoulders like a cloak. He felt a wave of fear pass through him, although he had no idea what he feared.

His lodge seemed deserted and throwing off his load of utensils, he called for Painted Shawl. She heard his voice and emerged from her mother's lodge. Her eyes were big and moist as if she had been crying.

"Oh Bear Claw," she spoke before he could ask what was wrong. "Something so bad has happened. Pawnee Killer has been murdered. It must have been during the night. Someone got into his lodge and hit him over the head. It is hard to believe, but his medicine bundle was broken open."

Bear Claw felt all the colour drain out of his face as if the blood had suddenly stopped flowing. He did not speak; he could not. His sister-in-law was saying, "Burning Fire and the Elks have been questioning everybody in the village, but nobody saw or heard anything. The place has been in an uproar of confusion. Who could have done such a thing?"

Bear Claw gripped her arm. The intensity of it startled her.

"What is missing from the medicine bundle? Is anything gone?"

"I don't know. White Arrow might. He has seen it because he was the one who found Pawnee Killer, but he did not say that anything was missing, only that all the things were scattered on the floor of the lodge. Lone Wolf and Burning Fire are in the lodge now, sitting with the body."

Bear Claw ran across the camp, his heart banging against his rib cage as if it was trying to break out of his chest. He burst into the lodge of mourning with indecent haste. Lone Wolf, Burning Fire, White Arrow, He-Who-Runs-Fast and six others, sat around the body of the medicine man, which was covered by a buffalo robe. They were praying and chanting, but when Bear Claw crashed through the tent flap, startled, disapproving eyes were turned towards him. Lone Wolf raised his eyebrows.

"Bear Claw, it's good that you come to pay your respects to our old friend, but you were never taught to hurl yourself into a lodge where a man lies dead as if you were a tornado."

He stopped for he had taken a good look at Bear Claw's face. It was a picture of anguish.

"My son, Pawnee Killer's death is a shock to you. Come and sit beside me and pray."

"Forgive me Lone Wolf for my bad manners, but I must know something. I must know if anything is missing from his medicine bundle."

"We collected it all together, at least White Arrow did. He did not notice anything."

"Are you sure?" Bear Claw turned to his brother. "This is important. Was the map there, the map that shows the way to the sacred cave of Sweet Medicine?"

White Arrow hesitated. There had been several pieces of buffalo hide, but he had not looked at them closely.

"I think so, but I am not sure."

"We must be sure. I must look in the bundle."

"No." It was Burning Fire who spoke. "It has been tied up ready to lie with him in death. It has already been violated once. We must not do it again."

"I beg you to let me open it. If it is there it should be passed on to someone for safe-keeping, but if the map has gone, then I know who has done this thing."

He -Who-Runs-Fast sat forward attentively, but he did not speak. Lone Wolf, moved by the anguish that he saw in the man he hoped would be the next peace chief of his people, stood up.

"If this is true my son then I think we can open the bundle once more." Burning Fire protested, but the chief raised his hand to silence him. "We must know who murdered Pawnee Killer. We do him no dishonour to open the bundle for this purpose and if the map is there he would wish us to preserve it."

He pulled back the buffalo robe and Bear Claw

stiffened as he saw the wound on Pawnee Killer's head. The blow must have been dealt with tremendous force for the skull was almost cleaved in two. He saw that picture again, that mental image of a gun barrel pointing at the centre of He-Who-Runs-Fast's back. Even before Lone Wolf opened the bundle, Bear Claw knew that the map was gone. He waited without hope as the chief began to untie the rawhide thongs. Lone Wolf laid the bundle on the floor, searching through the bits and pieces that had been part of Pawnee Killer's life and must now accompany him in death.

"There is no map," he said.

Bear Claw in one swift movement tore from his throat the pendant that symbolised his name and threw it on the floor. Then taking his shirt at the neck with both hands, he ripped it apart so that it hung from him like a loose waistcoat. He felt as if he had rent himself in half with it.

White Arrow jumped to his feet, dismayed by his brother's violent expression of grief.

"I do know who killed him. It was a man I trusted as my friend, a man I called my brother, a man who has sat by your side as a guest and eaten in Pawnee Killer's lodge. I am responsible for his death because I brought that man here." He turned to Lone Wolf, his eyes desperate. "Oh father, I have killed a brother Cheyenne, not with my hands, but with my blindness. I have flecked the arrows with blood and shamed my people."

Lone Wolf put out his hand to comfort him, but he was blocked by He-Who-Runs-Fast, who pushed himself in front of Bear Claw.

"Barnett," he demanded, "Barnett did this?"

"No, not Ben. When will you learn about Ben? He has been with me since yesterday morning. No, it was Lothar Klein!"

"How did he know about the map?" asked White Arrow, puzzled.

"I told him, that's how he knew. Like a fool I told him everything he wanted to know because I trusted him. He said he was my friend and I believed him. When he sat in Pawnee Killer's lodge the night of the wedding feast, when he shared his drink and laughed with him, he was studying the position of the medicine bundle, how he could get into the lodge and steal the map. It's all so clear now and yet my eyes were blind because" He stopped, not willing to formulate the words. He was blind because he had loved his mother so much. It was Hannah Marchak who had veiled the truth about Lothar Klein from him. Her revenge against White Bull had fallen hard on her son.

"I know why." He -Who-Runs-Fast did not hesitate with his explanation. "It is because you are a white man in your heart, not a Cheyenne. I have always said so and now we have proof. I knew these stray whites you bring to us would harm us one day. You are not worthy to be called a Cheyenne. Leave us in peace son of a white woman. Go back to your mother's people where you belong. It was a bad day when my sister married you. I am glad she did not live to see you now. I do not wish to speak with you again, ever."

So saying, he turned his back on Bear Claw, the formal expression of ostracism, to reinforce his intention of excluding all speech and walked to the back of the lodge. Bear Claw could not look into his brother-in-law's face as he spoke; he felt the words too deeply. His face flushed and he lowered his eyes. He did not know what hurt him most, the pain of Lothar's deceit or his own foolishness in not seeing through it. A true Cheyenne would not have told the German about the map. Perhaps He-Who was right; he was not worthy to be a Cheyenne.

"We don't all feel like He-Who," White Arrow reminded his brother. "I don't blame you for this. You were deceived. He behaved like a friend. But what I don't understand is why he wanted the map to the cave."

"He had heard a story that it is a gold mine, big pieces of gold encrusted in the walls. I told him that it was not so and he seemed to believe me, but that must have been part of his design. He must have been planning this almost since I saved him from that pit in the woods."

"The ways of a deceitful man are hard to penetrate," murmured Lone Wolf, his hand resting on Bear Claw's arm. "They twist and turn like a snake. You have a clear and honest heart that would not suspect a man of such things. You are not to blame for this death, although it speaks well for you that you feel responsible."

Burning Fire agreed, but he pointed out that something must be done quickly to stop Klein from reaching the sacred cave. He was ready to call out the Elk members to track him down and He-Who backed this up eagerly. Bear Claw knew he must make a decision, one that would bind him wholly to the Cheyenne way of life. Now he must prove he was worthy to live among his father's people or else he must go to his mother's kin and look for acceptance there, but he had been a Cheyenne too long to imagine he could live any other way.

"I will track him down. I caused this disaster to fall on us, so it is my duty to avenge Pawnee Killer."

"It will not be easy for you," Lone Wolf warned. "It is never easy to kill a man who has been your friend, no matter what he has done." "It will be easier for me than to live here in shame. No one can deny that it is my right to do it and I swear I will not hesitate. If I succeed and return to the village, I will stand pledge for the sacred Arrow renewal ceremony, so that the stains can be washed from the arrows. I will ride around all the bands of Cheyenne on the plains and announce my pledge."

He took out his knife and incised a small cut on the inside of his forearm, squeezing the blood from it with his fingers.

"You are witnesses that my blood seals my pledge."

They all knew that he could not be denied the chance to avenge Pawnee Killer. No true warrior would have challenged his right. Even He-Who-Runs-Fast spoke no word against it.

"We are witnesses." Burning Fire affirmed and Bear Claw left the lodge.

He went to the sweat lodge, to purify himself, burn away the dross of bitterness, disappointment and self-pity. He sat in the steam, rocking from side to side, trying to concentrate on his prayer for guidance, but as the sweat glistened on his body and the heat made his pulse race, he could not clear his mind. Over and over he saw himself offering his friendship to Lothar, telling him things from his heart, precious things that Lothar had received with that affable smile, that show of interest, but which could have meant nothing to him. Bear Claw hated the feeling of being used. If only he had not been so entranced with the notion that Klein's being German was a link to his mother. If only he had tried sooner to understand Benjamin's dislike of the man.

These thoughts went round in his head making any attempt at ritual preparation impossible. He pushed his way out of the sweat lodge, ashamed of his inability to exclude these thoughts from his mind. When he had dried himself off, he found White Arrow and Painted Shawl outside his lodge packing his bag with provisions. His brother handed him his shield and lance. Bear Claw studied the shield's design, the forbidding sword between two feathers. His dream vision had been a true one.

"I shall not need these," he said, handing them back to White Arrow. "You keep them safe for me."

In the dark lodge he dressed in silence, fitting his arrow quiver over his shoulder and taking his bow down from the lodge pole. His nieces stood in the doorway, their faces solemn. He stroked their hair and they clung to him, eager to show that they did not blame him for what had happened.

Outside in the dusty, yellow air White Arrow handed him the reins of his horse.

"I wish you would let me come with you. Your heart is so sore. It would help you to have company."

"White Arrow, could I stay with you when you caught your eagle?" His brother shook his head. "Well then, this is something that I must do alone, but I appreciate your wish to come with me."

"Aren't you going to put on your paint?"

"No, not yet, not until I find him. I will go to Ben first and tell him what has happened. He will not be so surprised. He never trusted Lothar. You keep an eye on all the women folk here for me. I don't know how long I shall be gone. If I don't come back, do your best to provide for them, but I'm sure Lone Wolf won't let them go hungry."

He took Painted Shawl's hands in his, embraced his brother and began to lead his horse out of the camp. He had gone only a few yards when he saw Tall Woman standing in his path. She was carrying a blanket which she held out to him.

"To keep you warm from the night wind. May you return to us with honour."

He was so astonished to hear her speak to him that he just stared, not attempting to take the blanket. She laid it across his horse, a faint smile on her face, amused by his astonishment, then she walked on towards her lodge, proudly unheeding of who might have heard her break taboo. One imperious look from Tall Woman could silence all criticism. She could have chosen no more positive way to show her regard for Bear Claw. It gave him strength and heart.

When he reached the Barnett cabin he saw the

chickens Ben had bought in Baker scratching around the yard. A rooster with a vivid red comb, perched on the fence contemplating the hens with a beady eye. It was very quiet. Bear Claw stood on the veranda, wondering just how he was going to tell the story to Ben and Frances, as if Lothar's shame rubbed off on him. Klein must have left in a big hurry once the deed was done.

The cabin door was open and as he stepped forward he could see Ben sitting in the rocking chair. One look at the Englishman's face told him something was wrong. He walked into the room. There was no one else there except Caesar, who was lying in his favourite position beside Ben's chair. Ben did not hear him come in. He was totally absorbed in staring at the fireplace, rocking his chair absently. The purchases from Farmer's store were dumped on the table. He was holding the rag doll he had bought for Sarah, running the soft, woolly hair between his fingers. In his other hand was a glass of brandy. A bottle stood on the table, more than half empty. There was weary despair in his eyes that made Bear Claw feel cold.

Caesar sat up wagging his tail at the sight of his old friend, but there was no reaction from Ben. Bear Claw spoke his name twice before he turned to look at him,

"Oh hello Bear Claw. You're earlier than I expected. I'm sorry if you were hoping for a meal. There isn't any. My wife had to leave suddenly it seems and she appears to have taken all the food with her. What's more, it doesn't look as if she will be back."

"Lothar!"

"Yes, Lothar. Lothar, my wife, my daughter, my horse, my pony trap and enough food to feed an army, all gone, vanished. She didn't even leave me a note."

"But Frances will be back, she would not go with Lothar."

"No, she will not be back. They haven't gone on a picnic Bear Claw. She has left me. Her clothes have gone and all Sarah's things, her toys, her cot, everything."

He was struggling to keep his voice even, to maintain some dignity. When he had come home to find the place deserted, he had run around the farm like a madman, calling for her, refusing to admit to himself what he knew had happened. Then his frenzy of agitation had changed into a suppressed despair. He had calmly unhitched the wagon, fed and watered the horse, let the chickens loose and then opened the brandy. It cushioned his despair at first, now it only increased it.

"But why Ben?" Bear Claw could see the emerald necklace on the table. It had been taken out of the box and spread to advantage.

"Ah, why? Now that's the leading question, the one I am afraid to ask myself because I know I shall hate the answer."

He held the brandy glass against his cheek for a moment, then he took a long drink. The Cheyenne picked up the bottle and gave it a thoughtful look. "This helps you?"

"What else is there to help me?"

Then, without warning, he hurled the glass against the chimney breast, shattering it into splinters that fell into the fireplace, covering the grey ashes with tiny stars.

"No, by God, it doesn't help me. It only makes me worse."

He buried his face in his hands and wept. Bear Claw could see the tears working their way through his fingers and running down the back of his hands. He stood in silence, sharing his grief, yet not knowing how to help. He wanted to hold him in his arms, as he would a brother, but he held back, afraid that the Englishman would be embarrassed by such an unreserved display of feeling. Instead he touched his arm lightly. Ben sat back in the chair, wiping his eyes with the back of his hand.

"I apologise. I didn't mean to behave like that. The brandy wasn't such a good idea-makes me maudlin. But I just keep thinking how desperate she must have been. I'm sure she loves me, but I had no idea how unhappy she was here, not until that night you fished Klein out of that pit. I saw it that night written on her face- fear, frustration, loneliness. For three years I have kept that woman locked in a cage of loneliness and boredom. Because I was happy, I refused to see it, convinced myself she was happy too. I didn't want those shadows back, but I hadn't got rid of them. Those damned shadows will pursue me to the end."

He was hugging himself as if he was cold, just as he had when he first confessed to Bear Claw about the shadows.

"You did not sleep last night. This morning you did not eat and now you drink too much. You are in a bad state to face this."

The Cheyenne was grateful to forget the urgency

of his mission for a short while, to sink his own pain in his concern for Ben. He began to unpack the supplies they had brought from Baker and was soon offering him a cup of black coffee and a crudely cut slice of one of Ellen Farmer's meat and onion pies. He sat on the floor, his face sombre, watching Barnett as he drank the coffee, waiting to tell his own story.

Ben regained his outward composure very quickly. He had always been taught that it was the mark of a gentleman to bear adversity with stoicism and dignity and although he often mocked the social mores he had tried to escape, he just as often found himself reacting instinctively in accordance with them.

"That coffee was appalling Bear Claw, but thank you, I think it will help."

"I must go soon," the Cheyenne said in a low voice, " After Lothar. You see I too have something to bear. I share your grief, now I know you will share mine."

He told Benjamin the story in an unemotional voice, almost as if he were an impartial observer instead of a principal actor in the drama, but Ben was well aware of what it mean to him.

"You are going to bring him back?"

"I am going to kill him. I must, there is no other way. I must act like a Cheyenne if I want to live among them and I do want to live among them. They are my people. I do not know my mother's people and they will not want to know me. It was because of my foolish yearning after my mother's people that Pawnee Killer died."

Ben stood up with a sudden air of resolution.

"Your story may explain why Frances left so abruptly without leaving any message. If Lothar told her what happened she would have been terrified for Sarah's safety. Perhaps she did not leave so willingly as I imagined."

He realised that he must sound like a man clutching at straws, but he preferred a slim hope to no hope. It was too easy to slip into melancholy acceptance, allow the shadows to engulf him. Bear Claw had chosen action and he was prompted to follow suit.

"I'll come with you."

"You will not stop me from killing him. I am sworn to it. You are a man of peace and it is not the way you would choose, but I must be true to the Cheyenne way. When I strayed from it these bad things happened."

"I do not know how I shall react if we catch up with him." Ben was taking his rifle down from above the fireplace. "Right now I have a mind to kill him myself, but I certainly have no right to interfere with your duty to your people. I must go for Fran and Sarah's sake. I have to find out if she went willingly. If there is any chance that she did not, she will need me when you catch up with Lothar. Even if she chose to go with him, she is going to be in trouble if you kill Klein. I can't let her face that alone. I want them back Bear Claw. I want my wife and daughter back."

Bear Claw could not deny Ben's right to join him any more than the warriors of the camp could deny his right to go. He nodded his assent. Ben looked pale and strained, but he was full of energy now.

"They can't be travelling very fast in that pony cart. If we go now we have a good chance of overhauling them. Now Lone Wolf has given you directions on how to reach the cave, we will catch up with them there anyway."

Bear Claw noticed that Ben put the necklace back in the box and slipped the box into his pocket.

It was not until he was saddling his horse that Barnett remembered the animals.

"I forgot all about the animals. We don't know how long we'll be gone. They could be without food for days and I can't leave them free to graze. I'd never see half of them again."

"No problem," Bear Claw swung himself onto his horse's back. "Our way to the cave leads us past the horse pasture. The sons of White Arrow are on duty there today. I will tell them to take a message to him. He will come every day and feed the animals if I ask it of him. He will see the house is safe, he and his sons. He wanted to come with me today, but I could not allow it, so he would be glad to help in another way."

"I like your brother."

"He is a good man. I am fortunate to have such a brother."

They rode through the woods without speaking, both occupied with their own thoughts. Caesar ran behind them, forcing jack- rabbits out of their hiding places in the undergrowth and driving them skittering through the brambles. The wolfhound had great stamina and could run for miles beside a horse without tiring.

They passed a massive tree trunk, gnarled and twisted like a piece of sculpture. Bear Claw reined in, looking back over his shoulder at the mossy turf below the tree.

"What are you looking at?"

"It was here I buried the wolverine. The grass grows over the digging already, there is no sign the earth was turned. I bury him very deep Ben, but his power reaches beyond the earth. He makes it bad for us now. If he did not frighten Lothar's horse that night, Lothar would not have fallen in the pit and I do not bring him to your house. I hope his evil finishes here and does not follow us to the Sweet Medicine cave. If it does, I fear one of us will die."

Benjamin stared at the earth dotted with white convolvulus and yellow coltsfoot. Nowhere could look less likely to emanate malign power. All was serene, shaded and full of growth.

"Well, we must make sure we are strong enough to overcome it," he said, coaxing his horse to walk on. "The power of evil is only as strong as we allow it to be. The monsters that stalk us are often of our own making, reflections of our own darker side that we prefer not to recognise as a part of ourselves. I think I know that wolverine Bear Claw and I intend to lay his ghost."

The Cheyenne hoped his friend was right for he still felt the power of the wolverine and was relieved to pass out of the woods.

It was dawn. The high plains wind that never rested moaned around them. It was cold before the sun came up. The wind had a bitter edge like the thongs of a whip. Ben watched the blue wisps of smoke curl up from beneath the can, where the water boiled over a sluggish fire. He pushed Caesar off his feet and got up to fetch the tin mugs he had prepared, pouring the boiling water on to the coarse-grained coffee. He took a mug to Bear Claw, warming his hands on it as he went. The Cheyenne took it gratefully. He was gazing out over the long vista, his attention fixed on two specks in the distance, increasing in size. The light was wan and indistinct.

"Somebody is coming this way," he said.

Ben strained his eyes and could just make out the smudges that Bear Claw saw as riders. He sipped his coffee, feeling the hot liquid warm him. He had woken that morning stiff and cold, surprised that the wind should be so sharp this late in spring. He had never camped in the open on the high plains before.

"Perhaps they may have passed Lothar and Frances and can tell us how far ahead they are. It's damnably cold this morning. I'm worried about Sarah. You know how unwell she was when we left for Baker. It can't do her any good travelling in searing hot sun by day, then camping in the cold at night."

"Frances will look after her," Bear Claw assured.

He could now see the riders clearly enough to

perceive that they were Indians, but he could not yet tell which tribe. They had ridden a long way and were into Dakota. The Black Hills were now visible on the horizon, looking sullen and smoky in the dawn. Even allowing for Lothar's head start, both men had expected to have overtaken the pony trap by now. Klein must have set a punishing pace.

"Sioux." The Cheyenne could now recognise the approaching horsemen. "Teton Sioux. Be on your guard Ben, have your gun where it is easy to reach."

"But I thought the Cheyenne and Sioux were now brothers. You told me about the treaty that was made."

Bear Claw shrugged. "That is true, but no man is safe in Sioux territory. If they are two young warriors looking for glory, one man will do as well as the next. We must show no sign of mistrust. Come and sit by the fire and drink your coffee as if you do not see them."

Ben took his rifle from behind his bedroll and placed it near him as he sat down by the fire. Caesar accompanied the visitors into the camp with wild barking, but the two men by the fire did not even look up. They could hear the jingling of bridle ornaments, bells and trinkets tied all over the horse ropes. The Sioux dismounted steering clear of Caesar and walked to the camp fire. They too jingled for bells were sewn all down the outer seams of their leggings. Bear Claw gave them a cursory glance, then motioned them to sit down.

They were both young men in their early twenties, handsome and powerfully built, with the classical, hawk-nosed look of the Sioux. They did not wear war paint, but they were extravagantly ornamented and groomed to perfection according to tribal fashion. One of them had hair braids that reached to his knees and he had woven, with meticulous care, yards of fur strips in with the plaiting.

Bear Claw took the coffee mugs and made fresh coffee for them, whilst they sat with deadpan faces, waiting. Not a word was spoken. The silence began to make Ben nervous. There was a fierce, predatory air about these two mute guests.

They offered their coffee to the four directions, then drank greedily, smacking their lips over the strong flavour. When they had finished they asked for tobacco and Ben parted half the contents of his tobacco pouch between them, grateful to find that it was still in his inside pocket. Bear Claw had a brief conference with them, but could learn nothing about the location of Lothar Klein. They had seen no one, at least so they said.

They rose thanking Bear Claw for his hospitality and mounting their musical horses, began to leave the camp. Both men were relieved to see them go and the Cheyenne suggested it was time to continue their pursuit. He ambled over to the horse and Ben went to put out the fire. As he did so, the Englishman realised that the sound of bells was growing louder again. The Sioux warriors had ridden a few hundred yards, then turned sharply round and were now charging back into the camp like knights at a tourney, their lances poised.

Bear Claw was nearer to them than Ben and he had little time to prepare, but he snatched the blanket from off his horse's back just in time to take the point of the lance in its folds. The impact of the blow knocked him off his feet and the Sioux, screaming his war cry, hurled himself on top of him.

Benjamin stood and faced a charging warrior with a lance for the second time in his life and this time he knew it was not a case of counting coup. But his opponent was over-eager, lunging too soon and Ben dodged the stroke, grasping the haft of the lance and jerking the Sioux off his mount. The moment he hit the floor Caesar was on him, mauling and shaking him, tearing at his leggings. The man was trying to protect his face with one arm, while he groped frantically for the knife at his belt. Ben pulled Caesar away and drove the Sioux's own lance through his heart. Blood spurted up all over him, splashing his face and staining the front of his coat, but he did not have time to dwell on what he had done.

Bear Claw was locked in a deadly struggle with the second warrior. The Cheyenne was strong, but the young Sioux was half a head taller and a stone heavier. He fought like a maniac, cleaving the air with his hatchet and snarling through clenched teeth, as if he would have bitten the flesh from his enemy. He caught Bear Claw a blow in the stomach with the back of the hatchet, winding him. He dropped to his knees, gasping for breath, his eyes fixed on the hatchet, now raised above his head. His mind recited his death song, for he had no breath to sing it, but instead of striking down towards him, the hatchet spun backwards out of his opponent's hand.

Ben had snatched up his gun and fired twice in rapid

succession. One shot would have been enough. It caught the Sioux in the forehead, burning a round hole between his eyes. The second shot buried itself in the man's body as he fell jerking in front of Bear Claw.

Barnett ran towards Bear Claw and helped him to his feet. He was still struggling for breath and Ben was not sure if he was wounded.

"Are you alright?"

"Yes, the breath is knocked from me, nothing more."

He began to cough, relieved to find his lungs filling with air. He straightened up and turning to the dead Sioux at his feet, rolled him over on his back, murmuring his approval.

"You shoot true. I have you to thank for my life."

Ben looked down at the body, the small, scarlet-edged hole in the man's forehead that he had put there. He turned away, only to see the other Sioux sprawled by the campfire, the lance protruding from his chest. It was then that he became aware of his bloody jacket and the sticky warmth of blood on his face. He rubbed his cheek with his fingers in an effort to wipe it off, a sense of disgust in the movement. It was the first time he had killed a human being. When he and Fran had come to Montana he had reasoned that he might be required to kill to protect them both. The very wildness of the place had made the thought seem reasonable, but accepting the theory was a far cry from doing the deed. The enormity of it threatened to overwhelm him. He struggled to hold down the wave of sickness that engulfed him.

"You fight well today," Bear Claw was saying, " If you are a Cheyenne, you have a good story to tell in the village. You must feel proud."

"No, to be honest I feel sick."

He could hold it down no longer and walked swiftly away. The Cheyenne listened to him retching and coughing. He had not considered that it might be the Englishman's first kill. He had been brought up in a society with the image of death as a nurse. It was inevitable that a warrior had killed before he was thirty, often many times. Bear Claw was a compassionate man, but he knew nothing of the guilt that comes with taking a human life. Paradoxically, he felt shame when he shot an animal to feed his family, yet when he slew an enemy he felt pride and no shame at all. When the opponent had died with honour, the two of them, the living and the dead, were welded together, both increasing in stature, one going to great praise in his village, the other to his respected place before the All-Father. The courage of the dead lived on in the man who vanquished him. In this Bear Claw was pure Cheyenne.

Ben came back wiping his mouth with the back of his hand, his face grey.

"This is your first killing?" Bear Claw asked simply.

"Yes, they say it gets easier. I hope I don't have to prove that theory."

"I see for you it will never be easy. You are not a warrior, you are a man of peace, but your courage is great. I can ask for no better man to be here with me this day.

Tell me, in your country is there no fighting, no killing? Do all men live in peace?"

Barnett shook his head. "There is no country in the world where every man lives in peace. It is human nature to fight and squabble, of course there is murder in England. People kill for greed, out of hate and jealousy or for revenge. Society condemns this and if they are caught, they are punished for it."

"Yes, it is bad to kill for these reasons amongst the Cheyenne also and punishment follows. But you have soldiers in England, men in red coats. I have been told about them. They go to war like the Indian."

"They go to war yes, but not like the Indian."

It was 1860. The Crimean war had ended only a few years before. Benjamin thought of the long letters he had received from his brother Phillip from Sebastopol. Phillip had been a regular soldier all his adult life, but he was appalled by the conditions in the Crimea. Inhibited by the necessity to maintain discipline, he could say little to his companions, but he poured out his feelings on paper to his brothers Ben and Sam.

To the plains tribes war was a game, a murderous half-hour played within a framework of rules, then away to lick wounds or glory in triumph. It was part of the fabric of life. War had become much more than that to the white man. He was learning to use all the fearsome weapons at his command to annihilate a whole race if the need arose. Bear Claw would never be able to conceive of the carnage that the white man's war would wreak.

"Do you not believe that it would be better for the

native population if you weren't all at your neighbours' throats continually? If the time comes when the white man becomes a real threat to you, I don't mean a few settlers like me, but whole waves of people, gold miners, railroad builders, cattlemen, all protected by the army, building settlements, cultivating the land, grazing large herds of stock, pushing you farther and farther back, how will you be able to stand up and say 'This country is ours' when the tribes are fighting each other constantly? You won't have a leg to stand on. No cohesion, no organisation, piece-meal treaties agreed by one tribe, rejected by another. It will be chaos and you won't stand a chance in the long run."

"You believe the white man will want to drive us out?"

"I don't want to believe it, but I am ashamed to say that I fear he will. He is not satisfied with small pieces. He must have everything."

"If that time comes, I will be sad, but I will fight and die if I have no choice."

Ben gave him a wistful smile. "You have no problem of identity Bear Claw. You are a Cheyenne."

Bear Claw was standing over the warrior who had almost killed him, staring at him with concentration. For a moment Ben thought he might be going to take his scalp. The experience for him had been traumatic enough; that would have been the final straw. He caught hold of the Cheyenne's arm. "Bear Claw , don't," but he did not finish the sentence for he saw what his friend had been studying so intently. Tied to the Sioux's belt was a silk scarf, cream coloured with orange flowers printed along the edge.

"I see that somewhere before," said Bear Claw.

"It's Fran's. Oh dear God!"

Ben untied the scarf and held it, all manner of hideous fears running through his mind.

"You must be calm Ben. It does not mean anything has happened to Frances. Maybe she dropped it. It is very light, blows easily in the wind, or maybe they call at their campfire too and are given this as a gift."

"Can you imagine Lothar offering gifts to those two? He would have blown their heads off with that Spencer rifle of his before they got within twenty yards of him. They would have to come upon him unawares and if they did, what did they do to my wife and daughter?"

Bear Claw heard again in his mind, his mother's voice, telling the story of how the Cheyenne murdered her parents. He thought of the wolverine, but all he said was, "Do not think of these things. They did not look like men who had just killed. There would be more trophies. They carry none, that is why they attacked us. We must ride now."

They left the camp as fast as they could, the horses' hooves thudding on the hard ground and Caesar stretching his long legs to the limit to keep abreast of the horses. Already, from a sky that moments before was empty, the carrion birds were gathering to reap the harvest of death by the ashes of the campfire.

CHAPTER EIGHT

Sarah was crying. She had cried on and off for the last
half hour and the sound grated on Fran's raw nerves
like a saw. The child was tired of this constant bumping
along. She wanted to toddle around the familiar cabin,
play with Caesar, rock in the rocking chair on her father's
lap. She missed her routine, so she protested in the only
way open to her, keeping up a constant litany of grizzling.

Lothar looked over his shoulder. The crying did
not bother him, he was too elated, too filled with the
notion that his ambitions would soon be fulfilled. They
were driving through a narrow defile that led higher up
into the hills, the horse picking its way with sure feet over
the uneven ground. Bushes grew out of the crevices all up
the face of the rock, their foliage thin and meagre, their
stems twisting into grotesque shapes in the effort to reach
the sunlight in the dank, shaded defile.

Klein glanced at the map that was spread out over
his knees. This passage way into the Black Hills was
clearly marked. They would be at the cave in less than an
hour he was sure. The next landmark to look out for was a
boulder the shape of a diamond, lying in the middle of the
track. Then they must veer left.

He was pleased with the progress they had made

since the hurried night flight from the cabin. They had seen no one, except in the distance, all the way down into Dakota. At a river crossing, a fisherman in a canoe further upstream called out and waved to them, but Lothar had driven on through the water as if he had not seen him. He knew this was Sioux territory and was grateful to have avoided any harassment so far. He did not discuss this with Frances. She was tense enough already.

"She has good lungs, the little one," he said. "I think she will be a singer when she is grown."

"Well I'm glad you take pleasure in it, for I certainly do not."

Fran was hot and sore. The light springs of the cart did little to protect the traveller from the rough terrain and he had been driving at an insane pace. She had moved off the driving seat to sit amongst the luggage in the cart,

hoping that this would be more comfortable, but there was little to choose between them.

Sarah was playing with her mother's hair, pulling out long strands of it and twisting it around her fists. Frances slapped her daughter's hands with fraught impatience to force her to let go of the hair.

"Please stop now Lothar. We have been travelling such a long time without stopping. Sarah is bored and I think she has wet herself. That's why she is so fretful. She wants to get out and run around and I need to dry her. I would welcome a rest myself."

"We cannot stop now my pretty one. We are almost there. Wait until we reach the cave, then we can rest and eat. Give Sarah one of her toys to play with."

"It's pointless. Whatever I give her she only throws it out of the cart. She has already disposed of her toy monkey, a bag of bricks and my scarf. It was my favourite scarf a present from."

She stopped, afraid to speak her husband's name. All these long, grinding miles she had fought to keep Ben out of her mind, tried not to imagine his reaction to her disappearance or dwell on the danger he might be in once Lothar's deed was known to the Cheyenne. Every moment that she lost concentration, she saw his face, heard his voice and felt a desire for the security of his arms around her.

Lothar, not indifferent to her agitation, had talked incessantly while he drove, all his plans for the future, all the things they would do together. They would go to Boston first, he told her, have the gold weighed, valued and banked. They could spend as long as she liked in Boston for he knew how fond she was of the city.

But to Frances, crouched in that cart trying to amuse Sarah, the lure of Boston was not as it had been. Visiting Boston as Benjamin's wife was one thing, but fleeing there with another man, having deserted her husband was quite another. Some might consider it the behaviour of a whore. She would never be able to face Henry and Jane. They had considered Benjamin's plan to move to Montana as the height of foolishness, but they were very fond of him and she knew they would be on his side. Her actions would be seen as a disgrace to the family. On no account must she be seen by anyone she knew in Boston. In fact it was now the last place on earth she wanted to go.

Her fears were doubled when she thought of London. Her only hope was to persuade Lothar to head for New York, so they could embark for the Continent directly. Perhaps in Paris or Vienna they could live undetected. The prospect gave her no pleasure. There was an aching emptiness in her when she contemplated the future. She was sure now that she had committed an act of pure folly and she should have had the courage to wait for Benjamin's return. But it was done and her pride prompted her to bear the consequences.

"There it is!" Lothar shouted, standing up and pointing forward, "The boulder on the map, just as it is drawn."

He gave a sharp jerk on the reins and urged the horse to the left, throwing his passengers hard against the baggage in the cart. Sandy, Ben's chestnut stallion, tied to the back of the cart, struck sparks from the rocks with his hooves as he was forced to change direction so quickly. He fixed Frances with a baleful glare, as if to suggest it was all her fault.

"Lothar," she asked, "Who did you steal the map from? Was it Lone Wolf?"

He did not expect the question. This was the first time she had pressed him on it, but he saw no reason to lie to her now.

"No, the old medicine man, Pawnee Killer. He had it stored away in his bundle. It was not so easy to get my hands on it, I am telling you. That old man was sleeping with one eye open and he was at me with a knife like some young buck."

"You killed him didn't you?" Her voice was flat. There was no accusation in it, but he felt accused.

"I have to hit him, or he tells the whole camp I am there. Then I am so full of spear holes, I make a good cabbage strainer. I get out like hell when I have the map. I do not stop to look at the old man. Maybe he is not dead."

His attempt to be candid had petered out. He knew Pawnee Killer was dead for he had made sure of it. He could not leave the old man as a witness. The longer the Cheyenne pondered over who had committed the crime, the better chance he had of reaching the cave. He stretched back and ran his hand over Fran's hair in a gesture of assurance.

"Do not worry. It cannot be helped. Maybe they do not suspect me. We get this far safe enough."

She wanted to be comforted by his assurance, to welcome the touch of his hand because her chance of any happiness in the future depended on it. His admiration was genuine enough, but she feared she would never believe he loved her, not after the way he had used everyone else. How could she be sure that she would not be abandoned once she became inessential to him? The thought stopped her from responding to his touch. He felt the coldness, the edge of hostility in her and took his hand away. He was disappointed for he had been sure she would turn to him unreservedly for support.

He was beginning to want her very much. The anticipation of the pleasures of Fran's body was now interwoven with his dreams of great wealth and all it could bring. Every inch of her spoke of class and good breeding.

It would be good to possess her and equally good to show her off. She would put the finishing touches to the figure he meant to cut in European society. If that society tried to deny his right to enter the charmed circle, it could never deny hers. She was quite wrong to imagine that he had any thoughts of abandoning her.

It was over an hour before they reached Lothar's goal, the cave where Sweet Medicine had received the arrows from the Old Ones, the spirits of the ages past. The track grew rougher and steeper as they travelled, the horses stumbling often as they scrambled for a footing on the rock strewn path. Undergrowth and thick stands of timber made their progress slow. Brambles caught in Fran's hair and scratched her arms as she tried to protect Sarah from them.

They passed several caves with hostile mouths that seemed to be inviting the bold to risk the dangers that lay in wait in the depth of shadow. Lothar knew none of these was his Eldorado. Marked on the map was a rivulet of water than ran down the rocks to form a shallow pool beside the cave. It was the water he heard first. He was weaving a path through a clump of trees growing close together, with straight trunks like sentinels forbidding the cart passage, when he heard the sound of running water. Beyond the trees was a clearing and he could see the stream wending its way down the rock face, eroding a deeper channel with every year that passed.

Green moss and clumps of pink flowers grew over the rocks at the edge of the stream and the water fell with a bell-like ring into the hollow that formed the pool. Two squirrels drinking at the rim of the pool scampered away as the cart disturbed the stillness of the clearing. There was a tranquil atmosphere here, something immutable. Frances was struck by the beauty of the place. Compared with the rugged terrain behind them, it was like some enchanted glade from a fairy story.

Lothar had no concern for the beauty around him, his eyes were fixed on one thing only, the great cave at the end of the clearing. It was bigger than the others they had passed and the mouth was sealed by a massive boulder. He leaped from the cart and ran to the cave.

"I knew we would find it."

He put his shoulder to the formidable obstacle, pushing with all his considerable strength, but it would not budge. He pushed until his face was scarlet, cursing in German. Frances climbed out of the cart, her limbs stiff, cramped by the long journey in that narrow space. She lifted Sarah down and both of them stood watching Lothar's desperation.

"I cannot move it. This is crazy, I must move it."

He paced up and down, his hands moving jerkily at his sides as he tried to think of a solution. Then he realised that all he needed was some kind of lever. There was no need for this display of panic. His initial excitement had prevented him from thinking clearly. There were plenty of tree branches lying on the edge of the clearing, several of them thick enough for his purpose. He smiled self-consciously at Frances.

"I forget the simple principles of engineering in my eagerness. I will soon shift this if I use my brains as well as my muscles. But first we sit down and eat eh?"

He had resumed his familiar, easy-going manner and strolled back to the cart to search for some food. They ate bread and cold meat with hungry relish, except Sarah, who had no interest in food. She was happy to be out of the cart and ran about the clearing, splashing her hands in the pool, fascinated by the falling water.

Frances watched Lothar wiping his moustache with satisfaction after he had consumed half a loaf and washed it down with clear water that he cupped from the stream in his hands.

He played with Sarah for a while, lifting her above the pool, pretending that he was about to throw her in, bringing her down to a few inches above the water, so that her soft shoes with their round toes just skimmed the surface. He was pleased that her squeals were of pleasure, not fear. He carried her over and dumped her in her mother's lap, then he kissed the top of Fran's head.

"Cheer up my pretty one, not much longer to wait. Now is the time to open Aladdin's cave."

It did not take him long to find the right piece of wood for a lever. He honed the end to the flatness of a spatula and slid it underneath the boulder, then put his whole weight on the thick end of the lever. He could feel the rock shudder and roll forward. Engrossed in his task, he had no idea that he was being watched.

Benjamin Barnett would have been hard pressed to describe the intensity of his relief when he first saw his wife and daughter sitting in the clearing. After finding the scarf at the belt of that Sioux warrior, he had travelled in an agony of fear, knowing that every dark outline in the trail ahead might be the bodies of his family sprawled across the unpitying plain. When Bear Claw picked up the tracks of the cart, he had felt a stirring of hope, but was afraid to be too optimistic. They had made good time and now found themselves in the wooded area beyond the clearing.

Ben first saw the burnished hue of Fran's hair as she sat on the grass in the centre of the clearing, with Sarah on her lap. In that soft, green glade, the fire of her hair cascading down her back, Frances looked incredibly beautiful. He could see Lothar straining away on the lever. He glanced at Bear Claw, who was leaning forward over his horse's neck, his face set, immobile, his eyes fixed on Klein.

At that moment Lothar's efforts came to fruition as the great stone rolled away from the cave mouth. He jumped back out of its path, letting out a shout of triumph. He almost expected to see light radiating out from its golden walls, but it was as dark and forbidding as all the others they had passed. Fran was coming towards him, her daughter in her arms. The cavernous blackness frightened her.

" I don't want to go in there Lothar."

"You don't need to, but there is nothing to be afraid of. That is our path to paradise."

He ran back to fetch the lantern and lit it. He also took his gun from the driving seat of the cart, for despite his bravado, he did not relish stepping into that cave unarmed. He was standing at the cave mouth, holding up the lantern, when there was a rumpus in the trees behind them, which made him spin around. Caesar, who had been lagging behind investigating a host of tempting smells, had now caught up. He saw Frances in the clearing and loped out to meet her, barking a welcome. Lothar was not sure what was bounding out of the trees. He thought at first that it was a wolf and took aim.

Ben acted on impulse as the barrel of the Spencer rifle was levelled at Caesar. Before Bear Claw could stop him, he urged his horse out of the cover of the trees in an effort to distract Klein, calling the dog back. He was in the open and exposed before he realised it. Lothar took his eye off what he could now see was Benjamin Barnett's wolfhound and drew a bead on his master. Ben was turning his horse's head, now fully aware of his mistake, when Klein released a hail of bullets. One nicked his hip, tearing a piece of flesh away, but another buried itself deep into his side beneath the rib cage. He gasped, surprised by the extent of the pain. Blood was spewing down his thigh. Frances was screaming his name; he heard that with great clarity as he fought to remain upright in the saddle. She had put Sarah down and was running towards her husband, but she did not reach him for Lothar grabbed her arm, dragging her back.

"Damn you woman, what are you doing? Get out of the way." She tried to get free and he threw her back towards the cave, where she fell to her knees, still calling out to Ben.

"Do you want to get hit? I finish off that husband of yours once and for all."

He groped in his pocket for more bullets to reload

the rifle, but by this time Benjamin with a tremendous effort of will, had turned his horse and ridden back into the trees out of sight, Caesar in close attendance.

All this had happened so fast Bear Claw had no chance to prevent it. Once he saw Ben had control of his horse and was riding back, he remained hidden, unwilling to reveal his presence to Klein. He rode forward to meet Barnett, his face anxious.

"Ben, you are a fool, why do you do this?"

Ben was clasping his hand over the wound, but he could not stop the blood leaking through his fingers His face was the colour of chalk and his eyes still held a look of surprise, as if he could not quite believe what had just happened.

"I could not let him shoot Caesar," he said with a faint smile of apology for his rash instinctive action. "Bear Claw, did you hear? She called for me, Frances called for me."

The trees around him were beginning to spin and his sense of balance suddenly deserted him. Before Bear Claw could reach out to catch him, he pitched forward out of the saddle and hit the floor hard. He struggled to get up, but the Cheyenne prevented him.

"No, lie still. Let me look at the wound."

He could see at a glance that the bullet had penetrated deeply. His primary concern was to staunch the bleeding. Aware that Lothar might come into the woods to check on the results of his marksmanship, he decided to move back to a secluded canyon he had spotted on the way there. He tore a strip off the bottom of his jacket to make a thick pad to cover the wound, binding it in place with the tail of Ben's shirt. Then he helped his friend on to his horse and climbed up behind him, holding him firmly in the saddle. He clicked his tongue at his own mount to follow him, whistled to Caesar and began to ride back to the chosen retreat.

In the clearing Lothar had reloaded his gun, but was hesitating, torn between a desire to make sure Barnett was dead and a desperate longing to explore the cave. He stood undecided, his rifle balanced in his hands. Sarah was wailing miserably, frightened by the shooting and her mother's distress and Lothar looked around at Frances. She was lying on the ground, a heap of hair and voluminous skirts. She made no sound, but there was something about the way she lay there that spoke her despair with great eloquence. He put down the gun and lifted her head gently.

"Please Lothar, I want to find Benjamin. He may have been hurt badly. He could be out there bleeding to death. I must help him."

"Oh yes, I hit him alright. I do not miss. I find him if that is what you want, but what I do is put him out of his misery."

She turned her head away, but he took hold of her chin, forcing her to look at him.

"You listen to me. You chose to come with me, you are mine now, not his. I will not have you thinking of him all the time. It is best for you if he is dead, then there is no going back for you."

He stood up, taking hold of the rifle again, looking

out towards the woods, but when he took a step, he found he was being tugged back. Frances had taken hold of his jacket in both hands.

"No, don't! I will stay with you Lothar and promise not to think of Ben any more. I will try to do what you want, just give him a chance. Don't kill him."

"And what if he is not hurt so bad eh? What if he is out there waiting for his chance to kill me?"

"He would never do that, Ben's not a murderer."

"Not like me huh? Well you better get used to living with a murderer."

There was another reason for Klein's hesitation to search the woods. It had struck him that Barnett might not be alone. The Englishman would have found it difficult to find his way to the cave without a map unless he had the help of someone who knew the way. That someone was likely to be Bear Claw. He remembered how the Cheyenne could hunt noiselessly, with stealth and skill. He stared into the trees, trying to pierce the gloom, feeling a prickly sensation down his spine. Now this verdant glade did not seem such a magical place to be. A whiff of death floated through it. He could hear nothing but the falling water. Perhaps he was foolish to be so nervous.

"Get up," he ordered Fran in a sharp voice. "bring that cart over to the cave mouth. We are too exposed in the open here and stop the little one from that crying. I do not like to hear her cry like that."

The crying did not sound the same now as it had on the journey, when he had joked about it with such good humour. There seemed to be a deeper, almost accusing note in the cry, which added to his unease.

The cart was backed into the cave mouth, the horses unhitched and hobbled. Lothar was so eager to take the lantern and explore the cave, but he could not risk being trapped in there by any Cheyenne. He decided to wait until the next morning. If anyone was out there, they would surely have made a move by then. He sat behind the cart, his rifle beside him, nursing his impatience broodily, while Fran tried to get Sarah to sleep, rocking her in her arms and praying for her husband.

❈

Bear Claw put the bottle to Ben's lips for the third time in the space of half an hour. Barnett found it impossible to quench his thirst. He was aware of a burning in his veins and a constricting tightness in his throat. He had convinced himself that if he did not move, he could stand the pain of the wound. He had been drifting in and out of consciousness, but for the last ten minutes his mind had been crystal clear.

A blackbird sat on the rocks above them, singing its last song in the fading light, before settling down for the night. The liquid notes had never moved Ben so much before. He had listened to countless blackbirds singing, but never had one sounded so distinct. The bird's black plumage, set off by the startling yellow beak, shimmered and became one with the song. He hoped it would never stop singing because while it sang he felt safe, but it took flight, disturbed by Caesar scrambling over the rocks. The silence it left behind was vast.

Bear Claw had done the best he could for the wound. He had made a tentative exploration for the bullet, but it was too deep for superficial surgery and it intensified the bleeding. He searched for any herbs that might ward off infection, but in the dry canyon he found nothing of much use. All he could do was bind the wound more firmly and he did succeed in checking the bleeding. He was building up the fire for the temperature was dropping and Ben was shivering despite the heat that was rising in his blood. The fire was reluctant and sulky, smoking a lot but not burning up. The Cheyenne took from his horse the blanket that Tall Woman had given him and spread it over his friend.

"You are cold. This may help."

"I'm alright, when the fire burns up I will stop shivering." Caesar lay down next to Ben and rested his long muzzle down the length of his paw. Barnett was grateful for the feel of the shaggy coat against him. "Caesar will keep me warm anyway."

His own voice sounded strange to him, as if it was coming from far away and did not belong to him at all. Bear Claw sat down beside him, his arms folded across his knees, He had come to take revenge on Lothar Klein on behalf of his people. He could not shirk that duty.

"You are hurt bad Ben. You need the bullet out, need healing medicine. You do not get that here in the mountains. My heart is troubled for you. I think the wolverine does follow us here as I feared."

Benjamin had tried not to consider that he might be dying, but he had never experienced a physical pain like that gnawing away in his stomach and it forced him to acknowledge the worst outcome.

"I realise I am in a pretty bad way, but I will not believe it has anything to do with that unfortunate wolverine. It happened because I was a damned fool. I brought this on myself and the seeds go back much further than today. If I die Bear Claw, you must not feel in any way responsible. You have a big enough burden already."

He felt a wave of faintness pass over him and closed his eyes.

"You talk too much," murmured Bear Claw, fearing to be drawn into that argument. "You must rest."

Ben lay listening to his heartbeat, which seemed loud and much faster than usual. The beating reverberated in his ears. When he opened his eyes again, Bear Claw was painting his face, daubing the blue tear drops down the side of his jaw and across his forehead. He ran his fingers down his nose to make the wide blue bar with a ritual deliberateness, a gesture of dedication.

"You are going to complete your task," Ben said. It was more a statement than a question.

Bear Claw nodded. "Yes, I must. I do not like to leave you here alone, but you have Caesar. Between them, Caesar and the fire will keep away prowling animals. The moon is rising. Once it is high enough it will shine some light into this canyon, but there will be no Sioux moving around here at night. But see, I lay your gun here."

He put the rifle down beside his friend, knowing

that he was barely capable of sitting up, let alone using a gun. Ben knew it too, but he smiled as he replied, his voice now a dry whisper.

"Thank you. Don't worry, I shall be safe enough. Take care, Lothar is cornered, makes him dangerous. Be as gentle as you can with Fran and Sarah. I want to see them more than – well you understand all that."

Bear Claw checked his weapons, the knife at his side, the bow that he had slung over his shoulder, then he was ready. He intended to run to the clearing. His feet were more silent than a horse's hooves. He stood looking down at Benjamin, a last flicker of hesitation in his eyes.

"Go on man, get out of here."

The Cheyenne inclined his head in mute acknowledgement and ran out of the canyon. Ben watched his sturdy figure moving over the rocks until it disappeared from his field of vision and felt more alone than he would have ever admitted to Bear Claw. He despised his fears. He had always hoped that when his time came he would be able to die with dignity. He knew he should be preparing himself with prayer for what might come, but all he could think about was Frances. When he had made his fatal mistake in the clearing, she had made it plain that she still loved him. He wanted so much to live when he considered that. Now he found that clarity of thought was slipping away from him again. The last thing of which he was fully aware was Caesar snoring by his side.

Bear Claw however was sharply aware of everything as he ran up the track in the darkness. Every movement and sound played a tune on his senses. He saw every pair of yellow eyes that watched him from the bushes and the unblinking stare of owls in the pines, heard the smallest rodent in the undergrowth. Far up in the hills a bear was groaning and he heard the pleading whine of young cubs. He felt one with the animals of the night for he too stalked his prey. He asked his brother creatures to lend him their skill, their unwavering sense of purpose.

He had determined to commit himself totally to the Cheyenne way of life, yet he had seen his purpose waver already when it clashed with his affection for Benjamin. He paused, asking himself again if he was right to jeopardize Ben's life to uphold his honour. He knew that if Ben died, his own life would be diminished beyond imagining, but he ran on driven by the years of training and absorption that had made him a Cheyenne. He had sworn before the honoured men of his tribe, there was no going back.

A soft glow emanated from the cave mouth at the far side of the clearing. Lothar's lantern still burned. Bear Claw could make out the silhouettes of Klein and Frances behind the cart that was drawn across the opening to the cave. Lothar was walking up and down, his rifle in his hands. Even from a distance Bear Claw could sense the tension in his movements.

The delay was telling on Klein, churning up a madness within him. The gold was there in the darkness behind him. A few days' work would make him rich for the rest of his life, yet he dare not go in there, not yet.

He was afraid that the madness would take hold of him, that he would throw down his gun and run into the cave to claw at the walls. The night was creeping by at a snail's pace; he did not know how he could bear it. Then there was Frances, sitting silently watching him, her beautiful amber eyes full of doubt and sadness. Sarah was asleep, curled up in the back of the cart. He would have welcomed some cheering conversation. He wanted to sit beside the woman, hold her in his arms and comfort himself, but there was something in her face, in the stillness of her body that kept him back. She had promised him anything he wanted providing that he did not hunt Ben down, but Lothar feared she would give him nothing.

"Well, can you say nothing?" he demanded. "Why do you sit there all the time, accusing me with those eyes."

"I do not accuse you. I say nothing because I do not wish to wake Sarah now that she has finally gone to sleep. First her crying bothered you, now the silence bothers you. I think it is you who accuse yourself."

Klein laughed. "You think to awaken conscience in me my pretty one. You God fearing English ladies talk much about a man's conscience. You waste your breath. I have no inner voice in me telling me to do God's will. I do what Lothar Klein says is best for himself and if others try to stop me then it is too bad for them. There is too much talk about good and evil. A man must do what he can to survive in such a world. Often he must cheat and kill to do that, to pretend it is not so is hypocrisy. Do you believe God will punish me, because if that is so, he punishes you too? I do not force you to come with me."

"I bear my punishment within myself already."

He clicked his tongue impatiently, walking away

from her out into the clearing. In the darkness the falling water glowed with a strange phosphorescence, lighting the rocks in the immediate vicinity. He thought he saw a shadow pass across the water and his finger hovered over the trigger of the rifle. Then he fancied he saw it again, dodging up through the boulders behind the waterfall. He hesitated, his first desire being to move back to the shelter of the cave, but he changed his mind and walked over to the water.

Bear Claw watched him from the cover of the trees. He too had seen something move up there. It was most likely a wolf or coyote.

Lothar was climbing up a little way, hampered by his efforts to make no noise. The Cheyenne glanced back at the cave mouth and saw Frances get up. She lifted her sleeping daughter out of the cart, wrapping her in an extra shawl and began to run towards the trees. Her feet made no sound on the soft grass of the glade.

It was an act of wild desperation, for she had no idea where she was going. She could bear no longer the thought that Ben might be out there in need of help, perhaps dying in the cold darkness with no friendly voice to comfort him. She had been seized with a terror that she would never see him again alive or dead. Not even fear for Sarah's safety held her back.

Bear Claw moved noiselessly into her path and waited. As she passed him, he stepped out, clapping his hand over her mouth to prevent any cry of surprise. He felt her body shudder, but she held on tight to Sarah and stood firm.

"No sound," he whispered. "Do not be afraid. It is Bear Claw. Listen to what I say. Ben is hurt bad, I do not lie to you, maybe he is dying, I cannot say. You must go to him, to see you is the most important thing of all to him now. I cannot come yet, I have a score to settle with Lothar Klein, but you must hurry. The way is straight. Follow the track until you come to a fallen tree all across the path. From the end of the tree go to the right, as the tree points and you will come to a canyon. He is there. You will see the fire. It is maybe one mile. Run and do not stop if you hear the night animals."

She could not see his face clearly, but she found his hand and held it, pressing it into the warmth of the shawl that covered her daughter. Then she began to run along the track.

The blackness was deceiving and she feared she might wander off the path. She feared nothing else; Benjamin was alive and he wanted to see her, this was her only concern. She wanted to cry with relief when she ran into the fallen tree, the trunk shining white in the gloom, stripped of bark by squirrels. Sarah stirred and murmured in her arms, but she did not wake. The end of the tree had split from the stump and a jagged spur was pointing like a signpost to the right, just as Bear Claw had said. She felt along it with her hand to make sure and walked on more slowly now because there was no clear path. Brambles snatched at her skirt and tangled about her feet, but she dragged on through them.

Eventually the undergrowth began to give way to clearer, stony ground which dropped down at an angle, rock cliffs rising on either side in dark silence. She saw the fire a few hundred yards ahead and began to run again. Caesar stood up snarling, but when he heard her voice calling his name he began to wag his tail. He would not leave Ben's side, but waited expectantly, glad to have company in his lonely vigil.

Frances put Sarah down on the ground beside the wolfhound and he snuffled around the familiar bundle. Then she turned, half afraid, to her husband. For a moment she feared that she was too late. He lay so still, his face colourless, the shadows of the truckling fire flames passing across it. She dropped to her knees, putting her head on his shoulder. During those days apart from him she had been living in an alien world, almost as if she herself had become another creature that she could not understand. Only now was she back in her own country.

As she pressed her face into his chest, she felt his shallow breathing and was filled with a sudden hope. If he had lived long enough for her to reach him, surely he could not die now? She rolled back the blanket with a nervous apprehension, looking for the wound. Bear Claw had bound it up well, but it was still seeping blood and even in the half light of the fire, she could see how stained were the top and thighs of his trousers. The bleeding had been severe.

She replaced the blanket and stood up, determined to do something useful and full of purpose. The fire was fading, so she set about building it up with more sticks from the bundle Bear Claw had collected. Her touch and presence near him had penetrated Ben's consciousness.

He opened his eyes and saw Frances bending over the fire, stirring it with a long branch, just as if she was in the cabin. Her hair fell in glorious disarray all over her as she leaned forward to stir the sluggish embers. He wondered if it was a chimera born of his fevered state, taunting him. But she looked so real that he could not help himself from speaking her name.

"Frances?" She dropped the branch into the fire and turned in an instant. "You are real. I thought I was delirious."

She stood there hands fluttering nervously, wanting to go to him but held back by her sense of the enormity of what she had done. She feared that she would never find the words to explain it to him.

He tried to sit up, but the pain forced him back. The sight of his distress overcame her hesitation and she sat down beside him, lifting him forward in her arms, tears scalding her face.

"Oh Benjamin, I am sorry. I am so sorry."

It was all she could say, all she wanted to say and she repeated it over and over, flagellating herself with the words. He wanted to comfort her, but was too weak for much emotion. He lay there feeling her tears dropping on to his chest and her hair brushing his cheek. When she was quieter he reached out to stroke her hair and she took hold of his hand, holding it against her face. It was so cold.

"I was afraid that I would be too late, but it's alright now. You will be safe now. I won't let you die. This is all my fault."

He blinked, trying to focus his blurred vision.

"No, it's not your fault. You are as bad as Bear Claw. He thinks it is his fault."

"I wouldn't have done it, I know I wouldn't, if you had come home that night from Baker. If only you had come home. I was lonely and afraid, afraid of what the Cheyenne might do to us after what Lothar did. I had to protect Sarah. Perhaps I also thought I wanted what he offered me, but now I know nothing is worth anything to me without you. How can you ever forgive me?"

"There is nothing to forgive. I am just as culpable. I should never have brought you out here. I have been so selfish."

She would not hear of it. She had allowed Lothar to call him selfish without defending him and now she would not let him condemn himself. She placed her finger on his lips to stop him.

"Coming to Montana gave your life purpose, but I was too weak to share it for long. It will be different when we get home. Sarah missed you so much; she cried for you."

He turned his head to see his daughter safely ensconced between Caesar's great paws.

"Lothar murdered Pawnee Killer. The gold is everything to him, he is obsessed by it. He thinks the cave in the clearing is full of gold, but after he shot you he was afraid to go into the cave in case you hadn't come alone and he might get trapped in there."

"Did he hurt you?"

"No, he was kind to us after his fashion and I think he would have continued to be so as long as he wanted to bother with me, but he does not love me. He doesn't love anybody."

She stopped her face flushing as she thought of the way he had tried to make love to her in the cabin.

"He did not- he kissed me- but nothing more. I would not let him. That is the truth Benjamin."

She dare not consider now the consequences of going on to the city with Klein. Ben also shut it out of his mind. She was here with him, that was all that mattered. A paroxysm of pain suddenly shook him, twisting up through him with a violence that made him writhe. Frances held on to him until it had passed and he lay exhausted with his head resting against her shoulder, his eyes closed.

"How did you know where to find me? Did you meet Bear Claw?" he asked, without opening his eyes.
"Yes, at the clearing. I was running away from Lothar. I kept thinking that you might be lying out there in the trees with no one to help you and I couldn't bear it any longer. So I just snatched up Sarah and ran. I suppose I intended to run until I found you. I didn't even consider what might happen to both of us if I never found you. Fortunately I ran right into Bear Claw. It was like a miracle to hear his steady voice. He told me where to find you. What is he going to do about Lothar?"

"Kill him, he has no choice if he wants to live among the Cheyenne."

He felt her shudder, but she said nothing for she knew it was inevitable. There was so much she had to learn about life and death in this country. She kissed her husband, a vigorous, warming kiss on the mouth, as if she was breathing her life into him. He could feel it flowing over him as he drifted away, an image of Bear Claw printed on his mind.

❊

Bear Claw had returned to watching the restless figure searching the rocks above the pool. He was waiting with the patience of a hunter for the right moment to strike, at least that was what he told himself. He might have considered also that he was doing what Lone Wolf had warned him against. He was hesitating. His eyes were accustomed to the dark.

The phosphorescence of the waterfall gave him enough light to put an arrow through Lothar Klein, yet his hand had not once reached for his bow.

The German had been in the rocks for almost two hours now. He had spent some time chasing the flitting shadow that had drawn him out of the cave and then he sat down by the pool where he had a good view of the whole clearing. It was only a few hours until dawn, he could wait that out now. But his restlessness got the better of him and he began to range about the rocks again. As he did so, he glanced over into the opening of the cave. The lantern glow revealed the horses, dozing on their feet, but he could not see Frances. He was surprised that she had withdrawn further into the cave for he knew it frightened her. A suspicion that something was wrong prompted him to walk back to the wagon. Sarah was gone also.

He picked up the lantern, stepping deeper into the cave calling for Frances, but only the echo of his voice came back to him. He began to search around the edge of the clearing, muttering to himself about the stupidity of women. He could hardly believe she had run off into the darkness with the child. They could be facing all manner of dangers. He held up the lantern, peering into the trees.

"Frances, are you out there? What damn nonsense do you play at? Do you try to get that baby of yours eaten by wolves? Come back here! If you are looking for Barnett you do not find him in the dark. Frances, do you hear me?" A figure stepped silently out of the trees behind him as he probed the darkness. An arm fastened around his throat like an iron band and he felt the thin, sharp point of a knife prick the side of his neck.

"Drop the gun Lothar."

Klein recognised Bear Claw's deep voice. His fingers loosened and the rifle fell to the floor. He considered trying to break away, but he remembered how the Cheyenne had bested him in all their friendly wrestling matches and it would only require a slight movement of that knife to cut his throat.

Bear Claw began to push him over towards the cave, the knife still pressed into his flesh.

"Do not try to break away or I will slit your throat like a whittling reed."

Klein believed it. He noticed that the Cheyenne spoke to him in English not German, as he shoved him up against the tailboard of the cart. He took with his free hand the lantern that Lothar was still clutching and held it up so he could see his face clearly. There was fear in the pale blue eyes that the man could not hide. It gave Bear Claw some satisfaction.

"Hey, my old friend," Lothar said in German. " Do you have to stick that thing into my neck? There's no need, I'm not going to run away."

"I do not speak the language of my mother's people to you," came the reply, still in English. "You are no friend to them and you are no friend to me."

"Oh come on Bear Claw!"

"I do not understand that tongue."

The knife bit deeper, nicking the flesh and Klein pulled back drawing a sharp breath.

"Alright, alright if you want to play silly games, we talk English. I am foolish not to realise that if Barnett comes, you are here also. What do you want of me Bear Claw?"

"I have come to kill you."

Lothar grinned broadly, shaking his head. He searched Bear Claw's face for any sign of weakness, but there was nothing to read, only a sombre mask.

"What is the need of all this?" He reached out and touched the tear drops painted down the Cheyenne's face. Bear Claw elbowed his hand away. "You will not kill me. You are not the kind of man to murder an old friend in cold blood. I know what kind of man you are."

"Yes," Bear Claw cut him short. " You know me to be a fool, who believed your offers of friendship. You saved my life only to bring this shame on me. You pulled me from the canyon's mouth only because I was useful to you."

"No, that is not true. You know that is not true. I saved your life because you were my friend."

There was indignation in Lothar's eyes, a note in his voice that rang true and Bear Claw looked away, not wanting to be seduced by reminders of what had been.

"You used me. You led me to betray my people and open the way for you to murder Pawnee Killer."

"I do not mean to kill the old man. I just hit him too hard."

"You are a liar. His skull is cleaved in two, such a wound is not made by mistake and you shot Ben. He takes you into his house when you are hurt, feeds you, helps you and you use him as you did me. You try to take his woman from him."

"She came of her own free will."

Bear Claw snarled, anger showing on his face for the first time. It was surging up inside him. Faced with death Lothar was just the same, evasive and lying. He should have expected nothing else, but deep within himself he had hoped to find some mitigating circumstances, something that would stop him condemning Klein completely. It was a forlorn hope.

"Do you hope to make her love you? She will never love you. Do you know where she is gone now? She is running to her husband, into the dark woods where there is danger and fear. She will face that rather than stay with you."

"He is alive then, that damned Englishman?"

"Yes." Bear Claw would not give him the

satisfaction of knowing how badly Ben was hurt. "But you live too long. If you have prayers to say, say them. I stop no man from singing his death song. You live life without honour, to die bravely is all that is left for you."

He twisted the knife so that the blade rested right across Klein's throat.

"No, Bear Claw please!" Lothar abandoned his efforts to bluff it out. All pretence was useless, he could only beg now, relapsing into German.

"Please you can't kill me. You must understand my dreams. I told you about my dreams. They are everything to me. That gold has been in my mind day and night for months. I like you Bear Claw. I wanted to be your friend, but you wouldn't tell me where the cave was, so I had to find it myself and to do that I needed the map. That map was the key to all I ever wanted. I didn't go that night to kill the old man, only to take the map, but he woke and saw me, so I had to kill him before he raised the whole camp. This is the truth, I swear it."

"But it is all for nothing Lothar Klein," Bear Claw was sticking resolutely to English. "There is no gold in that cave. The treasure is the treasure of the spirit that Sweet Medicine brought to the Cheyenne in the Old Time. I tell you this before, but you do not listen to me. This is not the place of your dreams."

Lothar could not believe that. The old prospector had seen it with his own eyes. He could not bear the thought of dying for nothing, that this cave was never his personal Eldorado.

"Let me look," he begged. "For God's sake let me

look. Don't kill me before I have seen it. I have come all the way from Germany for this moment. You can't be so pitiless as to deny it to me. How can I die well in this state?"

Bear Claw lowered the knife, aware that his hesitation could be fatal, but it was so important to him that a man be given the chance to die well. All the time he had spent with Lothar that spring he saw in a single image. There were many times of laughter and pleasure.

"Will it really help you to look in there? It can only bring you disappointment."

Klein saw a ray of hope. "Yes, yes I must go in."

He snatched the lantern from the Cheyenne's hand and Bear Claw made no move to prevent it.

"Come I will show you that you are wrong. Come with me and see the gold. See what your chiefs have been hiding from you all these years. See that they too are liars. What is the matter my friend, are you afraid eh?"

He was fevered with excitement, veering wildly between German and English, so that at times he was hardly intelligible. He hurried into the cave, beckoning to Bear Claw, but the Cheyenne hung back. He had been taught that only the spiritual leaders of his people must enter that sacred place.

"Come on damn you! You crazy Indians are always afraid of something. It's only a cave, a gold mine, there are no spirits in here. If there are, they do not frighten me. I have no regard for them. You find it easy to kill me, but not to come in here."

Bear Claw was beside him in an instant, holding

the knife to his ribs. He could not take the risk of letting Klein go into the cave alone in case he lost him.

"Do not think you are safe now," he hissed in Lothar's ear. "I still mean to kill you, but you must see how wrong you are. So take the lamp and show me this gold."

The deeper they went into the cave, the colder and danker it became. A leakage from the mountain stream penetrated the rock here, dripping endlessly from fissures above their heads. It smelt like wet iron. Their footsteps echoed, bouncing back off the walls and striking their ears like hammers. Bear Claw was afraid to speak, afraid that his own voice would strike him down. Lothar muttered to himself continuously. He held the lantern up to the sides of the cave as he walked, expecting to see the bright yellow winking in the seams of rock just as it had been described to him. He would not have been surprised to see great carbuncles of gold nuggets strewing the floor. All he saw in the lantern light was the smooth, uninviting face of the rock.

He told himself it must be farther back in the heart of the cave and stumbled on over stones made slippery by the dripping water. Then he tripped over something and went sprawling across the width of the cave against the far wall, almost dropping the lantern. Swearing, he held out the light to see what had caused him to trip. Bear Claw gazed at it too.

Lying close together were too skeletons. Remnants of their clothes hung on their bones, rough twill jackets and heavy boots. One of them was in a sitting position propped up against the wall, his fingers still gripping a pickaxe, as if he was about to get to his feet when he was killed. The other lay on his back. Scattered close by them was a collection of shovels, picks and a nugget pan. Bear Claw thought of the prospector Lothar had heard about, who went to join his brother in the Black Hills. He was certain they were lying at his feet now. Lothar had the same idea.

"So this is why the prospector I spoke to didn't see them anymore."

" I warned you that this is a bad place to be for such a reason as greed," said Bear Claw, eager to be back out in the clearing in the fresh air.

"Why? Who do you think killed these men, my friend, those spirits you keep talking about?" Klein bent over and picked up an arrowhead that lay between the ribcage of the man leaning against the wall. "I don't think spirits need to use arrows. These fellows were killed to stop them telling about the gold. We must be near the seams now."

"Show it to me."

"You still doubt eh? I'll show you alright."

Lothar broke into a shambling run, swinging the lantern dangerously close to the sides of the cave. The Cheyenne lost sight of him for a moment as the cave curved round a bend. Then he heard a shriek. Prolonged and stretched by the echoing vault, the sound curled around him in eerie agony. The despair in it was so palpable that it clutched at him. Klein's summary dismissal of the spirits of the Old Ones seemed ominous as the frightened Bear

Claw listened to that sound go on and on, as if it were searching for a way out of the cave. He forced himself to go on after Klein, around the curve of the bend. It was difficult to penetrate the darkness for although the lantern still shone, it was down on the floor where Lothar had dropped it when he came to the end of the cave.

Bear Claw now realised that the terrible cry had come from Klein. The German was faced with a blank, unyielding wall of rock. He had come to the cave's end, for him the world's end, for there was no seam of gold. He was scratching at the rock like a frantic dog, snapping his nails, rubbing the skin off his fingers, the tormented wail still coming from his throat. He beat his fists on the rock, cursing God, man, himself, the whole conspiracy of creation that had brought him to this point only to destroy him.

Snatching up the lantern, he hurled it against the far wall, smashing the glass and a spurt of flame illuminated the darkness as the last dregs of oil flared up. Bear Claw stepped forward to pull him away, for the flames licked over Lothar's shoe and his trouser leg began to burn, but Klein lunged past him and ran back towards the cave entrance, his arms whirling propeller-like as he tried to beat out the burning material now running all up his leg.

The Cheyenne ran after him, but turned his foot on a stone and stumbled. When he reached the cave mouth, the dawn was blue and misty. The freshness of the air made him gasp. Lothar was running towards the pool below the waterfall, tearing off his burning clothes piece by piece. He was almost naked when he threw himself into the pool, wallowing in the water to alleviate the scalding pain.

Bear Claw drew an arrow from his quiver and slipped the bow from his shoulder. Lothar was not aware of him. He was dancing and splashing in the water, making wild incoherent noises, laughing and shouting. It sounded as if there were twenty people in the clearing instead of that one, tortured lunatic.

Bear Claw fitted the arrow to the string and stretched it back to rub against his cheek. It did not seem like an act of revenge any more, but one of pity. An arrow sang, but it was not his arrow. He let the string go slack and his own arrow dropped at his feet, as he saw the vibrating, feathered dart wing down. It struck Lothar in the throat and the tip emerged at the other side of his neck. He did not fall at once, his hands frozen in the upward movement they had begun before the arrow stuck him, all his ravings silenced. It looked as if he was playing a macabre version of that old children's game of statues. Then a froth broke out on his lips and he fell forward, clutching at the shaft that transfixed his throat. He was dead when he hit the water. Two convulsive spasms and the body floated face down, thin streams of red trailing across the surface of the pool.

The Cheyenne looked up to the crags above the waterfall. The horse was black, gleaming even in the clinging mist. It seemed to him to be balancing on the very edge of the rock. In the blue dawn the rider was elongated, indistinct, changing shape like a restless image in water. It was an Indian certainly. Bear Claw had the impression of flowing hair, a brown feather, a white feather and a great beauty that stirred his heart.

It was all so insubstantial, ethereal and his eyes refused to focus properly. He was sure though that he saw the figure raise a hand to him in a gesture of farewell, then the horse turned and disappeared down the other side of the rocks. Where it had stood was a radiance, an aura of soft, trembling colours. A trick of the light, the sun coming up behind the mountains, striking colours from the mist- Bear Claw did not know, but he was seized by a sense of awe that he could not control.

He might have believed that a Sioux moving early in the mountains that were sacred to his ancestors had shot this sacrilegious, intruding white man and saluted his Cheyenne brother for his intention to do the same. But he could not shake off the belief that he had seen the Guardian of the Sweet Medicine cave, sent by the Old Ones to protect their secrets. If he had indeed seen this shining one, he knew his blunders were forgiven, for the Guardian had lifted the burden of revenge from his shoulders, had in his mercy relieved him of the duty of killing Lothar Klein. The path was open for him to return to his tribe. It was a confirmation that he was a true Cheyenne.

It was too comforting a message to disregard, whatever it was he had seen. The sign had been given him that the flaming sword was lowered and he could grasp the brown feather, sweet medicine for his spirit indeed.

He knelt in the clearing, praying his thanks to the Old Ones for their message. He did not want to look at Lothar, but he could not leave the body floating half submerged in the pool. He waded in and dragged him out on to the grass. The pale blue eyes were open and the lids would not respond to Bear Claw's efforts to close them. He watched the drops of water fall from the almost white eyelashes. The wet moustache clinging to Lothar's face reminded him of the day they went fishing, when he first told Klein about Pawnee Killer and the map.

He dare not remove the arrow in case it was the shaft of the Guardian, but he took two blankets from the cart, the blankets Frances had snatched from her bed the night they fled the cabin and wrapped them around the body like a winding sheet. On the edge of the clearing, with Lothar's own pick and shovel, he dug a grave and buried him. He now knew why white men marked graves with crosses because Ben had explained it to him. He bound two arrows from his quiver into the shape of a cross and stuck it into the mound of earth. As he did so, it entered his mind that he might soon have to do the same for Benjamin. He said a final prayer to the spirits of the Old Ones, hitched up Lothar's horse to the cart, tied Sandy behind and drove out of the clearing. He did not look back.

When he reached the canyon, the first thing he saw was Sarah Barnett chasing Caesar around the boulders, clutching at his tail. The dog was very patient with her, allowing himself to be grabbed, pulled and choked without so much as showing his teeth.

Over by the smoking embers of the fire he saw Frances sitting on the floor beside her husband. His head rested in her lap and she was bathing his face with water from the bottle Bear Claw had left there. He was not conscious and the fever was running high. He twisted and turned, murmuring incoherently. She tried to keep him still for his writhing had started the wound bleeding again. Her breast and the front of her skirt were damp with sweat and blood. She looked up at Bear Claw as he ran across the canyon floor, her eyes asking for some kind of assurance.

He looked at Ben's face, flushed with fever yet ashen underneath it. His face and hair were as wet as Lothar's when Bear Claw pulled him out of the pool. He did not like to acknowledge the resemblance.

"I'm so relieved to see you Bear Claw, to know you're safe. Lothar had that gun and I was afraid, " she stopped to speak soothingly to Ben. It was as much as she could do to hold him still. She hesitated for a moment before she asked the question.

"Is Lothar dead?"

Bear Claw nodded, one short movement of his head. She did not press him further, just lowered her eyelashes in acquiescence.

"We must get Benjamin home. He is burning up with fever and the wound is bleeding again. There's a good doctor in Baker, Doctor Sanderson. I am sure he can help, but we must get Ben to a comfortable bed, wash and disinfect this wound."

Bear Claw knelt down and put his hand on Ben's forehead. It was like touching a hot coal. His wife's forehead had felt that way the day before she died of smallpox. He recalled how the memory of it had burned in his fingers for days.

"The cabin is a long way from here, Baker even farther," he said. "The journey is rough, as you know. I do not think he will live."

"Of course he will, I know he will. I brought this on him and I won't let him die. I'll pray every minute of every hour and God won't be able to refuse me. He can't take him from me now."

Bear Claw had always believed that if it was a man's day to die, there was nothing anybody could do. No one could stay the beckoning hand of the All Father.

"The bullet is buried deep, if it stays there too long it poisons the flesh."

"Then we must go now. Dr Sanderson will be able to remove it. We must try. I can't sit here and let his life ebb away in my arms. You must think from the way I have behaved that I don't love him. I won't try to explain why I came here with Lothar, but you must believe that I love Benjamin more than my own life. Do you believe that?"

"I never doubt that you love him, neither does he. I love him too. Together we must try to keep him alive."

They dumped everything out of the cart except the water bottles, blankets and some food and the Cheyenne lifted Ben into it. The space was not big enough for him to lay full length, so Frances sat with him propped up against her, his head resting on her shoulder. Bear Claw, as he put Tall Woman's blanket back over him, put his hand on the box that was still in Ben's jacket pocket. He drew it out carefully and peered inside, afraid that the necklace might be broken. The box was crushed, but the stones were intact.

He shut down the lid and held the box out to Frances.

"Here, Ben buy this for you in Baker. It is not my place to give them to you, but I am sure he wants you to wear them for him now."

She held the box between her fingers, smoothing out the crushed corners as if she was caressing an injured creature. It was a pretty box, covered with dark, red satin. She was afraid to open it, fearing that at the sight of it, whatever it was, her courage would desert her and she would start to cry. She did not want to do that in front of Bear Claw. But he lingered, eager for her to look and she fumbled with the lid. When it sprung open at last, the faceted stoned flashed their brightness into her face.

"Oh how beautiful! Where ever did Ben get the money for these?"

"The money is paid. He will tell you about it when he is well. Wear them."

She could not lift both her arms up to fasten the rope of green and silver flowers around her neck because her husband resting against her shoulder prevented it. Bear Claw reached out and fastened it for her with a gentle reticence. She caught hold of his hand before he could withdraw it and held it for a moment.

"Bear Claw, when we get home and Ben is well again, I want to learn more about your people, become friends with them. I have always had a foolish fear of them in my heart because they are so different from me. I hope you will help me be a better friend to the Cheyenne and a better wife to Benjamin."

She could feel his discomfort, his desire to free his hand from hers and she let go, smiling at his confusion.

"We must go," was all he said.

It was an odd little procession that trekked back out onto the wide grasslands. Bear Claw sat on the driver's seat of the cart with Sarah trapped firmly between his knees, keeping her amused with songs and stories. He still wore his face paint and it fascinated her. She stared at it, touched it and drew copies of it on her own face with her fingers.

Loosely tethered to the back of the cart were now three horses. Caesar loped along, sometimes in front, sometimes behind. Now and then they would lose sight of him, only to spot him bounding along in the distance in hot pursuit of a jack-rabbit, but he would soon catch up with the cart.

Frances did her best to cushion her husband from the jolting and grinding of the vehicle. She could feel him growing weaker. Although the fever still burned, he was losing the strength to toss and turn. The journey seemed endless, much longer than the outward one with Lothar because of the insane pace he had set and his refusal to stop. Bear Claw stopped several times, to give them all the chance to rest, eat and drink.

When they finally reached the cabin, hot, sore and dusty it seemed to Fran that Ben was barely breathing. Everything looked so good there, the animals grazing peacefully, the flowers growing. It was home and she could not understand how she had ever felt this place to be a prison. She had created her own prison, but now she was determined to be free of it.

Once he had helped to get Ben into the cabin, Bear Claw stopped only to wash the paint from his face, before he rode like a maniac to Baker. He was back by late afternoon with a dazed Jeff Sanderson, who had never ridden so fast in his life. The doctor removed the bullet, but was not over sanguine about Ben's chances of survival. He had lost too much blood and if the fever reached another high point he might not be able to resist it. He regretted that there was nothing else he could do, although he would call again in a few days. He gave Fran some quinine to control the fever, told her it was now in God's hands, doffed his hat and rode back to Baker at a more leisurely pace than he had come.

After three days the fever abated, but Ben lay in a deep coma. If Frances had not trained herself to catch the rhythm of his breathing, she would have believed he was dead. Two more days went by and there was still no change in his condition.

Bear Claw refused to go back to his village until the All Father had made his decision. He paced about the farm, working harder than any squaw, work that a Cheyenne warrior would normally scorn. He hoed the crops, chopped wood, tended the animals, played with Sarah, doing all he could to free Frances from anything that kept her from Ben's side.

Some days Painted Shawl and her daughters would walk down from the camp to help him, defying

He-Who-Runs- Fast's displeasure. She refused to be ordered about by her brother and Tall Woman supported her. Bear Claw welcomed their company and his nieces were adept at devising games to entertain Sarah.

When darkness fell, he would pad into the cabin and sit on the floor beside Ben's bed, sitting with Frances for hours in friendly silence. She tried to make some conversation with him, but she was happy enough just to feel his presence. His love for Ben mingled with her own and gave her strength.

❀❀❀

It was Sunday. Sitting by the window with her bible in her hands, Frances watched Bear Claw by the barn, washing down the horses with a scrubbing brush that he dipped in a bucket of water. Now and then he flicked water at Sarah, who was sitting on the floor at his feet playing with her rag doll with the yellow woolly hair. Caesar lay on the veranda, his great paws lolling over the edge.

Frances had always read her bible on Sunday since she was a child, but this morning she had been searching for words of comfort, hoping that some particular phrase would leap up at her from the page and assure her that Benjamin was safe. Even she was beginning to doubt that he would live. She had slept little during the past few days and her spirit was falling to a low ebb.

She got up, putting her bible down on the chair and went to the bed. This was the ritual that she went through a thousand times a day, standing there searching his face for signs of life. His face was caught in the broad bar of sunlight that struck through the room. It was beautiful in its still, pale serenity, framed by the dark brown hair. It struck her the how thin he was. The skin drawn tight across his face seemed almost transparent, particularly around the prominent cheek bones, sharpening them all the more. She sat on the bed, but as she watched a great weariness came over her. The heat of the morning with its soft, lazy air lulled her to sleep.

When Benjamin Barnett first struggled back to consciousness, she was lying on the bed lost in a deep sleep, her freckled arm stretched out across him. The daylight was too bright at first and his eyes flickered shut again,

but he felt the brush of his own eyelashes on his cheek. It was a sharp sensation that forced him to open his eyes once more. He had been living in a tepid darkness, where everything was muted and dulled. There were shapes in the distance, but they never formed into anything positive, just grey masses that seemed about to become something more, then passed on. It was the same with sounds. He almost heard them, almost recognised them and then they were gone. He was floating endlessly on nothingness with no power or will help himself.

The touch of his eyelashes was so stinging a sensation in comparison with the state from which he had passed, that it brought tears to his eyes, like the sudden blast of icy wind on a winter's morning. He gazed at the beam of sunlight, watching the gad flies dancing in it and the horned beetles sliding down it like children in a playground.

Frances stirred and sighed. The sound was loud and startling to his ear, a mighty chord of music and he flinched, waiting for the echo to die away before he looked in the direction from whence it came. He saw his wife, her face tranquil in sleep. Around her neck was the emerald green necklace. Strands of her hair lay across her shoulder and they set each other off perfectly, the auburn and the green. He smiled at the perfection of it.

At that moment he had no recollection of anything that had happened. All he knew was the sensation that he felt. Frances was beside him; he was warm, drowsy, secure. He put his arm around her. It seemed to him that everything he did was in slow motion and audible. He could hear his muscles and sinews move when he lifted his arm. Then he was aware of some pain for the first time, somewhere below his ribs, a rawness that invaded his dreamlike state. But it was too diffuse to worry him; his mind was not clear enough to focus on it. Frances responded to his arm around her shoulder, reaching out for him instinctively in her sleep.

When Bear Claw came into the cabin with a squealing Sarah tucked under his arm, they were asleep in each other's arms. The Cheyenne knew then that he would soon be free to go back to his people. The All father had made his decision and the power of the wolverine was broken.

CHAPTER 9

Sarah reached out and grabbed for it as the wooden ball flew towards her, but with the lack of coordination common to young children, her fingers failed to grasp the ball and it bounced down the veranda steps into the yard. It was pounced on by two chickens, who thought it might be edible, but before they had time to be disappointed Caesar chased them off it and picked up the ball in his teeth with precision. He bounded on to the veranda, by-passing Sarah and dropped it on Benjamin's lap.

It was Ben who had first thrown it to his daughter. He was sitting in the rocking chair smiling at Sarah's frustration when she missed the ball.

"Caesar wants me to throw it for him Sarah. Will you let Caesar have your ball?"

She nodded, not in the least reluctant, her curly brown hair, identical in colour to her father's, dancing about her shoulders in springy profusion. Ben threw the ball across the yard, but because it was so light it did not go very far and Caesar misjudged the distance, over-running it and skidding to a halt a few yards beyond where it landed.

Frances looked up from her wood chopping, grateful to stop for a moment. She leaned on the axe, pulling back the strands of hair that fell across her flushed cheeks and tucked them up into the pins that held her chignon in place.

"I cannot sit here and see you do that any longer," Ben said, as he saw the weariness in the way she rested on the handle of the axe. "That log is much too thick for you to sever."

He pushed himself up out of the chair and came a little uncertainly down the steps, pulling at Sarah's curls as he passed her.

"No Benjamin, you aren't strong enough yet. You know what Dr Sanderson said yesterday that you mustn't attempt anything strenuous for another month at least. Besides, I can manage."

She swung the axe above her head with determination, but although it bit into the block, shaving out chips of bark and white wood, it made little impression. Ben smiled.

"If I wait that long you will have muscles like a prize-fighter and although it might come in handy, I don't want my wife to look quite like that."

He put his hand on her wrist as she made to lift the axe again and took it from her. He severed the wood in two blows and split half a dozen more, but the effort made him feel ridiculously weak and he was grateful to ease himself back into the rocking chair on the veranda. Frances said nothing, but she gave him a reproachful look before she began to gather up the wood.

Ben was growing impatient with the slowness of his progress. He knew he was lucky to be alive and that he should be thankful, but there was so much to do around the farm and he hated to see Frances struggle with it. Her determination and competence astonished him. Bear Claw, Painted Shawl and her daughters had been a great help, but they had not seen any of them for two weeks. Bear Claw had gone to fulfil his promise to announce to all the bands of Cheyenne spread across the plains, that he, Bear Claw, son of White Bull, stood pledge for the renewal of the sacred arrows. He-Who-Runs-Fast refused to let Painted Shawl go to the white man's cabin if Bear Claw was not there. When she tried to defy him he slapped her so hard he knocked her down and was taken to task by Tall Woman for treating his sister with disrespect, but she advised Painted Shawl to do as her brother wished this time. She always took her mother's advice.

Ben as he lay back in the chair, fighting off a desire to sleep, wondered how many miles his friend had covered since he last saw him. He found that he fell asleep suddenly, unexpectedly, sometimes in the middle of a conversation and it irritated him beyond measure. He was just beginning to be able to concentrate long enough to read for short spells, which went some way towards alleviating the frustration of his forced idleness.

Frances walked up the steps, the wood basket under her arm, her manner busy, almost aggressive. She was so determined to be the practical, uncomplaining wife that she was in danger of over-playing the role and he wanted to laugh. Then again, if he stopped to consider why she was so eager, he felt he might just as easily weep.

They had spoken very little about Lothar and that

momentous night she had abandoned the cabin. It was too painful for Fran just yet and she told herself she would wait until Ben was stronger. The excuse served. He did not want to hear her say sorry again in the way she had, when he lay in that canyon in the Black Hills.

Her distress could only heighten his feelings of guilt, so he was silent on the subject also. Both of them knew they must talk about it soon; there would be a need for it, but right then they were grateful that the bond between them had been strengthened by the threat of catastrophe.

Ben did not want Frances to sacrifice herself too readily as if the cause of her previous discontent had never existed. He knew he must do something positive to make the quality of her life richer here in Montana. He was not yet sure how, but he hoped that now she knew he recognised her loneliness, she might cease to feel so lonely.

He took hold of her hand as she swept past, forcing her to stop and he brushed his lips lightly over her fingers. They were red and chafed from wielding the axe.

"Why don't you stop working for just a moment? You behave as if there are only four hours in a day. Sit here for a while and admire the summer with me."

He drew her towards his lap and she sat on his knee, still hugging the wood basket as if to remind him that she could not stay there long, but he gave the basket a fierce look and she let it drop to the floor.

"Just look at that sky. Have you ever seen anything so blue? I really believe you have not stopped to look at anything since I've been ill. You have hardly taken a minute to breathe. There is a limit to how long anyone can keep up such a pace, even someone filled with such zeal as you. In your present mood you would make a marvellous missionary. You are wasted here. I think I will put you in a canoe and send you down river to convert all the tribes around the Mississippi basin."

"Now you are laughing at me Benjamin," but she was laughing herself. She remembered how she had confessed to Ben, not long after she had first met him, that her greatest dream in childhood and adolescence had been to become a missionary, influenced by the example of a cousin who had gone to China. It always surprised and pleased her how he remembered everything about her, even small, inconsequential details that she would never have expected him to even consider.

"Now there's something to rival the sky. Look there!"

He was pointing to the trees near the cattle pen where a kingfisher blazed, as it darted out of the trees into the open for a few seconds and was soon swallowed up again in the dark green shade of the woods, heading for the stream. Fran called for her daughter to look, but Sarah was occupied unpacking all the wood from the basket and laying the pieces in serried ranks. When she looked up the kingfisher had gone.

"You are right," Fran admitted. "I have been letting the summer pass me by and when I think how close I came to having to face it without you-" he motioned the thought away with his hand. " And it's so beautiful here Ben, nowhere more beautiful than our home."

"Frances, don't forget that wild animals like that wolverine still stalk the woods. You will still hear strange noises in the night. Men like He-Who-Runs-Fast will still resent us, perhaps pose a threat to us. Nothing has changed. It is a beautiful place, but it is also a wild, often dangerous place. Do you really accept that, or are you just pretending that you do?"

"There is no pretence. Things have changed, although I know the dangers are still there, I am not afraid when I look into the woods at twilight. I do not feel that dreadful sense of menace. I don't feel obliged to rush to bar the cabin door as soon as it grows dark. I think I know why. No fear can compare with the agonies I went through when I feared I might lose you. I am sure now that is the only fear I will ever have."

He sighed. " It is still something you may have to face. In this country a man is lucky if he lives into old age. It's hard on children too," he added significantly, his eyes straying to Sarah, playing so contentedly with the wood.

She fingered the green necklace at her throat as she considered her answer. She wore the jewelled petals all the time. It would seem strange now to see her without them.

"I have a certainty within me that we are destined to grow old together and Sarah will be there to see it with her husband and children. Not everyone is fortunate enough to be granted a second chance. I almost ruined our lives, but the future will be good, I know it. Now I must cook the dinner."

She stood up with resolution. "We must try and put some weight back on you. It pains me to see your shoulder bones sticking up through your shirt as if they had no flesh on them at all. It reminds me of the skeleton that doctor friend of yours, who was with you at Cambridge, used to keep in his lodgings to frighten the landlady when she came for the rent."

"Well that is flattering I must say, being told I look like old Jeremy."

She kissed the top of his head before she gave Sarah instructions to reload the wood basket and went into the cabin, leaving Ben to ponder on what she had said. He wished he believed that everything would be so easy for her as she imagined in her present state of enthusiasm.

He watched his daughter's laboured efforts to put each piece of wood back into the basket. Suddenly she let out a squeal of surprise as a splinter of wood buried itself in her finger. The pain from such an unexpected source caused great tears to well up in her eyes.

"What's the matter? Did you prick yourself?"

Sarah held up her finger beseechingly.

"Have you got a splinter in it? Come here, let me see."

He held out his arms to her and she clambered on to his lap.

"Oh, yes you have, a great big splinter. I bet you didn't know that bits of wood could bite you did you? Now I shall have to squeeze this out and that will hurt just a little bit, but when the splinter is gone, it won't hurt anymore."

She sat very still while he squeezed out the splinter, but it took longer than she had envisaged and when she saw the beads of blood spring up on her finger, she began to cry in earnest.

"Oh don't cry now, my sweet. It's out now. It's all finished."

He sucked away the blood from her finger and rocked her, trying not to dwell on the thought that if Lothar's luck had held, Sarah might have been in Europe by now, the daughter of Lothar Klein. He pressed his face into her hair, drinking in the pleasure and reassurance that holding her in his arms gave him.

"Why does Sarah cry? Maybe she thinks her old friend does not want to play with her anymore, he is away so long."

Ben looked up, startled by the voice and Sarah's muffled crying stopped. Bear Claw stood in the yard, resting his elbow on Caesar's shaggy head. The weeks of travelling on the open plains had tanned his skin until it was as dark as his full-blood brothers. He wore only a breechclout and a light waistcoat. Ben noticed that around his neck was the Star of David that he had always kept hidden in his medicine bundle. He looked lithe, fit and eager as he stood there fondling Caesar's ears, that broad grin on his face. Clearly he had enjoyed his travels.

"Look," he said. " I bring something for Sarah."

He was rummaging in the parfleche that hung over his shoulder and produced a carved, wooden dog on wheels. There was a collar around its neck with a lead attached. He rolled the dog along the veranda, demonstrating its squeaky walk. Ben lifted Sarah down from his lap so she could take possession of her new toy.

She had forgotten all about her sore finger.

"Wherever did you get that Bear Claw?"

"When I was amongst the southern Cheyenne, a man came from the east, an old man with a white beard. He came to trade with the tribes. He is a pedlar, like my mother's father and comes to the tribes every year. He has many good stories to tell. I tell him that he is welcome to visit the band of Lone Wolf if he wants to travel so far. He carries many pretty things that your wife would like to see."

He looked into the cabin searching for Frances. Ben called out, "Fran, Fran come here a moment. Bear Claw is back."

She was at the door in a moment, a mixing bowl and wooden spoon in her hands. She was so happy to see him safe and well. He really did look well, glowing with health and vitality. She wished he could have transferred some of it to her husband.

"I see you have brought Sarah a present. You should not spoil her so."

They all watched Sarah trailing the dog up and down the yard followed by Caesar, who was doing his best to flatten the unfamiliar, rattling object with his paw. When he started to bite it, Sarah smacked him on the nose with her balled fist. It was clear that he found this unjustifiable and withdrew, ambling back on to the veranda to lie against Ben's legs, mystified by the unpredictability of human kind.

"You timed your visit well," Frances told the Cheyenne, "I am just cooking dinner. You must have some with us, then you can tell us all about your journey."

When she had gone back into the cabin Ben stood up.

"Let's take a walk up to the top land. I want to see how the vegetables are coming on and I need some exercise, I spend far too much time sitting in this chair falling asleep for my liking."

As they strolled up the yard, Bear Claw could see the unsteadiness in Ben's walk.

"It is good to see you on your feet again, but you are not strong enough for much walking yet."

"I can't argue with that. A few hundred yards seem like twenty miles to me at present. I suppose I am impatient, but my progress seems very slow. I am not used to this inactivity and it throws such a burden on Frances."

The two men leaned against the fence and surveyed the rows of healthy vegetables, all expanding their leaves in the sun of early summer.

"Unless there is some form of blight, there will be a bumper crop this year. Your people shall share it with us. After all, you have helped to look after it. Frances tells me you tended these vegetables like a true farmer while I was ill. It is hardly a task expected of a Cheyenne warrior. Bear Claw, I have much to be thankful for. I am fortunate to be alive and without your help, I doubt very much if I would be. I have not had the chance to thank you yet, so let me do so now, for myself, for Frances and for Sarah."

Bear Claw shrugged, reaching down to pick a long stalk of grass which he ran through his fingers.

"It is the All Father you must thank for your life.

Because your life is precious to us, he does not take it for himself. If he had chosen to take it, nothing I do makes any difference. He shows great kindness to us both, for he sends his messenger to tell me I am welcome among the Cheyenne."

Ben raised his eyebrows questioningly. He had sensed a new joy, a serenity in his friend the moment he saw him. He had the look of a man who had come to the end of a long search and found what he had sought for so long.

"You had an experience while you were amongst the tribes?"

"No, before that. It was good to go amongst the other bands. When you live in a small band, you grow concerned with small problems and forget you are part of a big nation. Ben, I have a story to tell you. Sit down, you will grow tired standing so long."

His face had taken on that grave, concentrated expression that always came over it when he had something momentous to impart. Barnett sat down on the cross piece of the stile that he had set into the fence, keen to hear Bear Claw's explanation, but he was unprepared for what the Cheyenne said first.

"I did not kill Lothar Klein."

"You mean he is still alive? He escaped you?"

There was an astonished look in Ben's eyes. Frances had not told him Lothar was dead; he had not asked her, he just assumed it was so.

"No, he is dead. I bury him in the clearing by the cave, but I did not kill him. I was ready. My bow is in my hand, the string at my cheek, but it was not my arrow that pierced his throat. It was the Guardian."

"What guardian?"

Bear Claw told him the story from the moment he had sent Frances through the woods to the canyon. How he had felt the presence of the Old Ones in the echoing cave and how the discovery that there was no gold had driven Lothar frantic, as he fled out of the cave, his clothes on fire. He described how Klein had danced and raved in the pool below the waterfall. Sometimes the image of it would rise up before him as he rode across the plains, the sound lingering cruelly in his ears.

It was clear to Barnett that the memory of it affected him. He did not care to dwell on it himself. He had tried not to let any resentment of what Lothar had done rankle inside him. He wanted no truck with bitterness. He was eager to build on his strengthened relationship with Frances and bitterness could play no part in that. Yet he did wonder what he might have done if he had come across Lothar in that clearing when the German did not have his Spencer rifle in his hands. But to imagine the half-crazed Klein splashing in the pool, trying to ease the pain of his burns gave him no satisfaction at all. It was a tragic, macabre image that he pushed away from him.

Bear Claw was now describing what he called the Guardian and just how Lothar had died.

"I know you will tell me it was just another man such as myself, a Sioux maybe, angry to see a white man in hills which are sacred to their tribe also, but I know it is the Guardian Ben. The All Father sends him to kill

Lothar, to tell me I am fit to be a Cheyenne. The flaming sword in my dream vision is taken away. Do you believe what I tell you?"

Ben was chewing his lip thoughtfully. It did not matter who killed Lothar Klein. The message remained the same for Bear Claw.

"What matters is that you believe it and I can see that you do. There is peace in your face. You have become whole, at one with yourself. There can be no better feeling on this earth. I am very happy for you."

He reached out and shook the Cheyenne's hand with great warmth, as if he was meeting him for the first time and Bear Claw laughed.

"Lothar did you a service after all," Ben added. "Perhaps it will stand him in good stead eventually."

"I hope so. I fear his will be a troubled, wandering spirit for much time to come, unable to leave the earth. I do not want that."

"He did not hurt Frances you know and I do believe he was genuinely fond of Sarah." Ben was surprised to find himself defending Lothar, but he felt Bear Claw needed him to say it. "But tell me, is that why you are wearing your mother's pendant now, because you are an undivided being at last?"

"You understand much. I do not need to hide it away in my medicine bundle. It is part of me. I know very little about my mother's people, but I will learn more. I love and respect her as much as before, but now I see that she is wrong to teach me that I cannot be a Cheyenne and I am wrong to believe I must do all that she wished. I do not reject or despise her when I choose to be a Cheyenne. Her spirit will understand that. I hope you will teach me all you know about the Jewish people and about Christians also. If the Indian and the white are to understand each other, they must learn all they can."

Ben agreed, wishing he believed that the white man would be so eager to learn about the Indian.

"I will do my best to tell you all I know. Perhaps I might be able to help you to learn to read and write. You speak English so well, it seems ridiculous that you can't read it. If you could read, you would be able to learn so much more. In return you could help me get a firmer grasp on your language."

The prospect excited Bear Claw. He had always wanted to read the white man's books.

"I wanted to tell you all this ever since it happened," he said, "But you are too sick to take it in. Now I am happy it is all told."

He pushed his hand into the flap of his waistcoat. "I have something to give you. When I bury Lothar, I think he must have a cross for his grave, so I make one with my arrows. A thought comes to me that maybe soon I will have to do the same for you. I do not know then if you are still alive, your wound is so bad. It is good that I do not have to give you such a cross. So Ben, to hold our friendship in long life together I give you this other cross, to wear in life, not death. I will wear the symbol of my mother's people and you will wear the symbol of Jesus. This will bind us together."

He held out a small cross of fine amber on a leather

thong. The pedlar he had met amongst the Southern Cheyenne had told him it once belonged to a preacher who had drowned in the Mississippi. He had a yarn to go with every bit and bob in his pack.

Ben turned the cross over in the palm of his hand, searching for the right thing to say, but in the end all he said was, "I shall be proud to wear it." as he tied the thong around his neck.

"Now we all wear something with meaning," the Cheyenne remarked. He liked the look of the cross at Ben's throat. "I see that Frances wears the emeralds. I know you do not mind that I give them to her because it is important she sees the gift."

"I'm glad you did. The first thing I saw when I regained consciousness that Sunday morning was Frances asleep on the bed beside me, wearing that necklace. Nothing was very clear to me. I could not remember anything that had happened, but she looked so beautiful lying there and it seemed right that she should be wearing the necklace, almost as if she had always done so. It made me feel secure somehow."

"All is well between you?"

Ben hesitated, not wanting to give a bland answer. During these days of slow recovery he had often asked himself what madness had prompted him to bring Frances to this place. He loved it with a fierce passion, but the threads of existence here could be severed so easily. It needed only one extreme winter, trapping them in the cabin for months or a series of droughts that ruined the crops. The situation with the local tribes was bound to worsen as the threat from settlers grew. There were so many things from which he knew he could not guarantee to protect his wife and daughter. He hoped that it was his current physical weakness that sapped his confidence and when he was fully well again some optimism would return. He could not face the prospect of returning to Boston to live.

"Yes and I am hopeful they will remain so," he replied. "All the problems are not solved of course. Frances is so eager to be a good wife to me that she hardly seems to realise it. But we have both learned a lot about each other, that must be a good start. But how about you? Were you well received by the band when you finally got back to your lodge?"

Bear Claw was surprised that Ben was so ready to turn the subject away from his relationship with his wife. He did not understand why there should still be doubt. He had never seen a woman so much in love with her husband as Frances Barnett. He decided that deep down Ben must be sanguine about the future; it was just the Englishman's way to be guarded in his emotions. The Cheyenne did not fully perceive the complexity of Benjamin's nature, that kernel of despair that lurked within him that he constantly struggled to banish.

Ben stood up, suggesting they should go back to the house. He caught hold of the fence to steady himself and Bear Claw's hands hovered near him.

"It's alright, I just stood up too quickly. I tend to forget how useless I am at present. I find it hard to believe. Things will improve when I start eating properly again.

Fran has already accused me this morning of looking like a skeleton we both met once." He laughed at Bear Claw's puzzled expression. "Never mind. You haven't answered my question though. Do your brothers know you have become a true Cheyenne?"

"Those who know me well say they see a change in me. White Arrow says it shines in my face. Lone Wolf tells me that my experience is a sign that I will be a great peace chief one day. I hope this is true. I wish very much to be wise enough to help my people."

" You will be Bear Claw, don't doubt it. What does He-Who-Runs-Fast think of it all?"

"He still does not speak to me. He vowed it and he cannot break his vow, but I know he will come to the arrow ceremony at Blue Butte in three days' time and within it he will be one with me whether he likes it or not. The ceremony is long and solemn. I wish you to be there to see the dedication of the arrows to the All Father."

"I should very much like to be there, but if it is only three days away, I fear I'm not strong enough to travel out as far as Blue Butte yet. I can share it with you in spirit and perhaps there may be other ceremonies that Frances and I can share with you another time."

The Cheyenne nodded. "There is one soon, much nearer, at our camp. I have decided to take Painted Shawl as my wife. I have grieved for Crying Wind for a long time and all that time Painted Shawl has cared for me to honour her sister.

She is a brave woman with a warm heart, good to look at also. It is right that she has another husband.

Laughing Water and Red Dawn are like daughters to me already and maybe there will be more children, a son perhaps."

"I'm delighted to hear this, Frances will be too. Painted Shawl and the girls have been such a help to us. Sarah is really fond of them all. But I doubt if He-Who is very pleased about it."

Bear Claw made a dismissive noise. "I do not care what he thinks. It makes no difference to him, for she lives in my lodge anyway. The one to please is Tall Woman and she is pleased."

Ben smiled to himself, recalling the day he asked Fran's father for permission to propose to his daughter. Sir Gerald was clearly willing, but he dare not give his consent before he had consulted his wife. Ben had wondered often since, if they would have been so willing had they known he would take her thousands of miles away into the wilderness of America.

Bear Claw was saying, " Lone Wolf has said that you are always welcome in his camp. He says prayers for you when you are sick. When the summer buffalo hunt is over, I will bring you buffalo hides for the winter and we can sit and talk. Then you will teach me to read your language and I will teach you to speak my tongue like a Cheyenne."

He was so earnest, so full of his new-found joy. Ben could only hope there would be a good future for Bear Claw and his people, but the signs were not promising. As more settlers penetrated into Montana every year, friction was bound to grow. Dr Sanderson had told him yesterday of two families building cabins farther up river, about ten miles from them. The prospect could be good for the Barnetts, women for Frances to visit, children to be playmates for Sarah and support in times of hardship, but for the Cheyenne it could be worrying signs of things to come.

Ben realised that should problems arise he was in a good position to mediate because of his friendship with Bear Claw, but it could also be a dangerous position for some of the settlers might distrust his sympathy for Lone Wolf's band and accuse him of betraying his duty to his own kind.

It would not take much to ramp up the tension. A nervous settler, anxious for the safety of his family, need only take a shot at a passing Cheyenne and even if he missed, that would be enough to convince He-Who-Runs-Fast that retribution was necessary and hostilities could soon escalate.

Amongst the newcomers there would be families who had been fed stories of Indian atrocities, some of them true and who believed that the native population should be eliminated like any other vermin.

Barnett wondered if the uneasy political situation back East might prompt even more people to move westwards. Last winter the Baker Bugle, the newspaper rolled off on an ancient printing machine in a ramshackle office behind the livery stables, told the story in lurid detail of the fanatical abolitionist John Brown's October raid on the U.S military arsenal at Harper's Ferry in West Virginia. His objective was to provoke a slave uprising and establish a territory for freed slaves in the mountains of Maryland and Virginia. The uprising did not happen and Brown was forced to surrender. He was hung as a traitor, becoming a martyr and inspiration to many. Others regarded him as a madman and a murderer.

Henry and Jane's letters from Boston were full of worried speculation about political affairs. A campaign for the election of a new President was beginning and there was much support for the Republican senator Abraham Lincoln. Attitudes towards slavery would be a key issue in the campaign.

Slavery was illegal in most of the Northern states and Lincoln supported the introduction of a law to prevent the spread of slavery to any newly formed states. This was causing great alarm in the Southern states whose cotton economy was based on the labour of black slaves. They feared that it would lead to a total abolition and there were rumours that they would withdraw from the Union in consequence.

After years of campaigning against the suffering and injustice, slavery had been abolished in Britain in 1833. It struck Ben as ironical that many Americans who made so much of the notion of freedom after breaking away from Britain during the previous century, should still cling on to the institution of slavery. The Declaration of Independence stated that all men are created equal and endowed by their creator with certain inalienable rights. Ben had once caused a heated argument in a Boston drawing room, that almost came to blows, by suggesting that to truly reflect how things really stood, the text of the declaration should have added, "with the exception of black slaves." He pointed out that the man largely responsible for drafting the Declaration, the much admired Thomas Jefferson, had owned 500 slaves on his estates and seemed not to see the conflict between his beliefs on freedom and religious toleration and his support for slavery.

If conflict broke out over the issue of slavery, it was unlikely to reach as far as this remote corner of Montana, but Ben feared that when it was all over, whatever the result, it was inevitable that the Cheyenne's freedom to roam at will would eventually be challenged and curtailed by land hungry men backed up by the army. They would be forced to die fighting or submit to a way of life that to them was no better than slavery.

It was a bitter, painful thought and he did not voice his fears to Bear Claw, not wishing to cast dark shadows over his friend's optimistic mood. He decided he must concentrate more on the present, take courage from Bear Claw's natural, life-affirming philosophy and strive to make life as good as it could be for his family here in Montana.

"Well, before he goes off to take part in these great events, would the future peace chief of the Cheyenne honour a humble farmer by having dinner with him? Mind you, he might have to help me up the veranda steps first. They look a terrible obstacle from here."

He was grateful for Bear Claw's supporting arm around his back as they went up the steps together in that burning summer of 1860, confident that whatever happened in an uncertain future, their friendship was indissoluble.

THE END

Author's Note

Although she read newspapers and magazines, my mother never finished a whole book in her life. My father on the other hand was an omnivorous reader, often having his head stuck in a book at the meal table, much to mother's aggravation. He loved thrillers, adventure and war stories and westerns. I read everything I could find in the house from a very early age. Thankfully no one tried to prevent me by saying the books were too old for me. Many of the westerns were formulaic and poor quality, but for a six year old they were exciting. My imagination was fired by the background settings, the vast landscapes and as I grew older I discovered some good writers among them like Will Henry, Alan Le May and later Larry McMurtry.

I was always intrigued by the Indians. No one called them Native Americans when I was a child. If we played western themed games I always chose to be an Indian. I braided my hair in two plaits with ribbons interwoven and wore a sandy coloured, faux suede jacket that I fancied looked like buckskin. Willow trees grew in abundance on the banks of the mill pond and their flexible branches were ideal for making bows and arrows.

I enjoyed Western films the most when Indians

were involved and wanted to know more about them as human beings, not just as rifle fodder for the cavalry or beleaguered settlers. I was on their side long before films like "Broken Arrow" and "Dances with Wolves" portrayed Native Americans in a more sympathetic light. This led me to an extensive study of the North American tribes.

The semi-nomadic culture of the Plains tribes featured in this novel, flowered for a very short period, less than a century, roughly from 1750 to 1870. It was made possible by the horse and the buffalo. Early ancestors of the horse had been extinct in North America for thousands of years, but they were reintroduced by the Spanish in the 15th and 16th centuries. In 1680 the Pueblo rebellion against their Spanish overlords released many horses into the wild, whilst others were traded and had reached the Plains tribes by the 1750s. Horses transformed their lives, making travel, transport and hunting, particularly hunting the buffalo, so much easier.

Society amongst these tribes was far from anarchic. As I have endeavoured to show in this story, their lives were ordered by strict custom and ritual. Severe punishments were handed out to those who transgressed against the social code. Their religious beliefs were centred on the rhythms of nature and although full of superstition, also sustained a genuine mysticism that reached beyond the corporeal.

We are conditioned to accept the spread of mechanisation, agriculture, education and the growth of cities as progress, signs that we are civilised. A moral ambiguity arises however when progress destroys the culture of the native population. Even when intentions were good, the results were bad. Confined on reservations, with poor facilities, denied the right to hunt, reliant on government handouts, the spirit of the tribes was crushed.

I wish I could have seen the Great Plains before they were broken up by the plough, when they were still "the sea of grass." The Montana in this book is one of my imagination and research, not experience. The town of Baker is fictional, but typical of many small settlements growing up at this period. Some have completely disappeared, others grown into thriving towns.

I have always admired pioneers, people with the courage to start a new life in unknown territory, particularly those who managed to live in a spirit of toleration with the native population. I suppose many people today would consider the conditions in which I grew up to be akin to pioneering. The farm of my childhood, did have electricity, although I can just remember oil lamps, but there was no running water in the house. Water came from an underground spring and was fetched from a pump at the top of the garden. It was pure, soft, good-tasting water but in a severe winter the pump would freeze and boiling water had to be poured over the pump handle and down the pipe to get it working again.

We washed in a stone sink in what we called 'the back place,' which also served as a kitchen and had a weekly bath in a large tin bath with water heated in the copper. The lavatory was outside, a wooden structure with a tiled roof, where you did not linger long in the winter and my sister once found an adder curled up on the seat. Like the lavatory at the Barnett's cabin in my story, the bucket needed emptying regularly and the contents dug into the dung heap.

Of course we did not have to worry about attacks by wolverines, bears or cougars. Foxes were the only danger to our chickens. In the middle of one hot summer night, one bold fox snatched and carried off our little black kitten, Dicky Mint, from right beside his mother despite her valiant defence.

When you are young and strong you do not consider these conditions as hardships; only later did I realise that my mother often wished for an easier life. My upbringing has made me less liable to take things for granted and be less quick to complain about small things, than those born into the conveniences of modern life. I take pleasure in writing about pioneers, wild landscapes and skies free from light pollution because to a small degree, they are within my experience.

My parents passed many years ago now, but there are so many things about them that I will always miss. My mother's big, strong hands plaiting my hair with skill; her habit of quoting only the first two lines of poems she had learned at school because she could not remember the rest of the poem; the sight of her in the distance cycling back from town, the basket on the front and back of her bike loaded with shopping; her love of singing and antiques, both of which I have inherited.

I miss my father's old jacket hanging up behind the door with a treasure always in one pocket, a packet of boiled sweets, often pear drops, which we were permitted to raid. He was a heavy smoker, although he never did so indoors and I miss seeing the red glow of the end of his cigarette in the dark farm yard at night. Then there was his tinkering and swearing underneath the old cars that he bought, but most of all I miss choosing books for him at the library and seeing his pleasure when I brought them home. They always included some westerns. So this is for you Dad and if you were able to read this one at the meal table, I am sure Mum would forgive you.

Sue Boddington
March 2021.